RC LAKE PUBLISHING

Dakota Creed

A Tale of Post Civil War Texas

BERT LINDSEY

Dakota Creed
by Bert Lindsey

RC Lake Publishing
479 FM 416
Streetman, TX 75859
Email: texschutz78@gmail.com
Website: RCLakePublishing.com

Additional Books by Bert Lindsey
FICTION
Quick Tender
Razor Sharp
NONFICTION
Golly, Doesn't He Have Anything?

Author's Contact Information:
Email: lindz@valornet.com
Telephone: 936-675-1105

ISBN-978-1-7364791-0-0   (Print version)
ISBN-978-1-7364791-1-7   (E-book)

Cover image by DepositPhotos
Cover design by Mary Schutz.

Printed in the United States of America

DEDICATION

To the love of my life,
Kathy Gale Bridges-Lindsey
and
To Mary Neal Schutz,
My insightful and patient editor

Table of Contents

Chapter One

The Logging Camp

It was a freak accident. It happened so fast not even Quin knew how it happened. He was trying to protect himself from the second blow of the bull whip. He had held the crosscut saw over his head to deflect the tip of the whip from taking another piece of flesh from his shoulder.

Bull McElroy was still standing, with his left hand on the gaping hole in his throat and his right hand attempting to hold back the blood spurting from the right artery in his neck. The crosscut lay at his feet with the bull whip wrapped around the handle. Bull's eyes were wide open, staring at seventeen-year-old Quin.

Quin stood with his hand over the torn flesh from the first blow of the whip. Neither said a word. Bull lowered his knees to the ground and stared into Quin's eyes. Quin stared back, showing no remorse or fear. "I hate you, Bull, for stealing over two years of my life," Quin said as Bull bled out and slumped to the ground on top of the saw.

Quin had always been calm under fire. He had been called cold-blooded in the past, but to him it was just doing what had to be done to survive.

It was still early morning when Quin left the rest of the timber crew and returned to the logging camp to repair one of the saw teeth that he had bent. Bull McElroy used any excuse to inflict pain on his crew. He had felt the need to punish Quin for bending the tooth on the saw.

All the men in Bull's timber crew had been bought from guards at the Rock Island Union Prison for captured Confederate soldiers. The prison was located on an island in the middle of the Mississippi River near Moline, Illinois, and was accessible only by boat.

Quin was captured several days after his father was killed. Quin decided to give up his first name, Dakota, on that day. He was fourteen years old but looked much older when he entered the Rock Island Prison in December of 1863. The Union had drummer boys and helpers around camp his age, but they did not fight in the War unless it was to defend themselves. Not so with the Confederates. A lot of boys from the South were as good, or better, at shooting a weapon than their parents. Many had fought Indians at a tender age, and many followed their fathers into battle.

Bull McElroy illegally paid Union guards at Rock Island two hundred dollars for Quin in May of 1864, a year before the War was over. Three months after the War ended, several of the prisoners, including Quin, saw confederate soldiers walking on the west bank of the Mississippi River heading south toward a home that may no longer exist. The slave logging camp lay between the Mississippi and Ohio Rivers just north of Cairo, Illinois. The Ohio River merged into the Mississippi River several miles south of Cairo.

Word had leaked to the workers that the War was over, but they were still held prisoner. McElroy's excuse was that everyone had to work off the money he had paid for them to get released. It was now April of 1867, and they all knew Bull never intended to let them work off their debt.

Quin had thought about escaping the first day he had arrived, and every day since. The prisoners had all been chained to the floor, next to their beds at night to prevent escape. There were docks on the Mississippi River's east bank and on the northwest bank of the Ohio River. Steamships would pull up to the dock and load firewood for their boilers with their overhead cranes. The prisoners were removed from sight before each scheduled loading. Quin knew that the Mississippi and the Ohio Rivers were too wide and swift for anyone to swim across. Bull had shown all the prisoners the clear cut of timber on the north side of the timber camp. He also pointed out that the sniper guard armed with a Sharps .52 caliber could easily kill anyone who tried to escape.

Standing over Bull's body, Quin had to make some fast decisions. Should he try to overpower the other guards and free the other prisoners now, or should he escape, and once free, prepare to return and free them? He made the decision to do his best to escape and come back with a plan to free the others. The thought of abandoning them was never considered as an option. Some of them had saved each other's lives in the War.

After unbuckling the holster holding Bull's Colt .45, he removed a large Bowie knife from a scabbard on the other side as well as another Colt that was tucked in his belt. He wiped Bull's blood off the items with the tail of his shirt.

Once he'd made sure each gun was loaded, he slung the belt with one of the Colts and the Bowie knife around his waist and slid the other .45 behind his belt in front. Quin noticed another wider belt around Bull's waist. *Maybe this is a money belt!*

The possibilities of the belt's content thrilled Quin but he buckled it around his waist without checking. A quick search of Bull's pockets yielded only a few coins and greenbacks.

Vigilant and calm, he began to plan his escape. He knew monkey grapevines grew on most of the trees around here, so he ran to the harvested trees nearby and quickly found the vine he wanted. He cut two short pieces and lit one of them using a flaming stick from the campfire. After several puffs to make sure it was well lit, he placed it behind his ear and the unlit one under his hat as a spare.

He ran to the camp kitchen and knowing he could not trust the cook, Quin tied and gagged him. He filled two potato sacks with several slabs of bacon and Johnny cake. He made a quick dash through Bull's office and picked up several boxes of .45-caliber ammunition. He cut two feet off a lariat he found in Bull's office and used it to tie the two potato sacks together. He slung the two sacks around his neck. Leaving Bull's body where it lay, Quin sprinted to the eastern bank of the Mississippi in search of the log he had discovered months before.

The first time he had seen that log he thought it might be a possibility for escape. Several weeks back he found a board and slid it alongside the log as a possible rudder. Adrenaline kicked in when he saw it was still there. He pulled the Bowie knife from its scabbard; and in less than two minutes cut the log loose from its entanglement. The adrenaline made rolling the big log to the river's edge seem easy. It took only a minute to whittle the board into a large paddle. He straddled the log, looked back at the camp, and pushed off toward the middle of the river.

Everyone would know he had used the river for an escape route and so he had made no effort to cover his tracks. As he held tight, the swift current grabbed the log and swept it down the river.

He figured that he'd travel down river until near dark. He suddenly changed his mind when the water from the Ohio

River entered the Mississippi River and started pushing the log toward the west bank of the Mississippi. The water from the Ohio River was much colder than the Mississippi water and he realized he had to leave the river as soon as possible or run the chance of dying from hypothermia. He was several miles from the logging camp where he'd put in. Quin would rather have been farther down the river but felt lucky that the Ohio River current pushed him all the way to the west shore of the Mississippi, in the State of Missouri. It probably saved his life.

When he hit land, he tried to push the log back out into the water only to see it head back to shore less than fifty yards down the river. He would take what he had: on land on the west side of the Mississippi and out of the cold water. He paused, lowered his head, and thanked the Lord for his escape.

Being free overshadowed the misery of being wet and cold. It brought a happiness that he never remembered having before and a smile to his face. He couldn't remember ever smiling.

The grapevine from behind his ear glowed after he knocked off the ashes and puffed on it to make sure it was well lit. He then covered his tracks leaving the river and all the way past the first natural levy two miles away.

After traveling several miles, Quin found a small spring-fed creek. The sound of a steam horn coming from a steam ship on the river startled him. It sounded as if it was almost on top of him. Fear raced through his body. *Are they sending Union soldiers in search of me? Are they dropping off some of the guards from the camp?*

Quin regained his composure and decided there was nothing he could do about it if they were. *Union soldiers or guards surely would bring their horses. That's good! I need those horses.*

Quin stopped and gathered dry wood to build a small fire under a thick cluster of willows. Puffing on the grapevine and touching the glowing end to a pile of dry leaves started an immediate fire. Taking off his wet shirt and ringing the water out thankfully washed away Bull's blood. He moved around the fire in an attempt to dry his pants. He dared not take off his wet boots for they would shrink, and he would never be able get them on again.

Quin cleaned the Colts with his damp shirt and held the Colts over the fire to completely dry them. The Colts action was then tested and the action on both was harder than he liked. He then cleaned the torn flesh on his shoulder with the clean spring water He put the damp clothes on, buried the fire, covered his tracks, then took off and headed toward the southwest.

CHAPTER TWO

The Escape

Quin had chased the sun, moving southwest of it since around noon. The grapevine was puffed on occasionally, to keep it lit. Now that the sun was peeking through the tree line ahead, he began to seek a sheltered area where he could build a small fire. Bacon and Johnny cake would be a feast after this long day. Soon after eating he left to find shelter for the night, knowing someone would be on his trail. Quin could track a ghost to the gates of hell and knew there were others who could do the same but hoped none of them would get on his trail. He would hate having to kill them.

Quin continued southwest until he found water. With his Bowie, he dug a sump a couple feet away from a small creek and waited for it to fill and clear. He drank his fill of water and refilled the sump with sand and sprinkled leaves over the top. Working his way into the thickest cover of brush he could find, he cut an opening large enough to lie down in and covered himself with the cuttings and went to sleep with a Colt in each hand.

Before daylight, Quin awoke and listened to the sounds around him. The cold morning made him shiver but the wound on his shoulder drew most of his mental attention. The flexing of any muscle in the area brought immediate pain, but no sound from his mouth. His whole life had been riddled with pain and he had learned early that crying out about it never helped and caused further problems. He flexed his muscles to make sure he could move his arm and trigger finger until he felt the trickle of warm blood making a trail down his back. He didn't hear anything unusual. So quietly removed the brush from over himself, rose to his knees, and in the dim light patiently studied his surroundings.

He checked his two Colts and eased them close to his body and rested the butts on his thighs. Quin had many times witnessed animals freeze in mid stride and look straight at him for no apparent reason. He had seen this in deer cougar, elk, and other hunted animals. It had been discussed around the army camps, Rock Island, and the slave timber camp. Quin listened to every word they had said about the feeling they had, when someone was watching them. He had never mention that he had sensed that feeling all his life and had always felt hunted.

He eased the Colts to the ground and silently picked up a small green stick. Quin slipped his Bowie from his scabbard and trimmed the small limbs from it and cut it to length. He eased the stick to his mouth and bit down on it to suppress any chattering of his teeth that might occur brought on by the cold morning chill. He picked up the two Colts and again rested them on his thighs. He would not move off his knees until it got light enough to see any movement or strange shadows.

Quin froze in place. *Someone is watching me!*

After twenty minutes of daylight and detecting no sound or movement, the two pursuers gave up on bushwhacking Quin and decided to use another tactic.

"Hey, kid, this is Moe and Pike, guards from the camp. Come on out and let's fix some breakfast and talk. We'll holster our guns and come out in the open, and you do the same. Ain't no use in fightin' on an empty stomach."

Quin removed the stick from his mouth and placed his hand over one side of his mouth to throw his voice away from himself and answered. "I'd love to talk and have a good breakfast. I know I've got some explaining to do and I want you both to know my side of the story. Moe, if you will come out in the open first, I will come out and then Pike can join us."

Moe cautiously came out. Quin joined him and was as calm as a sleeping baby. When Pike joined them, he stayed a far distance away from Moe.

"I'm surprised to see you two so soon."

"Pike and me was supposed to meet up with Bull at the camp around ten o'clock yesterday. Bull was going to close a deal on buying two-hundred-thousand acres of hardwood timber land. The seller, Pete Simon from Carlyle, Illinois, had chartered the *Mississippi Rose* that was to arrive around 11 o'clock. He had papers to close the deal.

"When we got to the camp, we found Bull on the ground dead. He was where you left him after you killed him. We saw your trail entering the river. We figured you would be going to Texas and needed to get on the west side of the Mississippi. We hid Bull's body and told Pete Simons that Bull had a bad accident and would be laid up a few days. We didn't want any law snoopin' around. We paid the Captain of the *Rose* fifty dollars to drop us and our horses off on the west side of the river just south of the Ohio, and here we are," Moe said with a smirk on his face.

"Moe, Pike, I didn't kill Bull. He actually killed himself. He ripped an inch of flesh from my shoulder, and I raised the saw over my head to ward off the whip. The whip got caught up around the saw handle and Bull pulled the saw back into his neck. I left because the War is over, and we were being held as slaves. If you do run into any law asking questions, I would like for y'all to tell them what really happened."

9

"Hell, kid, we're not going to tell the law anything. We're going to run the timber operation and run it just as Bull did. We sure don't want them to know nuthin' 'bout you Rebs."

"That's fine with me, Moe. I'll give you two the money belt, and I'll head out to Texas."

"You're not too smart, kid. We're going to take the money belt and you're going back with us to work; or maybe we'll have to kill you and leave you here for the wolves.

"You're making a big mistake here, Moe, but I'm glad to hear there will be no law involved." Quin knew now he had to kill these fellas. He had to remember to pull the trigger hard and not let the aim of the Colts pull away from the targets.

"Let's fix breakfast and then you can give us your decision. Live and work for us or die." The same confident smirk was still on Moe's face as he spoke those last words.

"No use wastin' good food on you two."

Moe and Pike were knocked backward with a bullet in each of their hearts. Neither had cleared leather but Quin hadn't intended them to. He drew his Bowie and walked to each of them as they struggled to fire their weapons. Quin reached down and finished them off. He replaced the used bullet in each of his Colts, then emptied their pockets and took their money, guns, knives, holsters, and food sack.

Pike had a pocket watch in his vest. Quin wiped all the blood off it and slipped it into his pocket. He pulled the watch back and looked to see if it had markings. Seeing none, he slipped it back in his pocket. Quin said a quick prayer for the two's families. He was concerned that other people could have heard the shots but had no shovel to dig a grave; and even if he did bury them, it would take up too much time. He quickly covered the bodies with brush and hid their weapons. The brush would keep the buzzards away for a couple of days and by then he hoped to be miles away.

If these two left someone with the horses, they would have the northwest wind on him, and the horses would alert them of his presence, but he needed those horses. A half mile later he heard a horse nicker. He froze and waited.

He waited about five minutes in search of any clue there might be others nearby. He found a large rock and threw it hard. The rock drew no response other than nickers from the horses.

Both horses had been left saddled and tied to a tree. By the horse's actions it seemed they were glad to see Quin. They each had a lariat, bed roll, canteen, and saddlebag attached. A potato sack full of food was hanging from one of the saddle horns. Quin selected one horse to ride and the other as a pack horse. He led the pack horse to where he had hidden Moe and Pike's weapons and the other food sack.

Quin hurriedly opened both their saddlebags and found a pair of clean pants in Pike's. He cut a yard off one of their lariats and tied the end of both trouser legs and packed their weapons and holsters tightly inside and tied them onto the pack horse. Quin rode off trotting the horse to the southwest with the pack horse in tow. He never looked back.

After several miles of crossing back and forth over his tracks, Quin entered a shallow creek heading south. He looked back often to make sure the water was pulling sand into the footprints of the horses.

After riding several miles in the creek Quin decided to exit on the west side and ride into the tall thick grass. He meandered through the grass until he reached a dirt road.

A wooden sign that read "Charleston, Missouri, 10 Miles" with an arrow pointing straight ahead was beside the road. Quin rode on into the nearby oak-covered hills. After finding a spring-fed creek, Quin searched Moe's saddlebag and found a tin of Lucifer matches. He made a small fire then sliced and cooked the remaining bacon to prevent it from getting rancid. Staring at the last piece of Johnny cake, Quin's stomach turned as he forced himself to eat the disgusting last piece.

When he was young, it had always been a struggle for Quins family. After five years of drought and losing their crop each year, the bank had foreclosed on all his family's property and evicted them. Before that his father had been successful all his life but was now broke financially and spiritually. He had trouble making decisions and when he did it was with hesitation and doubt. Quin sought employment for his father, but no one would hire him because of his depression.

With guidance from Quin, the family had become squatters and were always fighting just to stay put. Quin's mother and sister Francie had been killed two years before the Civil War broke out. His older sister, Marlie, died a year later from an Indian's arrow. His father never had a slave, nor did he think anyone should be involved in slavery. Quin encouraged his father to join the Confederate Army so that they would have something to eat.

As early as 1820, men were lured to the Southwest, some by stories of free land while others were running away from something; often, from the law. Some had no family or land and had no means of getting either. In the Southwest, especially Texas, men were not judged by what occurred in the past and rarely were they asked about it. They were judged by their present actions. Some who fled the law back East became lawmen in the Southwest.

Many men who had no family became family of whatever brand they rode for. Be it a cause, a gang, a ranch, or something else. The brand demanded loyalty and to the others who rode for it, whether right or wrong. Lawmen were sparse and only a brand could ensure the protection needed in a wild frontier. Riding for a good brand gave these men pride and a family. They were willing to give their life for the brand and often did. Quin and his father would ride for the Confederate Army.

Quin thought of his father and how his horse was shot from beneath him when they were fleeing a battle. When the bugler sounded, the Confederate forces retreated and scattered back south. Quin rode in and snatched his father from the ground. He thought of killing the wounded Union soldier that shot the horse but figured the soldier had enough troubles being wounded. Instead, Quin said a prayer and left the Union soldier alone, knowing they had enough time to leave before the soldier could reload.

Quin didn't bother checking his father's horse. It was dead with nothing of value on it except the saddle, and they had no horse to put it on. They soon stopped to let his father get into Quin's saddle and for Quin to move to the rump of the horse. They had been riding double for five days, seldom stopping to water and rest the horse. Quin's father wanted to get as far south as possible and, Quin, against his better judgement, let his father ride the horse to the animal's death near a deep ravine. The exhausted horse stumbled and fell into the ravine taking the man with him. Quin had slipped from the horse's rump and avoided injury. Quin rushed to his father to hear his last word, *Wallanders!*

Totally alone in the world at the age of 14, the young man ate raw horse meat to sustain himself as he decided which direction he would travel. He buried his father in the bank of the ravine and said a long prayer over the grave and whispered. "Every one of them, Father. I'll get every one!"

He was captured two days later heading south and was taken to Rock Island.

Ten dollars and thirty cents. That's all he found on Moe and Pike. It wasn't a lot, but it was more than he had ever had, and it would certainly come in handy.

Bull's money belt was difficult to get open. The one-hundred-dollar bills he saw were tightly placed in one of the six pockets. He pulled out ten bills from off the top and left the others untouched. He would count later.

Quin bathed in the creek and dried off next to the small fire he had built. He found a clean shirt in Moe's saddlebag and decided to wear the shirt until he could buy a new one in Charleston. He covered the fire and buried his dirty shirt before he moved upstream for better cover.

While the hobbled horses grazed, he rolled out one of the bed rolls and placed his two Colts where he could find them in the dark. With his wounded shoulder off the ground, he curled into a fetal position, praying for a night of good rest.

CHAPTER THREE

Dakota Creed

Quin decided that he had to develop another mindset and name. No one in the Rock Island prison had ever heard his first name. He would start using Dakota. He thought about what last name he would use in place of Quin. He wanted one that he had never heard. After several hours of thought he settled on Creed. Dakota Creed. He hoped that any real Dakota Creeds had no relatives.

The War was over, and the law didn't seem to be on his trail. But he needed to leave his name and past behind. It would take some planning.

All his family members were dead and the only friends he had left were back at the logging camp. He valued their lives as much as he did his own. He would somehow work his way back and rescue them.

Missouri, a border state dividing north and south in the Civil War. Both the Union and the Confederacy claimed the state and it was represented by a star on each of their flags. Missouri had more than 1,200 skirmishes in the state during the War with most of the participants being Missourians fighting each other. Dakota was sure these feelings would still run deep, and he would attempt to stay clear of such.

He circled Charleston toward the southeast and planned to enter the town from the south. Five miles from Charleston, Quin left the road and traveled toward a hilly area covered with a grove of oak trees until he found a spring-fed creek. He removed the saddle from the pack horse and hid it along with Moe and Pike's weapons and food supply.

Nobody seemed to notice him as he entered Charleston from the south leading a horse without a saddle. He tied both horses to the hitching rail in front of the mercantile building. He stood for several minutes fiddling with his saddle as he discreetly observed the first women he had seen in several years. They were dressed differently from the women he had known as a youngster. The corners of his mouth moved outward, and he experienced his second smile.

Creed. Dakota Creed. Dakota Creed. I have got to think of myself as Dakota Creed.

Dakota bought a pack saddle and all new clothes including a hat, boots, and moccasins. The hat was a low-crown black with a brim that would cover his face with a little tilt of his head. He figured he would gain weight and maybe height now that he would be eating more, so he bought a size larger than presently needed on the shirts and pants.

He bought beans, tins of tomatoes, flour, corn meal, jerked beef and a large sack of hardtack. The hardtack would last forever without spoiling but usually had to be soaked in coffee or water to make it soft enough to eat. At least it had a slight flavor with the salt and pepper mixed in the flour before it was baked.

He bought two small animal traps. The traps brought back a few pleasant memories in his life that he had forgotten. Several waterproof tins of Lucifer matches, a small mirror, a pair of scissors, two towels, several bars of lye soap, and a lice nit comb completed his purchases.

Leaving the store, he rode back south and turned off into

the grove of oak trees. Locating the creek, he selected one of the deep holes along its path. The hole gave him the best view of possible danger and was secluded enough to hide his modesty. Placing the Colts on a rock in reaching distance, he stood to bathe.

After scrubbing himself from head to toe with the lye soap and rinsing his hair, Dakota used the nit comb until no head lice or nits were in the comb. He trimmed his hair to the top of his shoulders while it was still wet. He had not seen himself in a mirror for at least six or seven years. He had forgotten about his dark blue eyes. It was hard for him to quit looking at the hollow-eyed skinny face looking back at him. The face looked hard, and older than he was. A smile brought a more youthful look to his face and seemed to soften his demeaner.

At that moment he remembered that today, the fifth of May, was his birthday. *Cinco de Mayo,* a day that all of Puebla, Mexico, celebrated. A day that a rag-tag army of Mexico, outnumbered two to one by the elite French invaders, defeated the French in the battle for Puebla in 1862. He was now eighteen years of age. He related to their happiness.

Dakota changed into his new clothes and buried the old, then looked back into his mirror and tipped his new black hat at the stranger there and smiled. He remounted and rode back to Charleston with his pack horse in tow.

He was greeted at the front door of the café by a smiling girl that looked to be 16 years old. Dakota pointed to a table as another young girl rushed over and poured him a glass of water. She too had a big smile on her face.

The girl that led him to his table spoke up in a loud voice. "Barbra Sue! This is my table! You go and wait on your boyfriend; this one is mine." Two other girls were looking from the kitchen smiling and laughing at what was going on. Dakota finally realized what was happening. These two girls were fighting over the chance to serve him.

Dakota thought the café was wonderful. Just walk in and tell them what you wanted, and they brought it to you hot and ready to eat. There was no sand or dirt getting in the food and only an occasional fly or an ant to mess with. Another pleasing thing was that there were girls fighting to wait on you.

Dakota was sitting by the window so he could keep an eye on his horses when a cowboy rode up from the south with Texas written all over him. He looked as if he had been on the trail for several days. The cowboy dismounted and ambled in. He looked to be around twenty years old and had on a white high crown hat with a wide brim. His white shirt highlighted his face and hands that were weathered and dark. He wore a nine-inch Colt tied down low on his thigh.

"Been on the trail long?" Dakota asked as the cowboy was passing his table. The cowboy knew instantly that a Texan asked the question.

"Sure have, and you're the first Texan I've seen since I left home.

"My name is Dakota Creed. Sit down and let me buy you something to eat, and you can tell me what's going on back home."

"I'm Bob Randle and that's the best offer I've had in a long time. How long has it been since you've been in Texas?"

"Been six years."

"Your heart will be broken when you hear what's happened to Texas."

"Tell me. I need to know."

"The carpetbaggers are trying to take over all the land. Only carpetbaggers can vote, and they control everything. Every little town, road and especially a crossroad; they vote themselves in as a marshal, sheriff, or constable. Then if you have a penny on you, they trump up charges against you and fine you the penny. They reinstated four years of back taxes and are now adding a reconstruction tax on the land. The landowners are desperate and know they will not be able to pay all the taxes. The carpetbaggers own most of the banks and will not loan money to pay taxes when using the land as collateral. Most of the southern banks closed because they had no gold to buy the new gold certificates that the Union printed after the war."

"What's a carpetbagger, Bob?"

"I won't ask where you've been the last couple of years," Bob said, laughing. "A carpetbagger is a person from the North who rushed South to take advantage of the spoils of War. Most all of them showed up with nothing but a bag made of carpet."

"The Texas Rangers have been disbanded, and there is a state police in its place run by carpetbaggers. During the War, King Fisher moved into the Nueces Strip from Mexico and is stealing cattle from the Texas ranches and selling them in Mexico. A lot of the ranchers pulled out when the Texas Rangers were shut down. The new state police did nothing to control the rustlers and threatened the ranchers if they tried to prevent their own cattle from being rustled. A lot of Texans aren't taking all this well and are turning outlaw to survive."

"A clan near Marshall, Texas, has stolen everything of value and killed the folks they stole from and now that area is desolate. Seems as if no one wants to live there. Everything is falling apart in Texas. No farming, no ranching, and no jobs. I'm heading to Gage, Kentucky. I've been offered a job there as foreman on a thoroughbred horse ranch."

Hmm! A clan near Marshall, Texas. That's interesting.

Vengeance filled Creed's heart.

"How are you going to get over the Mississippi from here?" he asked Randle.

"There's a ferry at Wickliffe. That's in Kentucky. It's about twelve miles due east of here. A wide part of the Mississippi River where there is less current. Gage is about fourteen miles east of there."

"Do you think a man could buy some good horses there? I don't need thoroughbreds but do want twelve strong horses with staying power."

"Well, there's definitely a lot of good horseflesh in Kentucky. The thoroughbred ranches are always getting rid of accidentally bred horses to make room for the purebreds.

"Could I look you up say, six or eight days in Gage and see if the ranch you're going to would have any such horses?"

"Sure, I'll be at the Flying Dust Ranch northwest of Gage, Kentucky."

"So, what happened to all the cattle in Texas?"

"Nothing! There are thousands of maverick Longhorns. There's just no market for them in Texas. To my knowledge, two drives of Longhorns were gathered by Jesse Chisholm. One has been delivered and the other is on the way to the rail head in Dodge City, Kansas. He gathered more than a couple of thousand on his first drive from around Uvalde and just started his second drive a month ago with about the same number, gathered north of San Antonio."

"Are there any in East Texas?"

"Yeah, the Big Thicket and the Trinity River flats are full of them. It will take some tough cowboys to get them out of the Big Thicket, they're in there as thick as fleas on a cur dog's back."

Creed bid Randle farewell and asked the waitress for the tally. "My name is Clair Bridgestone, what's your name?"

"Dakota Creed; why do you ask?"

"You're new in town and I would like to get to know you better."

"I'd like to get to know you better too, but I'm just passing through and short on time."

"That breaks my heart, Dakota. I finally find a handsome man and he's just passing through."

"I'll try to look you up the next time I pass through and maybe I'll have more time." *Wow! She thinks that I'm handsome.*

Clean, well dressed, and newly wealthy, Dakota Creed walked into the local gunsmith and hired him to loosen the tension on the triggers of his Colts.

"I want you to look at the new Henry rifles I just got in. This weapon was available only to the Union soldiers toward the end of the War. They just now made them available to the public," the gunsmith said smiling.

"I've heard about the Henry. Does it hold fifteen rounds of ammunition like they say?"

"Sure does! It has a range of a hundred and fifty yards. I only have two and I don't know when I'll get more. You should buy one of them."

"What do you want for one?"

"I'd have to have $75 for it."

"Hmmm! Does that include a scabbard?" Dakota asked with a non-committal tone.

After hesitating, "Okay, I'll throw in the scabbard," said the gunsmith.

"What would you charge me if I took both off your hands?"

"Oh! I couldn't cut the price any more," the gunsmith said with a grim look on his face.

"I'm goin' into the Indian Territory and I need more fire power than I have. Do you have a case of the .44-caliber ammunition for the Henry?"

"Yeah, I have plenty."

"If I buy the two Henrys, what price would you give me on your two Colt .45s with the nine-inch barrels?" Dakota asked as he was picking them up and checking the tension on the triggers. *Just right.*

"I can get plenty of the Colts. I usually get $45 for them, but will let you have them for forty."

"Holsters included?"

"Yeah, I'll throw in the holsters."

"Deal."

"Here is something you are going to need if you are going into the Territory. A brass telescope. Take a look. It's yours for another $20."

Dakota walked away.

"You don't need the scope?"

"I need it, but not for $20."

"Give me $10 and it's yours."

Creed bought it all. Plus a few items that were bound to come in handy. He loaded everything on the pack horse and rode to the public stable.

"Lookin' to buy two good horses," Creed told the hostler.

"You want to trade those two in?"

"Nope, just need two more."

After several minutes dickering, a deal was made.

Dakota had a smile on his face and two fine horses in his possession. One was a big black gelding with a white blaze on his face and the other an equally tall buckskin.

Dakota wanted to get rid of Moe's and Pike's horses. He dared not leave them in town, sell, or trade them, and give a bill of sale on horses he did not own. Instead, he decided to lead them back to the camp with him. In Texas and most everywhere else, anyone having a stolen horse was usually hung on the spot.

He headed to the grove, where he changed his clothes and decided it was the perfect place to break in his new weapons. He would need to carry the new Colts with the nine-inch barrels a little lower on his hips to clear them from the holster when drawn. The Henry rifles were deadly accurate at a hundred yards but struggled for accuracy with anything over 125 yards. He loved the fast lever action.

The two shots he fired to kill Moe and Pike were the first shots he had fired since he was captured. He was 14 years old then. He had fired hundreds of rounds by the age of ten, many at people trying to kill him and his family.

Creed caught a large swamp rabbit the first night he set the trap. He skinned it, salted the skin down and rolled it tight and tied it. *That rabbit is gonna make a right nice breakfast.*

After breakfast he worked on the rabbit pelt. He nailed it fur-side down to a stump, scraped all the flesh away and rubbed salt into every crease. He repeated the process over the next two days then washed the pelt in the creek until it was soft.

Three days later Creed left the grove of trees astride the black gelding and leading the buckskin, with Moe and Pike's horses following along. He was well-rested, fed, and confident in his ability to handle his weapons as well, or better, than the day he entered the Union prison.

With his leather-working tools, he attached the Henry scabbards on the saddle, one pointing toward the horse's head, the other toward the horse's rump.

Creed had been pleased with the sight he received from the mirror before he left. He looked as if he had gained five pounds in his face alone. *I look better when I smile.* He thought of that waitress Clair and how she said he was handsome. Maybe he'd try to look her up when he had time.

Plans for how to rescue the other prisoners at the timber camp began to take shape in his mind. He hoped to capture additional weapons from the guards at the timber camp. He would not take the chance on how many horses would be available or how good the horses might be. He had to find good horse flesh before making the rescue. He would keep and take the guns he had taken from Bull, Moe, and Pike but would leave Moe and Pike's horses off the trail just before reaching the ferry at Wickliffe. He couldn't chance someone recognizing them in his possession.

CHAPTER FOUR

The Flying Dust Ranch

Creed received several glances as he waited to board the ferry. *Was it the black horse drawing all the attention? Was it his black shirt and black hat or was it the two Colts?*

Creed was surprised to see as many people as he did on the road to Gage. Most were well-dressed and riding beautiful horses and showed their friendliness with waves and smiles when they passed. Some held their heads down and didn't meet his eyes. Maybe they had burdens heavier than his own.

Up ahead Dakota noticed movement at the side of the road. He opened the tube case and withdrew the telescope. *I knew I would need this.* The most beautiful girl he'd ever seen was trying to unhitch a team of horses from a four-wheel carriage that had a broken back right wheel. The horses were not cooperating. Two men were grabbing her arm and trying to lead her away from the area. It would have made no difference if she were pretty, ugly, old, or young, in Texas women are treated with respect. One of the quickest ways to die is to show disrespect to a woman.

As he rushed forward, Creed could hear her sobbing her pleas "leave me alone." The dirty and unkept men both had Colt .45s strapped on their right hips.

"You give us a little and we will help you," said the one who was closer to her.

"Leave the lady alone!" barked Creed.

"Who the hell are you?"

"I'm the one who told you to leave her alone. Now!"

"Who the hell's going to make us?"

"I am," Creed replied.

The two reached for their Colts. Creed lunged his horse forward putting the horse between them and the girl, then fired his Colts before the men cleared leather. The bullets fired into their right shoulders sent them reeling against the carriage and to their knees. Creed jumped off his horse and searched the two for other weapons. He removed their Colts and knives and threw them into the brush.

The girl was so terrified she could not speak.

"You're safe now. No one will hurt you. Give me a few seconds, Miss, I'm going to get those two back on their horses and send them on their way.

"Go find a doctor. I don't want y'all to die," Creed instructed.

"We'll kill you for this."

"I'll remember that and the next time I see you, I will not be as easy on you. Now get!" Creed yelled as he slapped the horses on their rumps.

Creed turned back toward the young lady. She was wearing black riding boots and gray riding pants that fit firmly on her lanky body. Her bright white silk blouse had been soiled by her attackers and the top button had been popped off in the scuffle. Creed reached out and held her for a moment by both shoulders to steady her. When she looked up at him his knees weakened when he saw her teary-eyed, light blue eyes looking at him and the ruffled blond hair hanging part way over her face.

Sobbing, she reached out and wrapped her arms around

Creed's neck. "I don't know what I would have done if you had not come along." Between sobs she loosened her grip and looked back into his eyes. "Please don't leave me!"

After several minutes she settled down enough to talk. "I slipped off from home and went to Gage to buy a new pair of shoes. Those two men followed me when I was leaving Gage to head home. They tried to get me to stop and when I wouldn't they forced me off the road and the wheel broke."

"Are you okay?"

"I'm not hurt but I don't know what to do about the carriage or how I'm going to get home."

"Miss, nothing is broken that we can't fix. Let's figure this out."

"You don't understand," she sobbed.

"I know I don't, but if you will tell me, I'm sure we'll figure out how to solve this problem."

"I know I am in big trouble with my father for slipping off and if I don't get home, I'm going to miss the first dance at the ball tonight," she said with a sobbing, jerking voice.

"Miss, that is a dreadful problem. How far away do you live?"

"At least five miles. I'm Kathy Ann Fairchild and my parents own the Flying Dust Ranch."

"Nice to meet you Kathy Ann. My name is Dakota Creed, and I'm pretty sure I can solve your problem. Then I'll take you home, so you won't be late for that first dance."

"I don't think anyone one can fix that wheel," she declared.

"Trust me, I can get you and the carriage home. Stay here and I'll be back in a few minutes." Creed mounted and before he knew it the girl grabbed the back of his saddle and swung herself up behind him.

"I'm going with you," she exclaimed. Creed was pleasantly surprised by her action. *This girl is not only gorgeous, but she also knows her way around horses.*

Creed found and cut the long pole he needed to make the wagon portable. He cut a notch in the big end of the pole and trimmed it to slide under the back axle, letting the notch fall over the front axle. He tied one of his lariats around the back axle and attached it to the front axle to keep it from sliding back. The pole created a skid that kept the back axle off the ground and in place.

"Let's get going. You can show me the way." Dakota's two horses followed the carriage as he knew they would.

"Do you know Bob Randle?" Creed asked her.

"Sure do. Bob is our new foreman."

"When we get there, you run in and get ready for that dance. I'll stay with the team, and you just get word to Bob that Dakota Creed will be at the stable. I met Bob a few days ago and he told me he would be here. I need to buy some horses."

When they got near the ranch house, Creed began to realize that the house and stables were gigantic and beautiful. The house, barns, corrals, and fences were all painted white. The house was a mansion. The word "empire" entered his mind. *It is an Empire.*

Creed had never seen such beauty. All his life he had thought only of survival, his friends, family, and food. He had been hungry all his life and not just for food.

Earlier in his life, he realized he caught on to things quicker than most. He learned to read, write, and do arithmetic by the age of four. He was trapping, curing hides, firing a gun, and tracking by the age of six. Seeing the house, barns, corals, and fencing, Creed knew what he wanted. He would have his Empire, somewhere, someday.

The puppy she called Rascal met them as they rode up. His tail wagged, and his barking ceased with the raised hand of the girl.

"Dakota, thank you so much. Talk Bob into bringing you to the dance tonight."

"Don't know 'bout that. I would have to wash up my clothes before I could do that."

"What in the world happened to you, Kathy Ann?", said the stern muscular man rushing out the door.

"Don't have time to tell you now, Daddy. I've got to get ready for the dance tonight. Have Dakota tell you," she said as she rushed into the house.

"I'm Paul Fairchild," said Kathy Ann's father to Creed. "Tell me what happened."

"Mr. Fairchild," I'm Dakota Creed; just call me Dakota, if you like. I'll tell you what she told me."

After telling Kathy Ann's part of the story Creed told his part. "When they went for their guns, I had few choices other than killing them and I didn't want to do that. In Texas, that would have been the expected thing to do but I was not sure about here in Kentucky. I did not want to cause Kathy Ann any stress over my actions."

"Dakota, I'm not from Texas but I probably would have killed 'em."

"Yeah, I probably should have. They promised me they would kill me for wounding them. I hate having to look over my shoulder. I put them on their horses and sent them to get medical attention."

"Dakota, if you see them, point them out to me, and I will solve that problem for you."

"Mr. Fairchild, I appreciate that, but I like to fight my

own battles."

"I know that, but I'd sure like to make it, so they never scare or hurt another woman, especially someone like my daughter."

"I understand that! I think she's okay now, Dakota said. "I had previously agreed to meet Bob Randle here today to see if he had any horses for sale."

"Well, hey, come on in the house and meet my wife, Maude."

After the introduction, the telling of Dakota's rescue of Kathy Ann took only a few minutes.

"We insist you stay in the guest room and take your meals with us." Paul said. "Isn't that right, Maude?"

"Absolutely, we will have it no other way," Maude said smiling.

"I'm not going to the dance tonight, Mom. I think it would be rude of me to leave now after Dakota rescued me."

"I think you're right 'bout that," Maude confided.

At dinner that night Dakota quietly observed gentle manners of formal dining. He asked questions of all present. Kathy Ann couldn't take her eyes from him. After dinner Paul led Dakota to the sitting room for coffee while Maude and Kathy Ann straightened up the kitchen.

"Kathy Ann, that young man who helped you today has the most beautiful eyes I've ever seen," Maude said, smiling.

"I think so, too Mama," Kathy Ann said as she reached out and squeezed her mother's hand.

Dakota had never seen or been in a finer bedroom but opted to sleep on the floor with the bed roll between his knees. He just couldn't mess up the beautiful bed. It was his awakening to how comfortable his life could be.

During the three days he'd been at the Fairchild's home, Dakota recovered the two Colt .45s he had thrown into the brush and added them to his stash of guns. He spent time with Bob, Mr. and Mrs. Fairchild, Kathy Ann, and Rascal, who tagged along at his heels or by his horse at every opportunity. Rascal had taken a liking to Creed.

Bob and Mr. Fairchild helped Dakota pick out twelve strong, young, and fast horses with staying power. Creed questioned the low price of the horses. "These horses are worth much more than you are quoting me."

"Ah, forget about that, Dakota. I want you to have them at that price because I'm indebted to you for keeping Kathy Ann safe. We want you to be our friend. You will always be welcome here.

CHAPTER FIVE

Love and Death

Creed had learned from Mr. Fairchild about a ferry that crossed over the Ohio River at Ballard County, Kentucky, into Mound City, Illinois. *The Cairo peninsula and the logging camp were only 20 miles south of Mound City. That would be the best route to free my Compadres*!

"You know, Dakota, we were pretty fortunate during the War," said Fairchild. "There were no ferries crossing the Mississippi or the Ohio near here until a year ago. You couldn't pass through Gage to go anywhere. We were blocked off from the War by the Mississippi on the west and the Ohio on the north. Kentucky was a border state and voted to stay neutral in the Civil War. The flow of troops from the south drifted eastward toward Louisville, bypassing this area. We still don't have mail service or the telegraph, but we hope to have 'em soon."

Dakota had breakfast with the Fairchilds before his departure. He planned to leave at daylight to make his trip to the Ballard County Ferry and cross into Mound City before dark. Maude had the cook prepare food for Dakota to take with him, including a large sack of hardtack. Paul added several sacks of oats for the horses.

Dakota had worked on the large swamp rabbit pelt each night until he turned it into a soft fur-covered piece of leather that he made into a purse with a small gold button. He gave it to Kathy Ann before he left. Tears of happiness flooded her face and brought smiles to the faces of her parents. Kathy Ann leaned up and kissed Dakota on his cheek.

They invited Dakota to stay and although that would have been a distinct pleasure, he explained he had to take care of some important business. He promised to stay in touch and that he would return sometime in the future. Rascal had to be held back as Creed rode off. He whined, whimpered, and even howled. His new best friend was leaving.

He rode the big black and led his pack horse. The other twelve were divided and rigged on two lead ropes tied to Creed's saddle. After he was on the road to Ballard County, Dakota untied the horses from their lead ropes and trotted his own horse. The others followed dutifully.

Each time he looked back he longed for what he was leaving behind, but he had to rescue his friends. He checked again to see that all the horses were following. When he looked ahead something caught his eye about a hundred yards away at the tree line. He continued to look forward; and from the corner of his eye, he picked out two horses with two riders holding scatter guns, both with their right arms in slings. The road ahead curved to the west bringing him closer to the tree line.

Creed had taken his feet from the stirrups. When he was within about twenty yards, he saw the riders now on foot trying to steady their shotguns on a low tree branch. He raked his boots in the flanks of his horse. The horse jumped forward several feet. Creed had both .45s drawn and was flying to the ground just as their two scatter guns were being readied to fire. His two .45 bullets blew out the hearts of the two gunmen as their scatter guns fired into the ground at their feet.

Creed's horses had run off about twenty yards. He had fired each weapon and took the time to replace the spent shell in each. He was certain the shots would have been heard at the ranch and Mr. Fairchild would be investigating. He intentionally dropped the casings beside the road to leave a sign as to what happened.

Dakota stayed until both men, had bled out. He found the gunmen's two horses tied close by, remounted, and rode off leading the two horses. He whistled for the other horses, and they fell in behind the two horses, covering their hoof prints.

"What's that?" Bob asked.

"Bob, get our horses, I'll get a couple of rifles."

Kathy Ann hollered "Saddle my horse, I'll be there in a couple of minutes."

"You better stay here, Kathy Ann."

"I'm going. Dakota could be hurt!"

Paul could already see the threat of tears in Kathy Ann's eyes. "Okay, but stay back when we get close."

Paul saw the scuffed-up roadbed, dismounted, and picked up the two .45 casings and slipped them in his pocket. Paul suspected Dakota was asking for his help, which he would gladly give. He found the two bodies with a shot gun near their left hands and each with a hole in their heart. Each had their right arms in a sling. It was obvious to Paul and Bob as to what had happened.

"Where's Dakota, Daddy?"

"He rode on with the herd of horses. He had to catch the last ferry of the day."

"How do you know he's not wounded?"

"There's no blood on the road; and if he had been wounded, he would have come back to the ranch."

"This is all my fault, Daddy. I know those are the two men who attacked me. I don't want Dakota to get in trouble for killing them."

"I'll see to it that does not happen. You and Bob go on back to the ranch and don't mention this to anyone. I want to tell Maude about all this myself."

Paul buried the bodies in an area of the Flying Dust Ranch where no one was likely to find them.

On the way to the ferry, Creed discovered a trail that meandered along the south side of the Ohio River. There he released the two gunmen's horses and hid the saddles and bridles.

Creed reattached his lead ropes before he crossed the Ohio River on the ferry. It was a large ferry and Creed and his fourteen horses thankfully didn't attract much attention. He waited until all the traffic left the ferry area then headed south looking for a campsite. The one he found was on a creek about five miles farther southwest and a mile north of the Ohio River. He watered and fed the horses and built a rope corral in a thicket that reached the water in the creek.

Early the next morning he left the horses in the corral and rode southwest on the gelding until he found the clear cut. It was approximately 100 yards wide and brush was cleared another 100 yards or so into the thick timber. Looking west through his scope, he spotted the sniper's low tower. Creed looked at his watch. *I have time.*

Moving back north from the cut, Creed removed the money belt and took out the rest of the hundred-dollar bills slipped them into his pocket.

Chow would be served to the guards in an enclosed hall

at the logging camp. The prisoners ate outside seated on the ground under the watchful eye of a guard leaning against the only tree in the camp area. Eliminating the sniper guard quickly, without being detected, was crucial. He would give himself one hour in his plan to eliminate the sniper and would be at the logging camp by noon.

Creed had seen the small, low tower used by the sniper guard only one time. He mentally calculated the time it took to get back to the logging camp from the tower. The sniper was a muscular, big man who stood well over six feet tall. Creed had heard the other guards calling him "Sure Shot" Freeman.

When he was a prisoner here, Creed had questioned each of the other prisoners about the clear cut. Most agreed the cut was one hundred yards in depth and ran across the entire peninsula. It was rumored the sniper had been a buffalo hunter and used a Sharps .52 caliber rifle, with a firing range of 1000 yards. The tower was situated midway of the cut on the north side.

With the horses hidden in the corral, Creed began the next step in his plan. Creed carried one of the Henry rifles and wore both the nine-inch barrel Colt .45s on his hip. The Bowie knife was alongside the .45 on the left and he carried the scope around his neck. Creed didn't relish the idea of killing anyone, but he would not chance the guards, making noise and attracting attention before the prisoners' escape was underway.

Betting that the guard would be focusing on the clear-cut and not thinking of being attacked from the rear, Creed confidently crept forward toward the tower. He had a clear plan on how to kill the sniper without making a sound.

Creed crawled the last 200 hundred yards, getting in sight of the low tower, but the sniper was not there. He crept backward and located a secure location where he could keep sight of the tower. If the sniper did not show up in ten more minutes, he would call off the rescue for the day.

The sniper didn't show up. Getting the sniper out of the way was crucial to the rescue.

Creed slowly made his way back toward the horses. He was in sight of them when he heard a booming voice.

"Well, ain't you a purty sight, boy! Where's all that money you lifted from Bull?" The big man asked as he stepped from behind a tree holding a Sharps rifle pointed at Creed.

"I've got most of it. I was bringing it back to exchange it for the other prisoners."

"I saw a flicker of movement from the tower and investigated it. I didn't know it was my lucky day. Where is the money?"

"I have a bunch of it in my front pocket," Creed said grinning.

"Let me see it," the big man said as he lowered the rifle and stepped slightly forward.

Creed pulled the wad of hundred-dollar bills from his pocket and dropped them at the big man's feet. The guard instinctively bent over to pick them up as Creed retrieved his Bowie and drove the sharp blade through the big man's neck.

"Sure Shot" Freeman dropped the rifle and went to the ground, taking his last breath of air.

Creed looked at his watch. He didn't have enough time to do the rescue as he planned. "Sure Shot" was dead, and it had to be done now. When the sniper didn't show for lunch, they would come looking for him. There was not enough time to walk or run to the logging camp to arrive by noon. He would have to run his horse to make it before the guards left in search of Freeman. Creed left the money, except for a hand full, on the ground and ran to the horses. He saddled the first Flying Dust horse he came to and raced toward the logging camp. He didn't look at his watch. It made no difference what time it was. He would get there as fast as the horse would take him and decide what to do when he got there.

Creed took short cuts to the camp as he remembered, and the horse responded gracefully to his signals. He slowed and stopped about 300 yards out from the camp. Any closer would alert the guards, and horses. Creed loosely tied his horse and ran the remaining distance. He looked at his watch. The guards would be leaving the chow hall in five minutes.

The cook was taken by surprise when he slipped in the back door of the kitchen. A swift blow to the head knocked him unconscious; and seconds later, the cook was gagged and tied securely. Creed went out the back door of the kitchen to find the guard who would be sitting against the tree watching the prisoners.

Creed knew all thirty-five of the prisoners by name. He silently walked to the tree with one finger over his lips and held the Bowie in his left hand. Several of the prisoners saw him and their eyes got bigger, but none made a sound. He reached around the tree with both arms. His right hand went over the guard's mouth as he cut his throat with the Bowie. He motioned the prisoners to sit tight as he held the guard until he was still. Creed wiped the blood from the Bowie using the dead guard's pants and eased it back in its sheath.

He motioned again for the prisoners to sit tight as he moved toward the chow hall. Creed took the Henry that was slung from his shoulder into his hands.

He again placed his finger over his lips and walked into the chow hall. Creed had the Henry waist high, pointing at the guards who were eating. He asked for their attention. One of the guards jumped to his feet. "It's Quin! Get him! He's the one that killed Bull."

Creed pulled the trigger. "No! I didn't kill Bull, but I will kill you." His bullet struck the guard at the base of his neck and he died instantly before the guard's pistol cleared leather.

"Now, anyone else want to say something?" There was no response. "Listen up and listen well. Your life depends on it. The War has been over for two years. These men outside have been held as prisoners by you and forced to work as slaves.

"I had nothing to do with Bull's killing. It was an accident. His whip got tangled up on the handle of the saw and he jerked it back into his neck. But I didn't shed any tears when he died either."

"I'm taking the prisoners out of here. I'm sure you don't want to get the law involved. The War is over, and we don't want any trouble with the law either. Anybody got a problem with that? If you don't agree, you still have your weapons and now's the time to reach for them." No one moved.

There were eight guards left alive and Dakota gave them each a hundred-dollar bill. "This is to pay you for your horse, saddle, weapons, and the shirt on your back. Anyone not satisfied with that amount, speak up now." No one spoke.

"One at a time walk up here and lay your weapons and your shirt on the table, then sit back down." The process took less than three minutes.

Creed backed up to the door and motioned for several of the prisoners to come in and select a weapon and a shirt. "If you find a shirt that works for you, put it on but keep the one that you take off. Gather up all the horses and saddles you can find and bring them out front.

"Half of you go into the kitchen and gather all the food that you can carry. Saddle the horses and load what you can on the horses."

"Darrel, you and Tyner go into Bull's office and gather all the weapons, ammunition, logbooks, and pencils you can find and bring them with you."

"Donny, you keep a horse and stay outside here for a couple of hours. I'll leave my fifteen-shot Henry rifle with you. If any of them sticks his head out of this door before then, blow their head off and kill the rest." Creed had spoken these words loudly, making sure everyone heard them.

Donny whispered to Dakota, "Quin, several of the men want to kill them all before we leave!"

I'll take care of that. Donny, stay here a few minutes then slip out and catch up with us."

"Listen up, men. I plan to get us all out of here alive. I promise you I'll kill anyone here who messes this up. If you have different opinions about this escape keep your mouth shut. We will settle after we are safely out of here. If any killing is to be done, I'll do it."

Ten horses had been rounded up. Some of the prisoners ran alongside and then switched out, riding double back to the area where Creed had left his thirteen horses. "Hold up here a moment and rest. Donny, you come with me."

Creed gathered the hundred-dollar bills from the ground and instructed Donny to drag Freeman's body away and find a good place to cover it. Creed was disappointed that "Sure Shot's" horse had not shown up, but he had no time to look for it. He went back to get the rest of the men and led them to the horses. It was obvious that someone had been killed there and dragged away, but no one asked questions.

"These thirteen horses here are my Texas compadres. The black gelding and the buckskin are mine. I'll be riding the gelding and one of you can ride the buckskin. I have six more .45s in my saddlebags. If you didn't get a gun back at the camp, take one of these. If you still don't have a gun, team up with someone who does have one.

"We'll be catching a ferry at Mound City and crossing the Ohio River back into Kentucky. There's a ferry that crosses the Mississippi at Wickliffe, Kentucky, that will take us into Missouri. When we cross the Mississippi, we should be safe.

"We're eleven horses shy of everyone having a horse. Some of you will have to ride double as we make our way to Missouri. I will buy each of you a horse and saddle as soon as possible. I have two saddles and bridles hidden out south of the Ohio I will retrieve. Remember, the War is over, and you should act like it. When we get to Missouri, I'll buy everyone new clothes including boots and hats. Only Donny and I will be giving the orders. If any of you have a problem with that, let's hear it now." No objections were made.

"I don't want anyone speaking a word to anyone but Donny and me until we get into Missouri. We have only about five hours to catch the last ferry of the day leaving Mound City. I'll be on that ferry. Those of you whose shirt is nothing but rags, I want you to walk on the ferry in the middle of the horses."

They arrived at the ferry as it was pulling into the dock for its last run of the day. Everyone including Creed was running on adrenaline as they walked the horses onto the ferry in Mound City. Creed was ready to pay the fare when the Captain questioned his own count. "I need to count everything again. Everyone stand still." After recounting, the Captain spoke up. "How far did all you guys that don't have a horse walk to get here?" Creed made a quick glare at his men letting them know not to say a word. Dakota's right hand was positioned on top of his Colt. "How much do I owe you, Captain?" "Uh, that'll be only four dollars, Sir." After they disembarked, Creed cornered the Captain and apologized to him. "We've had a rough week and have had some horses drown. My men and I are really worn out."

"No apology needed. I thought your men were fretful for some reason. Now I understand why."

When the other passengers were out of sight, Dakota led his men to the trail that should take them to Wickliffe, Kentucky.

When they came to the trail that turned south toward the Flying Dust, Creed motioned them on to the west. He stood solemnly and looked south for several minutes before cantering to catch up with them so some of them could help retrieve the two hidden saddles and bridles.

It was a short time before dark when Dakota led them a mile off the trail that would lead them to Wickliffe. "Donny, I want three outriders circling the camp. Change them out every three hours." He wanted everyone to have their fire out and buried before dark. He again wiped away all signs of leaving the trail. He hoped they would all safely cross over the Mississippi into Missouri late the next day.

CHAPTER SIX

The Plan

Creed would be less than 20 miles from Kathy Ann and Rascal when they crossed the Mississippi at Wickliffe. He wanted to go to the Flying Dust, but some people who had been locked up a long time might react to freedom in the wrong way. Young as Creed was, he knew some would need his guidance. Their safety was more important to him than his happiness, at least for now.

Creed knew his Texans trusted him and would be loyal to him. They would ride for his brand but there were a few of the others he was not sure of. Creed and Donny had discussed this at length. All of them had been selected by Bull. They were all young, strong, and had no kin in the prison at the Rock Island Union Prison that could ask about their where abouts. Creed was the youngest of all, but had shown leadership in the War, Rock Island, and in the timber camp. He wouldn't discriminate against any of them now. Being free could change those he doubted.

"Okay, listen up, Men! We lost the War and I'm not going to re-fight it. I have no family left. I'm going straight to the Big Thicket in Texas and am going to drag every maverick Longhorn in there out. I'll brand them and drive them to a railhead or to some market up north or northwest.

"I'll hire any of you who want to work with me at thirty dollars a month and will feed you and your horse. I know that some of you will want to go home first so that's okay if you want to join me later, I can be found around Nacogdoches, Texas. The offer will always be there for you and yours. If you bring others, make sure they will be faithful to you and our brand."

"You guys are the only family I have. I'm pretty sure that if any one of you had escaped, you would have tried to rescue everyone here, so you don't need to feel indebted.

"By the time we leave Charleston, everyone will have a horse, weapons, and be well-fed. I'd like to know your plans before we leave Charleston. Jack, you and Billy take everyone's hat, pants, shirt, and boot size and write it down. Make a list and add an inch to the waist band. We're going to eat high-on- the-hog on the way home. I want a count on all the weapons we took from the guards. If one is not of good quality, we need to replace them with new or used quality weapons. Make sure you each have a dependable weapon."

"We're leaving at the break of day to cross the Mississippi by ferry tomorrow. Those of you who are riding double switch out every hour. We'll be in the saddle most of the day. Put some hardtack in your pocket because we will not be stopping to eat. We will rest up after we get to Missouri."

Creed was worried that trouble would raise its head in Kentucky over his two killings there and was anxious to head west.

They reached the ferry in Wickliffe with time to spare. Creed slowed the horses and scoped the landing. He was relieved to see only the ferry work crew.

After crossing the Mississippi, Creed moved everyone off the road five miles south of the ferry and stopped for the first time that day. "There are thirty minutes of light left. I don't think we should have a campfire, until we all have proper clothing and weapons. Team up and make small cook fires. Cook what you want or what you have. Share with everyone and have your fires out and buried by night fall."

The excitement of being free masked all the exhaustion their bodies were feeling and left each wanting to talk, laugh, and smile. No one wanted to sleep.

"Donny, send out the outriders as we did last night." He had become Creed's most trusted friend. He met Donny early in the War and they had saved each other's lives on several occasions. His hair was sandy and his body lanky. He had a good way about him in the way he directed his men. He had been a leader long before he joined the army. He was a good marksman and an expert with a knife.

The next morning, Creed led everyone to his camp in the grove of woods along the creek south of Charleston, Missouri. "We're going to spend a couple of days here to rest and clean up. Jack, Billy, and I will be going into Charleston and buy the clothes for everyone. We'll buy two shirts and pants each. You will have no excuse for wearing dirty clothes. We will buy eleven horses and additional saddles and bring them back for those who did not get one. I have a saddle hidden out here I will retrieve.

"I want everyone here to dig a deep hole while we are gone. When we get back with the new clothes, I want each of you to bury all the clothes you now have on. Then, once we return with the other supplies, you're gonna bathe, shave, cut your hair and use the nit comb to clean out any critters that you might have in your hair."

"Tomorrow after you get your new clothes, I will give each of you a hundred dollars. You can ride into Charleston two or three men at a time and buy what you want. Don't associate with anyone other than the ones you rode into town with. Ride in and out from different directions. No one is to go into any saloons. Often, they're places where the War is still being fought, and you could wind up in a carpetbagger's jail. Also, none of you have had a drink in more than three years and you don't know how it will affect you, so stay clear of whisky. You should wait until you are farther south. If you do go into a saloon, you will be on your own, and you will not ride with me when we head south. Donny, post guards here when we leave and rotate them out every couple of hours. The rest of you, go get some sleep."

Creed decided to ride off alone to count out the money in Bull's money belt. He would need thirty-five one-hundred-dollar bills to give to the crew. The rest of the hundreds in the stack would be carried in his front pant pocket. He took out the next bundle and was surprised. They were not hundred-dollar bills; they were all five-hundred-dollar bills!

Creed had heard of the new currency printed by the Union after the War ended. Not only did the Union government print the usual one- and five-dollar greenbacks but they also printed the ten, twenty, fifty, one hundred, five hundred, thousand-dollar bills and ten-thousand-dollar gold certificates. These certificates could be surrendered for gold on demand.

Later that afternoon, Creed, Jack, and Billy returned from town with eleven horses loaded down with saddles for every horse. There was a large saddlebag for each of the men. In addition, there were clothes, lye soap, towels, shaving mugs, razors, mirrors, scissors, and lice nit combs. It was the first real bath some of the men had had in three or four years.

Early the next morning, Creed passed out the hundred dollars to each of them. "Remember, the War is over. Relax, enjoy yourself and keep your mouth shut. If any law questions you, tell them you came from the Flying Dust Ranch, near Gage, Kentucky, trying to buy a thoroughbred racehorse. Keep the name Paul Fairchild, owner of the ranch, in mind. None of you have done anything wrong. Don't act as if you have."

"I haven't done anything wrong either, but I'm the only one who killed someone, and they would be after me, not you. I hate to ask you to do this, but it is important to me. I want to leave my past behind and no longer want to be called Quin. My name is now Dakota Creed and I'd like to be called Dakota, or just Creed. There might be people looking for Quin and I don't want to have to kill them. The farther south we go, the safer you should be. I'm not so sure about Quin!"

I forgot all those who wished me and Dad dead when we left them behind to join the Confederate Army. At that point, there had been more dangerous perils ahead that occupied my mind.

"Don't forget what I said about the saloon!"

Crowder Gentry was a sullen loner from Tupelo, Mississippi. It was rumored that he sought out and surrendered to Union troops for fear that he would be killed in the War. Crowder had been bought by Bull at the same time as Quin. He had no friends at Rock Island nor at the timber camp. Quin had tried to befriend Crowder at Rock Island and the timber camp and was continuously rejected by Crowder.

I'm a free man and I'll go into a saloon if I want to. To hell with what Quin said. Crowder's narrow brown eyes were filled with jealousy as he looked at Quin's back. *Quin has a lot of money. I don't care how he got the money, but he is afraid of his past, and I plan to get my share of the money.*

Dakota spoke up and explained what a carpetbagger was. "Now is a good time for me to tell you of a conversation I had with someone who returned to Texas just after the War. He left recently after spending two years in Texas under carpetbagger rules. The carpetbaggers carried the statement "to the victors go the spoils of war" to the extreme. No southerners can hold political office or vote, and most of the banks were taken over by the carpetbaggers. In Texas, they have done away with the Texas Rangers and now have a state police made up of carpetbaggers.

"A lot of good people in Texas have turned outlaw. I'm sure it will be similar throughout the south. I know a lot of you are from Louisiana, Mississippi and Alabama and want to go home.

"There has been no one available to tend to the plantations in the deep south. The plantations will lay barren of crops and most of the game animals will have been killed and eaten. I think you should go home but don't think it will be the same. If you have anything, there are those that will try to take it from you, and it won't be just carpetbaggers. I suggest you stay quiet and get the lay of the situation. Remember my offer."

"Buy yourself some jerked beef in Charleston. You will need it on the trail going home. We will meet back here an hour before dark, this evening, and see who wants to go with me. For those who choose to go with me, we'll be leaving early in the morning."

Creed mounted his black gelding and rode off on his way to Charleston and headed to the gunsmith's store to see if he had gotten more of the new Henry rifles. Creed would like his whole crew to have one.

He had seen several of his men since he entered town. He ignored them as they ignored him. No nods, waves, or words were exchanged. He was aware that every woman he passed turned her head toward him and smiled. He also was aware some men turned their heads toward him, sizing him up and probably wondering who he was and where he had come from.

"Got in a shipment of the new Henry rifles," said the gunsmith when Creed came through the door. "How many do you want?"

"I don't need any more, just need more of the .44 ammunition."

"You might wish you had them Henrys when you get in Indian trouble in the Territory."

"How many do you have?"

"I could let you have ten."

"I don't need them but if you give me a good price, I will buy them all. I'm sure I could sell them at a profit to my partners if we are attacked."

"Think of it as *when* you are attacked; not *if* you are attacked," laughed the gunsmith.

"How much?"

"I'll let you have them for seventy each."

"That price includes the scabbards? I'll take 'em," said Creed before letting the gunsmith back out over the scabbards. "I'll get several pack horses. I'll need ten cases of the .44-caliber rifle ammunition."

Creed rented six horses with pack saddles, loaded the rifles and ammunition, and sent Billy back to the camp. "Give them to the other Texans and instruct them to give any rifles they now have to others who don't have a rifle.

The horses are to be returned to the stable here in town."

"Hey Quin! Need to talk to you."

Creed looked at the drunk struggling to push back the long brown hair in his face. It was Crowder Gentry.

"You are right Gentry; we do need to talk." Dakota looked around to see who might have heard Gentry.

Hatless, drunk, and brave, Gentry approached Creed ready to speak when Creed held his hand up to stop him from coming closer as he backed up to keep his distance. The stench on Gentry was overwhelming. "I think we should have this talk in a more private place. Get on your horse and we'll ride back toward camp."

Gentry, oblivious to Creed's reaction to his smell, seemed pleased with Quin's response. After riding a mile out of town Dakota turned and rode another mile toward an oak covered hill.

"Okay, what's on your mind?"

"Quin, you seem like a troubled man. You have a lot of money and you're scared of your own name. I don't know how much you have but I'll help you protect your name and your money," Gentry said slurring each word.

"What are you talking about, Crowder, why would I need your help? And assuming I did, what would it cost me?"

"That will depend on how much you have; I want half of it."

"How do I know you will keep your end of the bargain, Crowder?"

"You don't, you'll just have to trust me," Crowder mumbled grinning.

"Is anyone else in on this, Crowder?"

"No, just me."

"I want you to think about a question I'm going to ask

you. Stay with me and think it through. I know you've been in a swimming hole and came out of the water finding a leech on you, haven't you?"

"Uh, yeah."

"What did you do with the leech?"

"I jerked it off and killed it."

"Why didn't you just leave the leech alone and let it stay on you?"

"Because it would just keep sucking my blood."

"Crowder Gentry, you answered my question as to what to do with you. I always want anyone I kill to know the reason why."

"That's not fair. You must have stolen that money and I agree not to tell if you give me half."

"Get off the horse Crowder. Leeches always gather more leeches, and I don't want your blood on it."

Dakota rode into camp with the horse Crowder Gentry had been riding. "Gentry just had to go get a taste of cheap whiskey, so he won't be joining us. I brought my horse and saddle back because he will not be needing it," Creed announced.

He pulled Donny aside. "Donny, I had to kill Gentry. Have you seen any of the men talking to Crowder of late?"

"Crowder was different from the other men. No one ever talked to him much. Seemed that he didn't want to talk to anyone, and all the men believed the story going around about him deserting and surrendering for fear he would get killed in the War."

"Keep your ear to the ground, Donny. Listen for anyone complaining about Gentry not joining us and let me know about it."

"We'll keep a campfire burning tonight but let's keep

three outriders circling the camp. We will fill them in on anything they missed when they come in. Let's call the men together and have a meeting!"

The fourteen Texans and seven from Louisiana who lived west of the Mississippi would ride with Creed to Texarkana. From there those men would head to their homes or what was left of them. The others would go back to the ferry and cross the Mississippi back to Wickliffe then head south to Alabama, Mississippi, and Southeastern Louisiana. Creed again let them know where he would be. "Good luck and Godspeed! If all goes right, we'll see you in Nacogdoches."

CHAPTER SEVEN

Return to The Flying Dust

It seemed that Kathy Ann and Rascal were on Creed's mind constantly. He had never thought about love before, but he knew he was in love with Kathy Ann and didn't know how to deal with it. Most girls were married by the time they reached 16 or so and he figured Kathy Ann was about that age. He knew she had feelings for him, but he had plans that he needed to fulfill before he could think about asking her to marry. *Would she wait for him long enough for him to build the "Empire" that he dreamed about?*

Creed and his group left the camp and set out for Texarkana, which was approximately 411 miles away from Charleston. They were traveling at least thirty miles each day and were near Little Rock after eight days. Creed had visited with each of his crew daily. They all had expressed that they would like to visit family and friends for at least a couple of months. An agreement was made to meet him in Nacogdoches in sixty days.

He decided to ride the gelding and one of the Flying Dust mares. The horses would be switched out as needed on his speedy journey back to The Flying Dust Ranch.

Before he left Little Rock, Dakota located the Wells Fargo Office and set up an account. He had been shocked when he had counted all the Gold Certificates in the money belt, and it angered him all over again at Bull McElroy. With a mix of $500 certificates, $1000 certificates and even three $10,000 certificates there was a total of $91,000 in the belt that Bull had worn. He still had more than $1000 dollars in his pocket. Creed memorized his account number with Wells Fargo and kept the receipt which he sewed between layers of his belt leather.

Riding at least thirty miles a day, and switching out his horses as needed, Creed was less than 20 miles away from his destination after seven days in the saddle. Creed was tired of jerked beef and hardtack but with coffee at night it kept him going. He found a place to bathe and change clothes, then climbed back in the saddle. He arrived at the Flying Dust just before dark. He had been gone for 19 days. It seemed like a lifetime.

Rascal met him in the front yard. He barked and yipped, moaned, and chased his tail. Then he jumped into Dakota's outstretched arms and licked his face. Paul Fairchild opened the front door with a rifle in the crook of his left arm.

"It's Dakota, Mr. Fairchild. I hate coming in here just at dark, but you told me I would always be welcome so here I am."

"You get down and come in here, Dakota! You're a sight for sore eyes! We just sat down for supper. Hope you're hungry. Grab your rifle and I'll get one of the hands to take care of the horses. I'll have them bring your packed goods in and put them in your room. I'm so glad your back! Kathy Ann has been moping around here like a sick calf since you left. She wouldn't even go to the dance last week."

"Dakota! I knew you would come back," Kathy Ann squealed as she rushed out the door. She looked at her father and then reached up and kissed Creed on the cheek.

After supper, Kathy Ann helped her mother straighten up

the kitchen. Creed used this time to tell Mr. Fairchild that he needed to talk to him in private.

"Do you want to talk now?"

"No! It can keep until tomorrow."

"After breakfast be okay with you?"

"Sure," answered Creed. "I hate to be devious, but I do want privacy,"

In the morning Bob had two horses at the front gate saddled for the men. They rode off quietly, with Rascal in close pursuit. They rode to a spring-fed creek where they dismounted and found a log to sit on that had a view of anyone approaching.

"Mr. Fairchild, I was halfway to Texas when I stopped and turned around and rode here. I am young, and I know almost nothing about women. Circumstances prohibited me from meeting or even talking to a girl other than my mother and two sisters who are now dead. I realize that most girls marry before they reach eighteen years of age. You see I have plans for my life's work that I need to put into place. I have developed strong feelings toward Kathy Ann. I never told her that. The farther I got away from her the greater I feared she might marry someone else, never knowing my feelings for her.

"Dakota, has Kathy Ann expressed her feelings toward you?"

"No! We have never been alone except when I drove her home that first day."

"I think Kathy Ann had been looking for a mate before she met you. She never missed a dance and always talked to her mother about guys she had met at the dances. Why don't you talk to her and tell her your feelings?"

"That's what I wanted your permission to do. Do you

think that I need Mrs. Fairchild's permission also?"

"Maude and I have already talked about you. She's impressed with you and we'll give you our permission to talk to her."

Kathy Ann was standing at the front gate when they returned. "I should sic Rascal on both of you. You knew that I would want to go with you regardless of where you went."

"Hey, Dakota, why don't you and Kathy Ann ride out to the creek for a while and catch up on things. It's been quite a while since you've seen each other. Put her on my horse and you take her back to where we've been."

"What did you and Father do out here?"

"I asked your father permission to speak to you about the feelings I have for you.

"And?"

"He gave his and your mother's approval."

"So maybe you could tell me what this is all about, Dakota," Kathy Ann said with a sweet smile, making him just a little uncomfortable and a little nervous.

"Well, uh, from the first time I saw you, you—well, you excited my heart. The more I was around you the more I wanted to be around you. I mean—I was halfway to Texas when I turned around and came back to tell you how I feel."

"You're a beautiful girl and am sure you have other guys telling you how they feel about you. I was afraid you might marry one of them before I could tell you how I feel."

"Now, I need to explain. I have something I must do, and I will be gone for at least a year. I want to know; do you have any romantic feelings for me?"

"Of course, but how could I let you know? It broke my heart when you left. This is the first time we've been alone since the first day you were here, and that was a pretty horrible day. Mom and Dad think a lot of you Dakota, and that's important to me. Why do you have to be gone for a year?"

"If it's okay, that's something I want to tell you, your mother, and your dad together. Let's ride back to the ranch and see if we can catch up with them."

"You know what, Dakota? This is the happiest day of my life."

Back at the house, Paul and Maude were happy to see the smile on Kathy Ann's face. Dakota was the first to speak. "There is something I need to say while we are all here together. Kathy Ann and I have strong feelings for each other. But I have a previous commitment that I must complete. It will take at least a year; maybe longer. I know things change with time and I don't expect Kathy Ann to sit by waiting for me to return. I've told her my feelings for her, and she expressed feelings for me. As soon as I complete the task, I would like to return here and court her if she is still available."

"Is this task so important that you are going to risk losing Kathy Ann?" Paul asked.

Before Dakota could answer Maude asked, "What is this task that's worth losing her?"

"Let me answer both questions," Creed replied.

"Before you answer, Dakota, I will still be available. When you return, we will pick up where we left off."

"That means so much to me! Thank you, Kathy Ann."

"My commitment to the task was made before I met her. It was made to a group of friends that I fought with in the War. It's an opportunity for me to build a business that someday could make a tremendous amount of money."

"Is money more important than Kathy Ann?" Paul continued before Creed could answer. "Money would never be a problem if you married Kathy Ann. Dakota, I want to tell you straight out that Maude and I don't intend to let Kathy Ann marry and move away from here. We would want you to stay here and work on the ranch and raise our grandchildren. It would be a life of luxury for you. What more could you ask for?"

"No! Money is not more important to me. My commitment to the men who saved my life is more important. I have become their leader and am committed to taking care of them as I have for several years. Also, I would want to provide for Kathy Ann and depend on no one else. My coming back here was to simply let her know my feelings toward her and learn of her feelings. I will return in less than a year, Kathy Ann. I've got to go now. Someone hold Rascal to keep him from following."

After loading up his pack horse, Dakota turned and rode off without looking back or giving a wave. Although he didn't have full approval of Kathy Ann's parents on his decision, he did have Kathy Ann's and that was good enough for him. Kathy Ann, her eyes brimming with tears, watched Dakota ride away until he was out of sight.

CHAPTER EIGHT

Fort Smith

Creed rode as hard leaving as he did to get there. He decided to divert his trail away from Little Rock and go to Texas through Fort Smith. It was a little farther, but he could make up some of the time by crossing over the White and Arkansas Rivers upstream in more shallow water instead of crossing the rivers near Little Rock.

If they were to drive the Longhorns north through the Indian Territory, he needed to know more about the area and what they could expect there.

When he arrived in Fort Smith nine days after leaving Little Rock, Creed was alarmed by the desperate looks on the faces of many that he passed. *What is going on here?*

Creed stopped at the first public stable he saw. He paid the hostler for one day rent to board his two horses and to store his belongings in the tack room.

He needed answers. A person could get shot for just asking someone the wrong question. For instance, questions about how many cows and land you owned could get you shot. But he had to know some things.

Creed looked at several prospects until he picked one, a frail young man who looked hungry, worn out, desperate, and walked with a limp.

"My name's Creed. I'm new to this part of the country. I've got a silver dollar here for you and I'll buy you lunch if you'll sit down with me and let me ask you some questions."

"Best offer I've had in days, but I gotta warn you, I don't have many answers, or I wouldn't be in the shape I'm in. Name's Bo Brailey and I'm mighty hungry."

Creed extended his hand to Bo. "You pick the eating place."

"Bo, order anything you want. Chow down and we'll talk when we get through." Later over coffee, the two chatted.

"Bo, I don't want you to think I'm trying to interfere with your personal business. I've been away from this part of the country for a long time and am trying to find out what's going on in the Indian Territory, Arkansas and Texas. Can you fill me in on what's happened these last couple of years?"

"Well, since the War, the army has been kickin' the butts of the Indians and forcing them outta Texas and back onto their reservations in Indian Territory. Most all the buffalo have been killed by the white buffalo hunters and the Indians are hungry and ain't staying put. The ones that leave the reservation are raidin' and stealin' anything they can to survive."

"Isn't the government feeding them?" Creed asked.

"They're tryin' to get them to raise corn on land that couldn't raise a weed. The cattle they give 'em can't live on brush, and they kill 'em to eat before they can breed."

"What's happening in Texas these days, Bo?"

"The Yankee government disbanded the Texas Rangers. They now have a state police force made up of mostly carpetbaggers. They are a lot of desperate people down there and a lot of them have turned bad. A lot of theft is going on and a lot of carpetbaggers have started dying of lead poison since they disbanded the Texas Rangers. There is no law that can control the outlaws except the Rangers."

"Any news on the New Mexico Territory?

"A lot of Comanche have headed out there instead of going to their reservation in the Indian Territory. They're runnin' into resistance from the Mescalero Apache. You probably know the Comanche have been fierce enemies of all the Apache tribes for years."

"Yep, but I've seen some mighty desperate people here in Arkansas since I've been here, can you tell me about them?"

"Most of the desperate ones are from Texas and I'm one of 'em. The carpetbaggers are not interested in the poor patches of mountains in Arkansas. There are too many clans to fight to get any part of the mountains and they could not hire anyone to take them. The mountaineers now every nook and cranny, and they are as slick as greased marbles. The men, women, and kids have shot rifles from near birth. They are famous for bark shootin' squirrels so's not to waste any meat."

"I don't want to be nosey, but what's your story, Bo?"

"I got shot in the leg in the battle of Shiloh. Somehow, I got left behind by the Union and my own troops. I guess everyone thought I was dead. Dead soldiers were all over the battlefield, both Yanks and Rebs. Come nightfall I crawled toward the south and away from the battlefield and the dead bodies. I suspect I passed out for lack of blood. I reckon at least several days had passed when I finally woke up, and I was in a wagon. I guess the hard rain in my face refreshed me and cooled me down. I was burning up with fever.

"The wagon had stopped under a thick grove of trees. The driver of the wagon placed a tarp over me and crawled under the wagon to protect himself from the heavy rain. The next morning, it had stopped raining. The driver had carried wood in a sling under the wagon to keep it dry and he had a fire going. He handed me a cup of hot coffee. I drank it but what I wanted was something cold to cool down my fever. He told me that he was surprised to see me still alive. He had cut away my pant leg that covered the wound. Gangrene had set in. He told me he was a country doctor of sorts and said if the wound had been lower, he would have cut my leg off to save my life. He told me he had done all he could for me and did not give me much of a chance to live."

"I asked what he had done, and he told me he had left the wound open so that flies would swarm over the wound and lay their eggs in the wound. He wanted the maggots to eat all the infected, rotting, gangrene flesh. If they did, he would pick the maggots out and sew the wound up. If they didn't, he would bury me. Four days later he was sewing me up and left me a crutch he had in his wagon. He gave me a sack of food and wished me luck. He told me he had to get back to his troops. He turned the wagon and headed north."

"It was at the beginning of the War. I was a long way from home, and I could not walk without dragging my leg. I met up with our troops on numerous occasions. They fed me with what they had but could not offer me any transportation and I just couldn't keep up. I kept walking south catching any ride I could on wagon or cart. I trapped fish, birds, rabbits, possums, skunks and squirrels and I made jerked meat with most of it. I ate a lot of bird eggs. I exchanged my jerked meat for beans each time I caught up with our troops. Toward the end of the War, I was still making my way home. Our troops were being overrun and I was not going to burden them by trying to go with them. I finally made it home about six months after the War ended."

"Where is home, Bo?"

"Bowie County, Texas!" He said proudly. "My father, Tobe Brailey, had fought with Sam Houston at San Jacinto. He received the bonus grant of 640-acres from the Republic of Texas for his War efforts. My father bought another section of land from a neighbor. Twelve of his friends wanted to stay close together and picked their bonus land grant in the county. Most of them had bought additional land."

In what area of the county is the land?"

"We are near Old Boston; the county seat of Bowie County is in Boston. You can see some of our land from Glass Hill where the county courthouse sits. Our land runs eastward all the way to Rock Creek. Some of my father's friends are closer to Texarkana and others are near Anderson creek, which is west of Old Boston."

"Are all your father's friends still alive?"

"Nah, but their families still own the land. Before the War with the Union, everyone was doing well. After the carpetbaggers moved in and took over all the public offices and most of the banks, it has been pure hell. There had been no taxes charged or paid during the War. The carpetbaggers imposed back taxes on all the property with large reconstruction taxes and fees. It has taken all the money that the owners of the land could scrape up to pay those back taxes. They sold most of their livestock and used their savings, if they had any, to pay the taxes. Normally that money was used to put in their yearly crop. Now we all are scrambling to raise enough to pay this year's taxes."

"There are no jobs in Texas and people are desperate. We are all going to lose our land and we have no place to go. The land always provided us with plenty to eat. Most of the hogs, rabbits, coons, and other game have been killed off. I have lived off small perch, that I caught out of Rock Creek, and poke salad for the last year and a half I've been home. Not for that I would have starved. I've been here three weeks looking for something better but it's not here."

"Bo, let me ask you one question. Are your friends convinced, as you are, that they are going to lose their property; and they too, have nowhere to go?"

"Absolutely!"

"Okay, I want to make you a proposal. Hear me through then I will answer your questions. This proposal is for anyone who wants to accept it. They will lose their property, but they do not have to move. They will sell me all their property for one dollar. I will pay them back all the taxes and fees that they have paid since the War ended. I will pay all the future taxes. I will give them and their existing family a lifetime estate on the property for one dollar a year.

"They can grow their crops, hunt, and trap as they please. As owner, I will cut timber and run cattle as I please. They can protect their crops with fences as they do now. They cannot cut any timber except firewood or run any cattle other than those raised for your food or milk. I would expect them to protect the land as if it were theirs, against poachers, trespassers, fires, and thieves. All my livestock will carry the brand of the Empire Timber & Cattle Company, which is ETCC."

"What about us huntin' and trappin' hogs?"

"Absolutely, I know everything is open-range unless it's fenced. There will come a day when I fence all the property. I know we will not be able to keep the hogs out and you and your neighbors will continue to have your hog roundups and ear markings as usual."

"Under normal conditions no one would take that deal."

"I know but we're not in normal conditions. I want everyone to understand that I did not put them in this position. If any of them don't want to take the offer, that's okay. I will just try to be a good neighbor to whoever buys their land for taxes due, and they will move the families off. Do you want to take this, that will let you stay on the property?"

"I have another question."

"Let's hear it."

"There are about ten black families that live on my place. They have their community they call Arkadelphia. Immediately after the War and before I got back, they made a deal with my sister. She let them live on our property and would share-crop part of our land. She had no money and accepted their proposal. As a matter of fact, several had started share-cropping way before the War was over. They are good people, Creed, and I would vouch for every one of them. Would you let them stay?"

"Yes!"

"Then let's do it," Bo said.

Creed saw excitement in Bo's eyes and even his slight limp seemed to vanish at least temporarily. Also, Bo seemed to have grown two inches in height.

"Let's go to Bowic County, Texas, Bo, and let me buy some land. I'll pay you to take me around and introduce me to your neighbors. It may turn into a full-time job if you're interested."

"I'm interested. Creed, I'm embarrassed to tell you this, but I had to sell my horse and saddle a few days after I arrived in Fort Smith. I'm going to need a horse before I can go anywhere."

"Don't worry 'bout that. Let's make it a full-time job. I'll furnish you with a horse and saddle and I'll feed you and pay you thirty dollars a month. Bo, can you read and write? I need you to do something for me?"

"Yeah! I finished grade school."

"Make a list of all the people who are now owners of the Texas bonus land grants that you know."

Not only did Bo list his father's twelve friends and their families, but he also listed eight more families that he knew.

Before leaving Fort Smith, Creed went to the office of Indian Affairs for the Indian Territory in the Federal Building. He was seeking information about driving Longhorn cattle across the Indian Territory to the railheads in Kansas. He had heard about Jesse Chisholm, of Scottish and Cherokee descent, driving a large herd of Longhorns through the Indian Territory to Kansas. Chisholm was a Cherokee fur trader and had hunted, trapped, and had traded furs from the Indians for several years in that part of the country. Back then he traveled on a two-wheel cart. His fur trading gave him an advantage.

Creed met with Ryan Maxwell, head of Indian Affairs for the eastern sector of the Indian Territory to find out if they might be willing to contract with him. Maxwell was eager to talk to Creed.

It seems that the head of Indian Affairs for the western sector of Indian Territory had bought some Longhorns from Jesse Chisholm that were driven up from South Texas. He and Indian Affairs had a falling out over something, and he refused to ship any more Longhorns to them.

Texas Longhorns were the only cattle that could survive and reproduce on the sparse vegetation they would encounter in the Indian Territory. Maxwell had just learned that the army was forcing Indians onto the reservations in the Territory at a rapid rate. They needed cattle for the eastern part of the Territory.

The Indians needed a steady supply that they could harvest year-round. Creed walked out of the Indian Affairs office with a contract for one thousand head of Texas Longhorns each month on a steady basis at a selling price of forty dollars a head. Creed squeezed information from Maxwell that the reason Chisholm was not delivering any more was because of slow pay from the government for the Longhorns.

Maxwell promised to pay Creed upon delivery of the thousand head of Longhorns to the Red River crossing and had put it in the contract. Creed planned to drive branded herds and hold the cattle in Bowie County. On the first of each month, he would drive a thousand Longhorns to the banks of the Red River. Maxwell would meet the herd there, and the cattle would be counted as they crossed the river. The first one thousand were to be delivered in ninety days.

Creed gave Bo a hundred-dollar bill to buy an unbranded horse, bridle, and saddle while Creed went to the blacksmith shop. He drew the ETCC brand of the Empire Timber & Cattle Company on a piece of paper. "I want six sets of branding irons. How long will it take?"

"Six hours, and it will cost you three dollars."

"Get to work," said Creed, good naturedly.

He wanted to register his brand in Arkansas so if anyone stole any of his branded stock and drove them to Arkansas, his killing of them would be easier to justify.

"I want to register my brand, please," he said as he entered the registrar's office.

Creed was given a hand full of papers by the clerk.

"Empire Timber & Cattle Company? Humph, must not be a very big empire. Never heard of it. How much branded stock do you have in Arkansas now?"

Creed looked the clerk straight in the eye but didn't say a word. The clerk's shaken voice could barely be heard when he spoke. "That will be twenty-five cents registration fee, please."

Creed met back up with Bo who was leading a tall bay horse. "Good looking horse, Bo."

"Thanks, I knew you would want me to have as good a horse as you, so I could keep up."

"You're right Bo. I want all my riders to ride the best. I want them to dress better than other outfits and be proud of our brand. Creed picked up his horses and with Bo went to the blacksmith shop where he branded all the horses.

CHAPTER NINE

Killing Call-out

Five days later, they arrived in Boston and rode to the Bowie County Courthouse on Glass Hill. Creed registered his Empire Timber & Cattle Company brand at the courthouse and, with Bo's guidance, sought out and found attorney Desmond Duke. Duke was six feet five inches tall and weighed two hundred and eighty pounds. Bo had told Creed that Duke was a prominent attorney who stood up to the carpetbaggers; and not only threatened them with lawsuits, but his physical appearance alone intimidated them even though they were in charge.

After talking to Duke for just a few minutes, the two men signed an agreement for Duke to represent the Empire Timber & Cattle Company. Creed made an escrow consignment with a voucher from Wells Fargo for Desmond to use where needed. He also gave him a copy of the Indian Affairs contract for the Longhorns.

"Duke, I want you and Bo to go with me to the printer's shop. I don't want anyone to see this agreement but the ones who agree to sign it. I will insist on us staying with the printer while he sets the type, and we'll make sure no extra copies are left behind."

"Sounds good to me. This is going to upset the applecart of the carpetbaggers waiting to buy the land on the courthouse steps. I can assure you, Creed, that you will be a marked man in this county."

"Is there any way we can avoid filing these papers at the courthouse?"

"There is no reason that you must record your deeds in the courthouse as long as you have a dated deed signed by the seller and a witness. I will make sure all the taxes are paid in a timely manner. The lease agreement is a private matter. I suggest that we keep a signed copy of the deed and the lease transaction in my safe and you keep copies in Wells Fargo's safe. There are people in the clerk's office who will report any land transactions to the carpetbaggers. I have the list of properties you plan to buy and will stay in the courthouse until I have written out all the legal descriptions and make sure of ownership. I'll handle paying all the taxes and fees that are due to the seller."

When one-thousand blank deeds and lease agreements were printed, Bo gathered all scrap paper from the floor and wastepaper baskets. Duke took the printer by the arm and glared directly into his eyes. The printer looked away. Duke's big hand gently turned his head back straight and held it so he could not turn away again. With the other hand Duke dislodged all the type pieces, removed them from the tray, and dumped them in a pile. "If I hear a word about this, you will be the one I come to see."

Bo was the first to sign a deed and a lifetime lease estate agreement. With a receipt, he was reimbursed the taxes and fees he had paid the carpetbagger officials. In seven days, Creed had bought 22,880 acres of land. He had told the sellers not to mention the sale to anyone. To do so would diminish the image of their lawful authority and rights to the property under the lifetime lease agreement.

Creed turned Bo loose on the west end of the county and

he took the east. They were signing referrals as fast as they could get to them. He made a point to buy contiguous properties from the south along the Sulphur River to the north along the Red River. In two and a half weeks, they had signed an additional 70,800 acres.

Duke searched for Creed and finally found him at the courthouse looking at maps. "Need to talk to you now, in private! Let's go to my office."

"Creed, you know I mentioned to you that you would become a marked man by the carpetbaggers. I think you need to take heed on what I'm going to tell you. You may know some of the things I'm about to mention. Bowie County is unique. In downtown Texarkana you can step across a line in the middle of the street and be in Arkansas. In less than thirty miles you can cross over into Louisiana or cross the Red River to the north and be in the Indian Territory. It is a magnet for outlaws. If they get in trouble in one of the states, they simply go to another state, or the Territory The carpetbaggers use these outlaws to do their dirty work."

"You don't know Hitch McCoy, but he knows you. He is a friend and confidant of mine and is telling me that you are indeed in their crosshairs. They know you are buying up a lot of the county and they feel you're pushing them out. They have hired four brothers from Arkansas to call you out and kill you. You need to get out of Bowie County, Creed."

"When is all this supposed to happen?"

"Hitch doesn't know. I've asked him to look over your shoulder for them and he should let you know when he finds out."

"I'm not going to start running or I would be running the rest of my life. If anything happens to me, get in touch with

Donny Calloway who will be in Nacogdoches in six weeks and give him a copy of the contract for the Longhorns."

The next day Creed and Duke were having lunch in Boston. Creed looked up at the man who just entered. He had one of his .45s cocked before the man took a step. Duke placed one hand on Creed's arm as he waved to the man who walked toward them. He spoke to Creed. "One of the Carlin brothers is outside. I don't know where the other three are, but I assure you they are close by. He is sending someone in to call you out. I will back you if any of the other three enter the fight."

"Thanks Hitch," Duke said.

Before Hitch could be introduced to Creed, a small frame middle-aged man entered the room. "I have a message for Dakota Creed."

"I'm Dakota Creed."

"Milo Carlin says that you are a low-down, lying thief and you need to be killed. He says you are too yellow to come out and fight him like a man. He's going to give you ten minutes, or he will come in and kill you here. Anything you want to tell him?"

"Yes, tell him he won't have to come in here!" The man turned and walked out.

He was confident Hitch would back him if others entered the fight. Creed pulled out his pocket watch. "Desmond, you and Hitch ease out the back door and get situated out front. I will be out in eleven minutes."

The clock was ticking. Creed had never thought of his own death before. It used to not be important to him but now he had Kathy Ann to think of.

It was an unwritten law of the West that if you were called out, you had to answer or live the rest of your life in the living hell of being called a coward.

At eight minutes he could hear Milo Carlin plainly calling him a coward. Creed was cool and patient. He stood and pulled his hat low to shade his eyes. He checked his .45s and loosened them in their holster, then re-checked the Henry. Creed wasn't worried about Milo. He would be in range. His nine-inch barrel would give him more accuracy over a standard Colt. But he would have to watch for a rifle shooter. It was now ten minutes. Creed waited another minute, putting pressure on Milo as to what he was to do. Creed *knew* what he was going to do.

He eased toward the door with his Colt in his right hand and the Henry in his left. Milo was in the middle of one of his rants. Creed moved to his left when he exited the door and was now in the thin shade of the building. Milo was in the sun. Creed jerked his head up and Milo showed fear when he looked into Creed's eyes. Milo was still fumbling for his gun when Creed fired his first shot. The bullet from the Colt lifted Milo from his feet and back about five feet.

Before Creed could move, a rifle bullet whizzed past his head and tore splinters from the wall behind him. Creed dove from the entrance to a water trough at the edge of the porch. One bullet pulled at his shirt as it passed. Another bullet shot from a higher location entered Creed's body on the right side making him drop the .45. He was struggling to fire his Henry when something hit his head making him drift off into a dream world. Everything seemed to be in slow motion until it stopped entirely. His thoughts were hung up. Not going forward or backward. He wanted to fire his rifle. He wanted to be with Kathy Ann. He wanted to sleep. He wanted his Colts. He got nothing but another tug on his shirt. Then things went dark.

CHAPTER TEN

The Recovery

"I was supposed to be guarding a near-dead body. What are you doing awake? Hitch deadpanned and grinned.

"Where am I, Hitch?

"You are at the last place they would ever look for you."

"Where is that?"

"At a sharecropper's home in Arkadelphia."

"How long have I been here?'

"Well, what is the last thing you remember?"

"I remember dying by the water trough outside the café in Boston."

"Okay, let me tell you the rest of the story. You probably should be dead but as you know you aren't. We figure you killed Milo Carlin with your first shot. You moved a hair and missed a rifle bulled that slid past your ear. Jason Carlin fired that shot and I killed him. He was atop the hardware store. You were hit by a bullet in the right shoulder fired by Keith Carlin. Desmond killed him off the roof of the feed store. You were trying to fire your rifle with your left hand and were hit by a glancing bullet to the head. We didn't see where it came from until he fired again, hitting you in your left side. Both Duke and I shot and one of us wounded the youngest brother, Crib Carlin. He was jumping from the roof of the dress shop across from the café. That was six days ago.

"The Doctor removed two bullets and sewed you back together. He said if you had not been unconscious, you would probably have died of shock. Crib Carlin survived and is squealing on the carpetbaggers in court today on charges of murder for hire. You might better stay dead until the trial is over. Desmond is in court today trying to convict the carpetbaggers. He told me not to let him know until after the trial if you woke up. You had a little fever the third day but none since. You've been moving in and out of consciousness and we have been giving you water when you were conscious but no food."

"I thought my throat must have been cut for I'm starved to near death," Creed croaked with a feeble grin.

"I'll fix that. How about a mess of eggs, ham, biscuits, gravy, and grits?" Not waiting for an answer Hitch called to Maw Hickerson to fix food for the wounded.

Maw had a family of ten including her husband Clem. She loved cooking and eating and the cookstove was always hot. The smoke from the wood fire mixed in with the food on every occasion. Maw Hickerson got her large body busy in the kitchen and a few minutes later entered the bedroom with the food. "Here you be, Child! Been worrysum 'bout you. This'll fix you up good as new. The grits be the best ever cooked," Maw said in a jovial voice as she gently raised Creed up in bed and placed a large pillow behind him.

Creed thought he had died and gone to heaven. It could have been because of his hunger but he thought it was the best meal he had ever eaten. By the time he finished eating his thoughts were clear. He saw the large bandage on his left side and peeked under it. There was slight redness far away from the sewn-up wound. *It looked great.* He patted the bandage back in place. He wanted to look at the shoulder

75

wound, but it was in a difficult place to see so he would have to wait.

Creed heard a horse approaching the house. Hitch reached and handed Creed his gun belt and bolted toward the front door with a Colt in one hand and a Henry in the other.

"You know you could get your head blown off riding in fast and unannounced, don't you?" Hitch bellowed.

"You will forgive me for that when I give you the news. Is Creed okay?"

"He is conscious. He's eaten now. Come on in, Desmond, he will be glad to see you."

Duke rushed in announcing his presence. Creed lowered his .45 and placed it nearby. After greetings, Desmond was eager to tell his story. "Crib Carlin was trying to save his own neck and turned on the carpetbaggers. I had filed murder or attempted murder charges against the carpetbaggers, depending on if you died or not. I did this after learning Crib Carlin wanted to cooperate with me on the charges. I got lucky in convincing Circuit Judge Weatherspoon that the carpetbaggers were a flight risk being close to two other state's borders and the Territory. He decided he should hear the case immediately. After hearing Crib Carlin's testimony this morning, the Judge called a recess until one o'clock. The carpetbaggers didn't show up to continue the hearing and neither did their lawyer. There were witnesses that saw them heading north to the Indian Territory. The Judge put out a warrant for their arrest.

The doctor removed Creed's bandages the next week and instructed Creed to use his right arm as much as he could. Still not fully recovered, he put on his gun belt and worked through the pain until there was none.

Desmond filled Creed in on Hitch McCoy's background. "Hitch was from West Texas and entered the War with the Confederates at the age of 20, after his wife was killed in an Indian raid. He wound up in a no-win situation in the trenches of Vicksburg and had been there for over 43 days, wounded and out of food and ammunition."

"His Company wanted to surrender. Hitch would have none of that. He talked two of his friends into escaping with him. They left the trenches and headed south through the thick kudzu vines, and with his good arm, Hitch physically pulled his friends through the thick vines for over a mile when they could not make it on their own power. He found Confederate troops in Natchez, Mississippi, and joined their ranks. Hitch insisted that his friends be treated for their injuries before he was. This was told to me by the two men who escaped with him.

"After the War, Hitch and his two friends headed home. The two moved on when Hitch decided to stay in Bowie County rather than returning to the sad memories he had in West Texas."

Creed planned to leave the next morning. "Bo, find a friend of yours who you can train to sign up sellers and who will ride for the brand. When he's ready, turn your friend loose in any direction you need him. Here's a hundred dollars. Should keep you two eating until I get back from Nacogdoches."

"Creed, I've been meaning to tell you something that's got me a little worried."

"What is it, Bo?"

"I have been followed several times. I thought it would stop after the trial, but it hasn't. You know I have a good bit of money on me, given to me by Duke, for when it is time to pay the seller the money back on their taxes.

"You've said enough. I'm going to hire Hitch McCoy and he'll put an end to this."

Creed stopped by Duke's office to tell him he was leaving the next day and that he would try to stay in touch with him.

"I hate to tell you this, but there are several new carpetbaggers, and their cronies, that have moved in filling the void of those that fled to the Territory. Two of them have come to me wanting to talk to you concerning the Empire Timber & Cattle Company, and rumors they are hearing."

"Well, if they push too hard on you, tell them I am under a contract with the United States Government, which I am. Also, hire Hitch McCoy on a full-time basis and have him contact Bo. Bo has a problem and I want Hitch to handle it. Also make sure Maw and Clem Dickerson are well taken care of."

Duke followed Creed outside to his horse, then swiftly walked in front of Creed and softly spoke. "Look over my shoulder, across the street. Take a good look. Those two came to town a couple weeks ago and have been running rough shod over every Reb they see. If they have a conflict the carpetbag judge lets them off. Since they've been in town robberies have tripled. Keep an eye out for them.

Creed noticed that they had an interest in him as well.

CHAPTER ELEVEN

Jefferson, Texas

Near the Sulphur River south of Maud, Texas, Creed sensed that the two men Duke had warned him about were on his trail the moment they got on it. He checked his guns and backed his boots out of the stirrups. When he reached the river, he stopped, dismounted, tied his horses, and walked away a short distance. Creed picked up a piece of dead log, circled the log over his head and let it fly into the river. When the log hit the water, the splash changed his pursuers from their silent pursuit into two rushing riders trying to prevent Creed's escape across the river. As they passed, he stepped out from behind a tree and into the trail behind them and whistled. They turned, reaching for iron.

Both pursuers fell hard. He emptied their pockets and discovered they were from Cleveland, Ohio. They had thirty dollars and some change between them. Creed threw their weapons in the river and threw a lariat around their feet. He mounted one of their horses and dragged the bodies into the swift water. Creed cut the rope and returned to the north bank covering all trace of them.

Several miles farther south Creed found a good place to hide their saddles and looked for a place to leave their horses. It was almost dark when he stopped near a creek and watered the horses. He threw out a hat-full of oats and released the carpetbagger horses to search for the scattered grain. He tied burlap over the hoofs of his two horses and made a meandering retreat farther south eating jerked beef and chewing on a hardtack.

Creed reached a well-traveled road and removed the burlap and eased onto the roadway heading south. He rode all night by the light of the moon, then left the road and made camp before the light of day.

Having traveled all day and night, Creed was about forty miles south of Bowie County. He fell to sleep thinking of Kathy Ann and Rascal and slept until noon.

He rode into Jefferson after dark and checked into the Excelsior House Hotel with his bedrolls. The smell of magnolia blossoms brightened his expectations of seeing this Texas city in the morning.

Jefferson was built on the Big Cypress Creek. It was a port town for steamships that traveled Northwest out of New Orleans and enter the Red River to Shreveport. They would leave the Red River and enter Caddo Lake and get to Jefferson by going up the Big Cypress Creek. Before the War, steamships brought goods from all over the world to Jefferson and hauled mostly cotton back. It was the most northern and western port in Texas. Jefferson had one of the first telegraph lines in Texas and the only one in East Texas until you reached the gulf coast.

Creed checked on the horses he had left at the public stable, then returned to the hotel for breakfast. The sun was bright, and birds were singing. He chose one of the tables set outside on the sidewalk for dining. A soft breeze filled the area with pleasant sounds and aromas. Often, he could hear fish splashing in Big Cypress Creek and other times, from a different direction, he would hear squirrels barking from tall Cypress trees. The wonderful smell of coffee was everywhere.

Creed was surprised to see a paddle-wheeler steamboat

sitting idle in the port. After asking permission to board the steamship, he found that its captain was waiting for a load back to New Orleans or at least back to the Red River in Shreveport.

Creed had a long discussion with the knowledgeable young captain Lance Devereaux, a Frenchman from New Orleans. Devereaux expressed his fear that he may have to go back to New Orleans empty. He was waiting on a telegraph wire to tell him of any freight available for the trip. If he did not get a load back sometime today, he had decided to give up on Jefferson and deadhead back to New Orleans. Once there he knew he could get a load and go up the Mississippi.

Devereaux shared information about rates, contacts in New Orleans, and what could be shipped on a charter basis. After his long conversation with Lance, Creed expressed an interest in learning the French language and asked him if he recommended any books that could help him. Lance insisted he take one of his many books he had on ship. "This book translates English into French. You can use it and give it back when you come to New Orleans,"

CHAPTER TWELVE

The Wallanders

A straight trail to Nacogdoches would put Creed close to Marshall, too close for comfort. He wanted no trouble and would try to avoid the Marshall area for the time being. Creed decided to go out of his way westward and go through Gregg County. He was not ready to do some important business in the Marshall area but when he was ready, he would take care of it. Creed knew he was on the Wallander's list, but they were on his list also.

His thoughts wandered back to his youth. It had been difficult growing up without a real home and his family had been forced off several good spots where they had squatted. But finally, he and his father had found a spot where they truly wanted to stay. It was a two-acre hollow that had a spring. Water from the spring meandered out of the hollow on the lower west side, and it had an abandoned cabin that was entwined with wisteria vines.

The hollow was not quite deep enough to hide the whole cabin after the wisteria had been chopped from around it, the roof could be seen. There were no trails in the area leading to it. It took two years and many stubbed toes to cut all the vines that encroached the windows and door of the small cabin and from around the spring.

They'd worked hard to have enough vegetables to barter for other goods in Marshall. The vegetables were grown in a secluded area just south of the hollow that had been cleared for a garden and stable. Waste from the stable provided fertilize for the garden. He and his family were not bothered during the two years of peace the area provided.

Once it became a desirable place and all the hard work had been done, the hollow was found by the Wallander clan. The Wallanders were notorious in the area. They owned nothing other than the things they stole. They were known for trying to kill all witnesses to their thefts.

Far more boys were born in their clan than girls and incest was common among them. The boys ran off any suitors of the girls. They all looked alike, thanks to years of in-breeding. They too were squatters. As their clan grew, they would split up and branch out.

Their clan was so large the law avoided them if they could. The Texas Rangers had never been called in to control them for fear of revenge by the clan on those that did ask for help. Quin's father knew who they were the minute he saw them. When his mother and sister Francie recognized them, they both ran trying to get into the cabin.

They didn't know who the rightful owner of the hollow was, but knew it was not the Wallanders. The members of the clan were rumored to exceed fifty, and fifteen of them had attacked the Quin family.

His family had been outnumbered. The Wallanders had not asked them to leave, they just opened fire, killing his mother and Francie at the cabin door. Quin dragged them both into the cabin while Marlie, his older sister, gave him cover by opening fire. At the back of the cabin and near the spring, their father had cut out a camouflaged trail in the wisteria vines that would lead out of the hollow to the south. To get to the trail, a trap door had been built in the floor of the cabin giving access to the spring and the camouflaged trail behind it.

Quin opened fire on the clan while his father carried his mother and Francie and hid their bodies off the camouflaged trail. Marlie helped Quin hold off the clan until their father returned by firing and hitting anything that moved.

Quin knew they could not hold them off much longer and prepared to escape. The logs of the cabin would hold and keep any bullets that hit them but not the windows and door. A lot of lead was coming in. Quin's father packed the ammunition, guns, and food that they had and opened the trap door and took everything he could carry to the stable. He saddled the horses then returned while Quin and Marlie held the Wallanders off.

Quin rapidly fired from different windows and heard sporadic firing coming from the Wallanders. After firing a volley of shots, Quin closed the trap door on his way out and raced up the zig-zag trail. They rode off and hid in a secluded spot less than a mile from the cabin.

After dark, Marlie and Quin slipped back to the hollow to see how many Wallanders were present and to retrieve their mother's and Francie's bodies. Most of the Wallanders seemed unconcerned about their dead and wounded and were more interested in drinking 'shine. Marlie and Quin witnessed several fights break out among the Wallanders that were cheered on by their kin. They made the count of Wallanders present and then carried the bodies of their sister and mother back to their hideout and buried them.

Quin knew that he and Marlie had killed at least six of the original fifteen. They counted twenty-two. Thirteen Wallanders had joined the original group.

"Father, Marlie, I am going to Marshall to find an

equalizer. We're going to kill some Wallanders. I'm taking most of the money we have. You and Marlie sit tight until I return." Late the third day he returned with a saddle bag filled with dynamite. "Around midnight, we will go to the hollow. Father, you and Marlie go north of the hollow and set up there. I will go to the camouflaged trail and ease past the spring to the trap door. One thing, though. Do not raise your heads above the ridge of the hollow until after the explosion.

"I will prepare two feet of fuse line and attach it to the blasting cap here before we leave. I will not attach it to the dynamite until I get the saddle bag placed. Once I light the fuse, I will race back up the trail and get out of the hollow before the explosion. We will finish off any survivors. The explosion will draw a crowd from a long way off. We will come back here and hide out for a while. A lot of people and law will have a lot of questions and we don't want to be involved and entangled with the answers."

At midnight, Quin lit a grapevine twig; and when it glowed, he cupped his right hand around it and the three of them moved out with guns and ammunition. Quin had the two-foot fuse line with the attached firing cap in his shirt pocket. When they got close to the hollow, they could still hear a lot of loud talk and fussing. He again cautioned Marlie and their father to keep their heads down behind the ridge, outside of the hollow, until after the blast. Then, anything that moved in the hollow after the blast was to be shot.

His father and Marlie moved out and he puffed on the grapevine making sure it was lit. He pulled his Colt from its holster a couple of times and then made sure his Bowie was loose in its scabbard. He started down the trail under the thick cover of the wisteria vines with the lit grapevine cupped in his right hand.

A flickering light from the campfire danced around and inside the hollow. Quin paused at the exit of the trail just above the spring. He was going to take his next step when directly below him he saw someone was on their hands and knees drinking from the spring. As he was rising, Quin stepped forward with his Bowie drawn from its scabbard. He cupped his right hand that was holding the lit grapevine and covered the guy's mouth. He drew the Bowie and sliced the man's throat. The jugular veins were severed on both sides and blood spurted in all directions. Quin had to hold the man tight for a few minutes until he bled out. When he went limp, Quin lowered him to the ground and immediately started puffing on the grapevine. After several puffs, the grapevine regained its glow.

Quin made it to the trap door and took one of the sticks of dynamite out of the saddlebag and slightly raised the door. The loud noise from the drunks snoring must have forced others from the cabin. Quin placed the saddlebag of dynamite on the floor and lowered the trap door silently.

He turned his attention back to the stick of dynamite and the firing cap and the fuse line in his hand. To his dismay, six inches of the fuse line was dripping blood. He cut off the section, wiped his hands, stuck the firing cap in the stick of dynamite and touched the glow of the grapevine to the fuse. The fuse line sputtered, and he simultaneously puffed on the grapevine. Two more inches sputtered off the fuse before the fuse caught fire. Quin raised the trap door enough to slip the stick of dynamite with the lit fuse into the saddlebag and lowered the trap door. He turned and ran to the trail in the wisterias.

Quin had only made it onto the trail about fifteen yards before he tripped and fell forward. On the way down, he covered his ears and pulled his body into a fetal position and closed his eyes in preparation for the explosion. The earth shook around him and pushed his body three feet off the ground before dropping him. The wisteria bent over and acted as a springboard when debris crashed into it.

Bells in his head were ringing and every nerve in his body seemed frazzled. Gunfire brought Quin to his senses. He dared not move. He was in the hollow and Marlie and their father were again shooting anything that moved. He heard no shots coming from the hollow. When all the shooting stopped, he called out to Marlie that he was still in the hollow and was okay. It took him several minutes to get on his feet and take his first shaken step.

They counted 25 dead. They didn't know where the extra three came from or how many more Wallanders would come to the site of the explosion They searched their pockets and took every penny they had on them. It wasn't much but it would help them through until they could find another place to squat and bring in a crop. Quin was ten years old at that time. Marlie was fourteen and sweet Francie had been only eleven.

To hell with the Wallanders! I'm going to see Francie's and mother's graves.

CHAPTER THIRTEEN

Alazan

Three and a half days of hard riding after bidding farewell to his mother's and Francie's graves, Creed approached Alazan, a small Spanish community located on Alazan Creek ten miles southwest of Nacogdoches. Tall pine trees reaching sixty feet in the air were everywhere. Francisco Lazarine was the clan leader of a group that fought with Sam Houston at San Jacinto for Texas independence from Mexico. Before the War, when discussions were held about Texas leaving the Union and joining the Confederacy, Sam Houston was outspoken against the idea. He forecast the outcome and the consequences.

Lazarine did not speak out on secession but agreed with Sam Houston. He held his family clan together with a tight fist to keep them out of the War and moved them southwest to distance them from Nacogdoches.

They lived in isolation south of the Angelina River and north of the Neches River. They were renowned vaqueros. They were descendants of conquistadors from Spain, who had overtaken the Aztecs in Mexico and the Incas in Peru in the 16th century with the help of the distinctive world class horses they brought with them. The interbreeding of these thoroughbred horses created the wild mustangs in the southwest.

Creed stopped in a secluded area and made camp shortly after lunch. He washed and groomed his horses. He then bathed and laid out his best clothes for his arrival in Alazan. He knew Spaniards had an eye for horse flesh and respected the care that was given them. They also respected the person who gave the care. Dakota had spoken Spanish from an early age. He took every opportunity to carry on conversations in Castilian Spanish.

The next morning, Creed rode into Alazan. There was not much there except a few well-kept houses, one store, a large blacksmith shop, and a Catholic Church. There were flowers planted and cared-for around every building. Creed was getting a lot of cautious attention. As he was tying his horses to the rail in front of the store, two well-armed vaqueros appeared. One on each side of him. Creed kept his hands away from his weapons. With a big smile and in perfect Castilian Spanish he asked about their famous leader Francisco Lazerine and let them know he wanted to talk with him.

One of them asked. "Did you fight in the War?"

"Yes, but I have moved on and will never speak of it."

Creed knew why he was asked if he fought in the War. Often southerners who fought in the War were resentful of those who did not, and some wanted revenge.

"Why do you want to talk with Señor Lazerine?"

"I want to ask for his help."

"He has no money, Señor!"

That is not the kind of help I need."

After the questions, the vaqueros held their own meeting and agreed to take Creed to meet with Señor Lazerine. "You must agree to surrender your weapons and we will take you to see him." Creed was surprised to see guards posted along the trail that led him to Señor Lazerine's cottage.

They were greeted at the front door by Lazerine's wife Loretta and several teenage grandchildren. The esteemed gentleman was sitting up in bed. After the escorts whispered in Francisco's ear for several minutes, they introduced Creed.

"Señor Lazerine, thank you for seeing me. My name is Dakota Creed."

"Mr. Creed, they told me of your horses. I hope to see them in a day or so. I have been feeling unwell the last week or so and hope I will be better soon."

Creed recognized the look in his eyes. He had seen the look many times at the Rock Island Prison and the slave timber camp. The most terrifying was the look of his deceased father who once stood erect and strong. Creed had seen the progression of his depression starting with the drooping shoulders, not looking at who he was talking to, then to not being able to decide on anything. Worst of all was not getting out of bed. Creed had seen how devastating this kind of depression could be. The souls of many had died for no other reason.

"Is there anything I can do for you, Señor Lazerine?"

"I know of nothing anyone can do for me. I took Sam Houston's lead in not supporting the cessation from the Union, and now the carpetbaggers are punishing me and my followers as they do the ones who fought for cessation from the United States."

"Are they trying to take your land?"

"Yes! By selling everything we own, other than our land, we've paid the back taxes but have no way to pay the current reconstruction taxes or future taxes. We will lose all our land and there are no jobs where we could make enough to pay these taxes."

"Señor Lazerine, I have jobs. That is why I am here. I will hire all your vaqueros. I will feed them and pay them thirty dollars a month. These jobs will be permanent if they remain loyal to you and me and my brand."

"They will do as I say. The carpetbaggers will take the land and run us off. We now have nowhere to go. My vaqueros will need to stay here and find someplace to take our families. I wish now that we had fought for the Confederacy. We might be dead but that might be better than what we face now."

"If I show you a way for you to stay on your land, would you let them work for the Empire Timber & Cattle Company?"

"It sounds impossible at this stage that we could stay on our property. We have elders that will die from heartbreak when we must move. If it were not for our priest, I would entertain making a deal with the devil to stay on our land."

"Señor Lazerine, I am not the devil, and I would like the Priest to give his blessings on what I propose. Could you summon him here and any others that you like and let me make an offer to you? If you accept, it will enable all of you to stay on your property the rest of your lives and give all your vaqueros permanent jobs."

Creed could see Lazerine's spirit and strength rise as he realized a glimmer of hope was being offered. He gave orders to give Creed's weapons back to him. He told both vaqueros present to fetch the Priest and several others to meet him and Creed at the store in an hour.

Lazerine's wife helped him dress and the grandchildren hitched the horses to the coach. The grandchildren assisted their grandfather into the carriage and Creed volunteered to drive. Lazerine examined the horses that Creed was tying behind the carriage. "I want those horse's bloodline to mix with my remuda."

"I will trade you two mares for two of yours," said Creed.

The guards along the path escorted them to the store.

Creed used the travel time to fill Lazerine in on his proposal. By the time they reached the store he began to seem more the true leader he was. He stepped down from the carriage without assistance with his head held high and a glint of power in his eyes.

Creed was introduced to Father Raul Montoya, Priest of the Alazan Catholic Church.

"Father, I want your blessing on the proposal I will be making. I will not proceed without it."

All the deeds and leases were signed with Father Raul Montoya as a witness. Creed paid in gold all the money due them for the taxes previously paid. He also advanced gold coins to the vaqueros that would be joining him. Creed wanted their families to be taken care of while they were off working.

"Señor, I need twenty sets of branding irons. I have one that your blacksmith can copy. Could he have them ready before your vaqueros leave?"

"I'll see that he does." Lazerine said.

"Please give the blacksmith these five twenty-dollar gold pieces. I'll be needing more work done by him. Let me know when he needs more money."

"Father Montoya, I would like to talk to you in private." They retreated to a tree a short distance away. "Father, as an infant I was baptized into the Catholic Church to free me from the original sin I was born with. I have a question and I don't expect you to answer it now. Would you think it through and give me your answer the next time we meet?"

"What is the question, Son?"

"If a person thinks that what he has done in the past is not a sin, but survival tactics for him or his, is it a sin?"

Creed left Alazan for Nacogdoches with four vaqueros by his side: Juan and Jesús Lazerine, sons of Francisco Lazerine, and Hector and Pedro, his grandsons.

He had three deeds each in his pocket for each of the twenty-two tracts of land. The deeds described the 48,000 acres of land he purchased. He had everyone's pledge that no one else would ever see or divulge the content of the lifelong estate lease.

He had twenty other vaqueros heading southeast with twenty sets of branding irons, his two Henry repeating rifles and two cases of .44-caliber cartridges. In tow, they would have the forty mustangs bought from the clan for the remuda. They were branded with the Empire Timber & Cattle Company brand. Ten vaqueros would stop in the Trinity River flats and start branding every maverick Longhorn they found. A maverick Longhorn was one that was unbranded and was not with a branded mother. The other ten would stay there and help with the branding until Juan and Jesús caught up. Then Jesús's crew would go to the Big Thicket with two sets of the branding irons and get to work.

In Nacogdoches Creed bought two wagons to be used as chuck wagons. While the vaqueros stocked the wagons at the mercantile, Creed was buying Henry repeater rifles. He found only eight and bought them and eight cases of .44-caliber ammunition. He replaced his two Henry rifles and sent the other eight and ammunition with the chuck wagons. He would supply them all with Henrys when he found more.

Juan and Jesús left with the wagons and their sons to catch up with their crews. Creed went to Wells Fargo and withdrew enough money to replenish his supply and to pay the taxes that were now due.

When Creed tried to pay the taxes on the property using only the legal description the clerk refused to accept it.

"Why are you trying to pay these taxes? You must own the property before you can pay taxes on it. Anyway, Sheriff Mattingly is foreclosing on that property tomorrow morning and is going to buy it himself. It's his turn," the clerk said as he tilted back his head and looked down his nose at Creed.

"I do own the properties and I'm not letting them be sold to Sheriff Mattingly or anyone else. I have twenty-two deeds to show proof of ownership of the property."

"Have you registered those deeds here in the court records?" The clerk asked.

"No!" replied Creed.

"Well, we don't accept documents to be registered any time after noon of each day. The sale takes place in the morning before we would have time to record your deeds," the clerk confidently said.

"You have misunderstood me. You do accept payment of taxes today, don't you?

"Of course!" Replied the clerk.

"I'm not here to record my deeds. I'm here to pay my taxes," Creed said, smiling.

"If the deeds are not recorded, how do we know if they are not forged documents?" The clerk asked.

"If they are recorded, how do you determined that they are not forged documents?", Creed asked the clerk.

"We look and make sure their signature has been witnessed and been signed by the witness."

Creed placed the signed warranty deeds on the counter. The most prominent signature on the entire page was not that of the seller but that of Father Raul Montoya, Priest of the Alazan Catholic Church.

"Now, how much do I owe you?"

After paying the taxes, Creed thought it best to put the deeds in a safe place. He returned to Wells Fargo and deposited them there. He asked the teller, "Do you know Sheriff Mattingly?"

"Yeah, I know him."

"What can you tell me about him?"

"He was a detective from New York City. He brought eight thugs down with him. As you know, no one can vote and hold public office but Yankees. It was just after the War and they were the only Yankees here and the eight thugs voted him in."

"What does he look like?" Creed asked.

"Look out the window. See all the Derby hats? That's him on the left with his eight deputies."

"Does anyone else in town wear a Derby hat?"

"Nope!"

CHAPTER FOURTEEN

River Rats

Creed was a young man who would take every opportunity to avoid trouble. He would get out of Nacogdoches before Sheriff Mattingly came after him. *As soon as Mattingly finds out that he had been beaten out of his turn, he could turn deadly, and could end up dead. I do not want that, so I'll ride south.*

Creed forded the Angelina River and continued south to a community called Lufkin, a few miles north of the Neches River. The only thing there was a trading post and a few scattered settlers.

The four riders saw Creed at the same time Creed saw them. Smiles broke on everyone's faces. It was Donny Callaway and Erskine Philbrick on their way to Nacogdoches. Two riders were with them that Creed didn't know. The two others were introduced as cousins of Erskine's. It took only a few minutes for Creed to have an opinion of them. They were both hungry, strong, and willing. Creed knew by their demeaner that they would ride for the brand. They looked the same as Erskine the first time Creed had seen him. They were the kind you would want on your side if you were in any kind of fight.

Creed brought them up to date on what was happening. He asked them to go on to Nacogdoches and relay his message to them. "Donny, some of them may be late in arriving. Pick out someone to stay behind to tell them what's going on and where to meet up with you."

"Try to stay clear of Sheriff Mattingly. If you do bump into him, tell him nothing. If he wants to know where you got the horses, tell him you bought them from Paul Fairchild at the Flying Dust Ranch in Kentucky. I'm going farther south to the Trinity River and meet with the vaqueros I've hired. I want to make sure there are enough maverick Longhorns there to fill the first delivery. I'll come back here to the trading post in two weeks and wait for you."

Before leaving, Creed went into the trading post and introduced himself to the owner Ralph Tillman. Tillman was a big strong man and gave Creed all his attention. He was born in Texas, and it showed. His mannerism let everyone know what side of the fence he was on and this was important to Creed.

The Neches River was only twelve miles south of the trading post and Creed wanted to cross before dark. He had no idea how far Mattingly would pursue him. Even though he had broken no law, he knew Mattingly would be angry about his recent purchase and would want to talk to him.

After he crossed the river, it was still light enough to see two or three miles farther south. A large, high hill was visible. He would make a dry and fireless camp halfway up. Creed removed his saddle and pack from the horses, hobbled them and turned them loose to graze. Before daylight Creed was in a concealed position where he could see all the way back to the river. He sat motionless for two hours. He saw deer, hogs, and a few Longhorn cattle but no horses or riders. He casually gathered his horses and headed south chewing on jerked beef and a hardtack.

Creed was fifty miles from the Trinity River. With the pack horse loaded down with rifles and supplies, he would try to make thirty miles today and arrive at the Trinity River by noon the next day. He had hoped to catch up with the wagons and the vaqueros. The vaqueros were more familiar with the area and knew where to cross the Angelina and Neches Rivers. That knowledge let them be farther down the trail than Creed thought they would be.

The number of maverick Longhorns Creed saw astonished him. His progress was slowed with his attempt to count them. He gave up when the count rose to over a thousand. Maverick Longhorns could be claimed by anyone with a hot branding iron. The information Creed received from Indian Affairs convinced him of the importance of branding.

Creed saw the campfire well before dark. He made sure he was seen before getting too close to the camp. He held his hands high away from his weapons and when he was within hearing distance he hollered. "Hello, camp, Creed comin' in!"

When he mentioned the number of maverick Longhorns, they agreed that there were enough mavericks for both crews to work within 100 yards of each other. They turned in early and woke early, anxious to join the rest of the crew.

Before noon two vaqueros were seen racing toward them. Creed recognized the horses as being his and Jesús recognized the riders as part of his clan.

The news they brought was not good. The evening before, the crew had been approached by ten Ratas del Rio. River rats were common in Texas especially since the War. They were low-lifes who made their living on and along the rivers—fishing, hunting, and stealing. They drank, gambled and fought. They would even steal fish from other fishermen's lines, including those of other river rats, which often led to killings.

Antonio and Armando Lazerine said that the day before they had seen them at a distance and had them well covered. "When they arrived at the branding camp, they said they wanted coffee. We told them we had none to spare. We had them covered with the two Henrys as well as our other weapons. They seemed excited about seeing the Henrys and could not take their eyes from them. We showed enough force to persuade them to leave," Antonio said.

"We posted double guards throughout the night. When we spread out this morning and started our branding, the ten river rats swept in and shot Roberto and Edgardo from behind, hitting Roberto in the shoulder and Edgardo in the arm. The rats grabbed the Henrys and a case of ammunition from Roberto and Edgardo and rode off.

"Edgardo and Roberto should be okay. We cleaned up their wounds. Their only danger now is infection."

"Antonio, can you lead me to their trail?"

"I can, Sr. Creed!"

"Juan, you and Jesús go on to the camp and keep branding mavericks. I'll send Antonio and Armando back as soon as they put me on their trail."

"You can't tackle that bunch by yourself. Let's get the whole crew and we will wipe them out for good," cried Juan.

"Juan! Edgardo and Roberto got shot riding for the brand. The brand is not going to have a reputation that anyone can mess with us. They will learn that if they mess with the Empire Timber & Cattle Company, justice will be swift. Those who attempt such will be wiped out. I will let two of them live to spread a warning to others."

Creed left his pack horse with the wagon. He retrieved

one of the Henry rifles and a saddlebag full of ammunition transferred it to the saddle of the black gelding. He also gathered his scope, moccasins, a sack of jerked beef and some hardtack. Just before nightfall Antonio and Armando set Creed on the rats' trail and they headed back to the branding camp.

Creed had a hard time going to sleep. *Why was he so worried about the river rats?* He should have the advantage of surprise and he had never seen a river rat that was a better marksman than he. Most of them would be drunk, or hung over, but then there is always the risk of a lucky shot. Then it dawned on him why he was worried. When he was fighting the Comanches, Wallanders, or the Union soldiers, it mattered little to him if he lived or died. Now, it made a big difference. He could visualize his Empire in reach. His men and the Lazerine clan were depending on the success of the Empire. It was his dream for Kathy Ann and her family. He had everything to live for and now wished he had brought help.

When Creed awoke, thick heavy fog engulfed the flats of the Trinity River. Creed put on his moccasins and walked, leading his horse, to be closer to the signs on the ground. Creed was now on the river rats' trail and the fog was burning off. He got on his horse and, around noon, could hear the rapid firing of the Henrys, and laughter from the shooters.

Creed checked his weapons, tied his horse, and slung the saddlebag of ammunition over his shoulder. He cleaned the lenses on the scope and hung it around his neck. He stopped a hundred yards from their camp and looked through the scope toward the rats. Creed counted only seven men, all of whom were shooting floating targets in the river. Creed noted their weapon positions and determined their demeanor. Most of them acted like they had been drinking.

It bothered Creed that he located only seven men. Creed returned to his horse and made a wide loop to the north then to the west. He took another look with the scope when he was north of them. He now could locate only six men. They turned from the river and disappeared.

What are they doing? Finally, it dawned on him. Creed looked at his watch and it showed one o'clock. In Mexico, a siesta is taken each day throughout the country. The custom had hung on in Texas.

Creed decided he would have his first battle near where he was. He tied off his horse and moved forward to a location he could defend and escape from. He would be ready when they got up from their siesta. His plan was to pick off as many as he could before return fire from the rats would chase him off. Creed waited until he felt safe, then moved west looking for another place to do battle. Once he found a defendable place, he moved back to his northern position and waited.

Creed quietly moved near a giant fallen oak tree. The trunk was on the ground and had a large limb that was about four feet off the ground. Creed crawled into the crotch of the fallen oak with the large limb at his back and waited.

His mind wandered to Kathy Ann. He thought of her often, until thoughts of building the Empire Timber & Cattle Company gently pushed her aside. Creed felt guilty about that but thought Kathy Ann would understand.

They were stirring! Creed wanted to start shooting before they could get to their rifles, especially the Henrys. He saw only four, now five. They were standing close together. Creed took an extra second and aimed at the first rat's head.

When that one's head exploded, he took body shots at the other four before anyone returned fire. He knew he missed one. When they did return fire, it was with pistols, which were out of range. Creed could hear a lot of screaming. The return fire was coming from a wide area and not coming anywhere close. *Where were the Henrys?* Creed tried to get a count of those left. He reloaded his Henry and took shots at things he could see, a foot, arm, or where a head should be, then heard someone scream when he fired at two of his targets. Ten yards apart, two of the rats opened fire with his two Henrys they had stolen. They each rapid-fired the fifteen shots in the Henry. Creed had hunkered down behind the giant tree trunk. When the firing stopped, Creed let out a blood-curdling scream.

"We got him!" One of the rats shouted.

"Hurry and reload and let's make sure."

"Let's go, sounds as if he was hit hard, but we don't want him crawling off and getting away," one of them said.

Creed heard them running. He peeked over the top of the log, raised his Henry and fired twice. Even though the rats were running forward, when the bullet from the Henry hit their chests the force of the bullet pushed them backward and off their feet.

Creed ducked behind the trunk and rolled under the limb. He crawled through a leaning pine thicket, which gave him cover, and retreated to his horse. He replaced the two cartridges in the Henry along the way. He mounted and headed west to the location he had chosen. After getting out of rifle range of the rats, Creed ran his horse and made as much noise as he could. He wanted them to follow. When he first located the hideout, he nearly passed it up. The sun was high enough then to blind him as he looked west. The chosen location was near one of the many flats in the Trinity River bottom with no trees to block the sun. The location was nothing more than a small windrow of driftwood that was created by flood waters from the Trinity River.

Creed rode past it two hundred yards to the next timber. He jumped from the horse, tied him to a small tree in the open, and raced back to the windrowed driftwood. Creed let out the loudest pain cry he could muster and moved forty feet east toward the end of the windrow. He held the Henry in his right hand and one of his nine-inch Colts in his left. He saw three of the rats racing toward the driftwood.

"Hold up!" One of them shouted.

"There's his horse," another pointed out.

The three jumped to the ground and ran to the driftwood.

"He might be dead. I heard him scream. Let's wait him out. He's not going anywhere without his horse."

They were less that forty feet from Creed, and well in range of his Colts. He eased the Henry to the ground and palmed the other Colt.

All three of the rats were concentrating on Creed's horse when they heard his demand. "Put your hands up and don't move."

Even looking down the barrel of two Colts one of the rats could not resist going for his gun. He died at the feet of the other two rats with his gun still in his holster. The other two pushed their hands in the air even higher. Creed removed their weapons and led them to the tree line.

"Let's have a talk. My name is Dakota Creed and I own the Empire Timber & Cattle Company. Yesterday, you and your gang shot two of my vaqueros. How many were in the gang and how many got killed back there?"

"Ten—and you killed every one except us two," whined

one of the younger men.

Creed had killed four on the opening volley of fire. He killed the two that had the Henrys, and three are here. He must have killed one randomly firing.

"You both need killing also but I'm going to let you live because I want you to tell everyone you see that they better not mess with the Empire Timber & Cattle Company."

Creed took a thin hemp pigging tie from his waistband and unplaited it.

"Listen up! Lay on your belly facing me. Take off your bandanas and stuff them in your mouth good and tight. If I hear a sound out of you, I will kill you. Now roll over on your left arm, stretch out your right arm and spread your fingers. Any resistance will get you killed."

Creed tied the pigging tie tight behind the second joint of their trigger finger. There was no resistance but there were moans and muffled cries when they realized what was about to happen. Creed drew his Bowie and cut the finger off at the joint above the unplaited pigging tie leaving only a nub.

"I want you to never forget me. Every day of your life that you look for your trigger finger I want you to think of this day. These are the things that will happen to people who mess with the Empire Timber & Cattle Company."

Creed put the two on their horses. "If I ever see you two again, I promise you I will kill you on sight. Now get the hell out of here."

Their screams of pain could still be heard long after they were out of sight. He retrieved the two stolen Henrys and tied the Henrys onto his saddle. He stuffed the remaining .44 ammunition in his saddle bag.

A mile away Creed looked back. The buzzards were already swarming over the area he had just left.

CHAPTER FIFTEEN

Branding Camp

Creed arrived back at the branding camp in time to see what looked like magic occurring. A vaquero had his lariat pulled tight around the horns of a Texas Longhorn. As the Longhorn neared the branding fire, a quick lunge sideways by the horse made the Longhorn turn and kick his back heels high in the air. Another vaquero's lariat raced out from his hand, hit the ground, and bounced, or was pulled up, around the back legs of the Longhorn and was pulled tight as his horse backed up. The vaqueros pulled in opposite directions until the Longhorn fell to the ground. Another vaquero ran to brand the animal.

The vaquero raced back to the fire, reinserted the branding iron in the coals and reached for another white-hot iron. The vaqueros loosened their lariats and flipped them off the horns and the legs of the branded Longhorn. A herder had another Longhorn ready, and the process was repeated over and over.

There were four branding fires going about a hundred yards apart. Each fire had a crew of four vaqueros branding.

"Creed, it has been six years since any Longhorn has been branded on this range. Once we start moving the herd north, if any has a brand that is not ours, do you want us to brand them or try to cut them out?" Juan asked.

"No! Any branded cattle with someone else's brand that follow us will be accounted for in our tally book. The brand owners will be paid for their branded stock. The good part is that we will be eliminating the brand in the area."

"Juan, I would like for you and Jesús to ride with me early in the morning, and Let's see how many mavericks there are in the next twenty-five miles southeast of here. Be sure to pay close attention and look for any brands on the cattle. We will each take an extra horse from the remuda. It will be a fifty-mile ride. So, we'll eat a big breakfast and leave at the break of daylight. Load up on jerked beef and hardtack too."

After eating that night, Creed did as usual. He sat by the fire and studied the book Lance Devereaux had loaned him and thought of Kathy Ann and Rascal.

Early the next morning, they rode out, staying in sight of the Trinity, a meandering river rushing toward the southeast. They saw several groups of Texas Longhorns all moving northwest. The farther Creed, Juan, and Jesús traveled to the southeast, the larger the group size grew. By noon, they had counted two thousand head. The trio turned north for five miles then turned northwest. Within twenty-five miles, there were over five-thousand mavericks, and more were drifting northwest. None of the Longhorns they saw had a brand.

"Juan, Jesús, I am in awe of these numbers."

"Creed, six years ago, if there were two thousand head of longhorns within the twenty-five miles and fifty percent were mature cows, and the percentage stayed the same, how many cows and bulls would be on the same range if all the cows bred each year?" Juan asked.

"If everything went perfect?"

"Yeah!"

After a short hesitation Creed spoke. "Wow! If I figured right, there would be roughly more than 10,000 cows and the same number of bulls. Wow! Twenty-thousand head in twenty-five square miles. I need to sell some cattle!

"Juan, can you find more vaqueros?"

"We know at least twelve vaqueros who could come from Alazan. They have been on a job that they should be through with by now. We also could send someone to the lost pines near Bastrop along the Colorado River. We have thirty vaqueros of our clan that are trying to hold on there until things get better."

"Do any of them have the Texas land grants there?"

"They should if they haven't lost them by now," Juan replied.

"Juan, I will go to the lost pines myself and try to bring all the vaqueros back here. I have at least twenty of my men that are in Nacogdoches. They will be here in about two weeks. I was planning to meet them in the Lufkin community in twelve days. I will go there now and leave instructions on how to get here and then I will leave for the lost pines. We must increase our branding before someone else moves in and starts gathering these mavericks for themselves.

"Juan, Jesús, my men are not nearly as good with cattle as your vaqueros. But they are loyal to the brand and to all those who ride for it. Most of them have fought Indians and others. You and your men can't do your job if you are having to look over your shoulders for river rats or other intruders. My men will act as guards, day and night. Their foreman is Donny Callaway. You both can ask him for help in things that you need help with.

"Juan, let me know how many vaqueros do you reckon it will take to drive a couple of thousand head of Longhorns up to Bowie County? You will need to start driving the branded herd north as soon as possible.

"Creed, last year Jesús and I rode with Jesse Chisholm on the first trail ride to Kansas. We learned a lot on that drive. The cattle would move along at a pace of ten miles a day and could easily be pushed to make fifteen miles. This was done often when the trail boss felt it necessary to get the herd to water. Water won't be our problem. We were herding 2300 head. Chisholm thought 2000 head would have been better. With the distance we are going, we should be able to drive 2500 head fifteen miles a day. We can drive two herds at a time and keep them a mile or two apart. We will need two trail bosses. Then for each herd we will need two-point men out front, two swing men to turn the direction of the herd, two flank riders near the end and two drag riders at the back. You can make the decision on the outriders."

"Juan, you and Jesús will be the trail bosses. Pick your crews."

CHAPTER SIXTEEN

Lawyer Glad Mathews

Creed wanted to cross over the Angelina River before dark. Tillman had told him of a ferry that crossed at Marion about twelve miles east. Marion had been the first county seat of Angelina County from 1846 to 1854. The county seat was moved to Jonesville the latter part of 1854. The dwindling town of Marion still operated the ferry.

The ferry would keep his feet dry, and he could more easily enter Nacogdoches from the southeast. After crossing, Creed found a small creek that fed back to the river. He rode north until he found its origin. It lay in the middle of a long curving hill that slowly reached upward at least a thousand feet. Magnolia trees and numerous dogwood bushes sprinkled the hillside. There was no underbrush to interfere with his view.

Clear, cold water bubbled from the sand. The creek at its origin was three feet deep and had a diameter to match. He moved a small distance away and started a small fire, made coffee and cooked bacon on a green stick and ate it with a hardtack. After he finished eating, Creed buried the fire. The sound of the running water lulled him into the depth of sleep before he could finish his thoughts of Kathy Ann, Rascal, and the Empire Timber & Cattle Company.

The next morning Creed rode to the crest of the curving hill and tied his horses. He slowly walked near the ridge on the west, north, and east sides of the creek. He could see the spring and creek for the entire mile-long walk. He turned around and walked back. He had the same breathtaking view. Over the ridge, the ground gently sloped away for miles in all directions. Tall long-leaf pines could be seen the entire distance. He walked back over the ridge and again looked down at the breath-taking sight. *This is one of the special places in the world that God created.*

Creed rode toward the courthouse in Nacogdoches keeping a keen eye for anyone who looked like a law man. He saw the three shingles that lawyers had hung on posts in front of their offices advertising their trade. He asked a few locals about the attorneys and found that two were carpetbaggers and one was a bitter ex-confederate soldier.

"Are there any other lawyers in town?"

"No!" Came an instant reply.

Creed wanted nothing to do with the one they called a bitter ex-confederate. He was moving on, not backing up. The War was over. He would talk to the younger of the two carpetbaggers.

When Creed opened the door, the young attorney jumped to his feet and rushed to meet him. "Come in, I'm Attorney Glad Mathews."

"I'm Dakota Creed, owner of the Empire Timber & Cattle Company."

"Oh my! Am I glad to meet you! You are the talk of the town around here. Not only does Sheriff Mattingly want to talk to you but so do most of the settlers in this county. No one knows who you are or what kind of deal you made with the Lazarine clan, but they want in. I want to represent you."

"Mr. Mathews, I…"

"Call me Glad. I'm glad to be alive and I'm very glad you walked through my door. I will devote one hundred percent of my time to your needs and with Mattingly breathing down your neck you are going to need my help. I am the one who can handle him and anyone or anything else you might need."

"I can handle Mattingly, but I don't want to have to kill him just because I legally bought land he wanted."

"Mr. Creed, he didn't want to *buy the land,* he wanted to steal it."

"Call me Dakota, I like your attitude. Let's talk."

Glad put a "closed" sign on his door and pulled the shades down. Creed asked him questions about himself for almost three hours and was satisfied with his answers. After that, he filled the attorney in on his goals, without mentioning anything about the money or the life estate agreement that let the seller and his family stay on the land. Creed discussed only the deeds. He made a contract with Mathews and gave him a five-thousand-dollar gold certificate to be put in escrow along with a list of things the attorney was to do. It would be a full-time job. Taking care of Mattingly was at the top of the list. Opening the Empire Timber & Cattle Company Bank would be second.

Mathews was given payroll responsibilities until the Empire Timber & Cattle Company Bank opened. He was also to find out who owned the spring-fed creek and 50,000 acres around it with instructions to buy it.

Creed later ran into Donny, Erskine, and two of Erskine's cousins and told them of his planned trip to the lost pines near Bastrop and purpose for the trip.

"Donny, if you need more money contact Glad Mathews on the courthouse square. Mathews is an attorney and now works for our brand full time. There is a ferry southeast of here that will take you across the Angelina River to Marion. If you go twelve miles west of there you will find the place where we met the other day. Check with Ralph Tillman, the owner of the trading post, and buy all your food and feed supplies there. Twelve miles south of the trading post is a wide shallow river crossing on the Neches River. Keep heading south until you find the branding camp on the Trinity.

"The vaqueros there will be alert to anyone getting close so enter with caution. They were raided the second day they were there and are understandably antsy. Juan and Jesús Lazarine, the crew chiefs, will be expecting you. I want your crew to ride night and day as outriders around the camp. Ride as if you were riding around a herd of sleeping cattle. I want Juan and Jesús branding cattle and not having to worry about raiders. I want your crew to help them with any other task they might have. They will be shorthanded until I return with more vaqueros."

"Creed, do you want us to help the vaqueros with the branding?" Donny asked.

"Donny, I have a lot of confidence in you and all our crew but trust me, don't try to help them with the branding unless you want to embarrass yourself or the crew. Once you see them brand a couple of Longhorns you will understand what I'm saying. Your crew would only be in the way. They are all Spanish and have done this job all their lives.

"I should be back at the branding camp in a little over two weeks. If you, Juan, and Jesús want to head north with a herd, take them through Alazan and I'll catch up with you from there. Try to move as many as you have branded or as many as you can handle. We own most of Bowie County and we can hold them there until Indian Affairs is ready to take them."

Creed left his crew in Nacogdoches and headed to the lost pines near Bastrop. Antonio arrived back at the branding camp with the twenty new vaqueros two days after leaving Tillman's trading post. They were put to work immediately. Donny and Erskine arrived at the branding camp six days after Creed had left them in Nacogdoches. Twenty-two of the thirty-four former prisoners that Creed rescued and sixteen of their family members who wanted a full-time job, were with them. Three former prisoners came from Alabama, two from Mississippi, and five from Louisiana were among them. They had been expected by Juan and Jesús Lazerine, but they had not expected that many.

Juan and Jesús now had eight crews doing the branding. They had enough branded Longhorns to make two drives. Not long ago they started branding all the young stock and castrating all the young bulls. They drove the branded heifers east and the steers north. The bulls would grow faster as steers and the young heifers would be kept behind to replenish the ones taken.

At a short meeting, Donny, Erskine, Juan, and Jesús decided that Donny and Erskine would provide a wood crew that would rotate out each day. Their duty was to find dry driftwood and seasoned cow chips for all the fires in camp. The chips were plentiful and preferred by the branding crews. The chips burned slowly and would create a tremendous hot fire. The wood crew would make sure all the branding fires were started early enough that the branding irons were ready to go at daybreak, and enough chips were available to continuously keep the fires burning all day. The campfires were started each morning and had a ready supply of wood. A reserve of dry wood and cow chips were kept under the wagons to be used if rain occurred.

"Donny, Erskine, we need to drive a herd of branded Longhorns north and scatter them out on the way to give room for more unbranded stock to move in. The branded stock will let others know we are here and claiming mavericks."

"Moving the branded stock out and leaving room here for mavericks will be better than moving the branding camp," said Juan.

"Juan, I've talked to Erskine and we think we have enough hands for us to ride the river from the Big Thicket to Crockett. We will look for signs of anyone trying to join the hunt for Longhorn mavericks and try to encourage them not to. We think all the intruders will come from the south if there are any. Do y'all have a thought on this?" asked Donny.

"How many men do you reckon it would take?" Juan asked.

"We want to have two crews with at least five in each crew, each one of them armed with a Henry and two Colt .45s. We will have plenty of riders left here to guard the branding camp. The five in the crews riding the river will offer enough force to defend themselves and in the long run defend the branding crews. The branding crews must pay attention to their job or end up impaled by a Longhorn. The crew scattering branded cattle up the Trinity will be led by Jack Ranson. His crew can drive the herd northward as they go. Billy McBride will lead the crew that's going to the Big Thicket. We will switch out the river-riding crews each time they return to the branding camp. Jack and Billy will stay on with each new crew."

"That's a good plan, Donny," said Juan.

Jack Ranson and Billy McBride were two of Creed's closest friends. They had all fought together in the War before being captured. Both were older than Creed but respected him as their leader in the War, prison, and the logging camp.

Erskine and Donny divided their crew and Erskine went with his men to be outriders for Juan, Jesús, and their vaqueros. Donny stayed at the branding camp with the rest of his men. They moved the two 2400 Longhorn herds and half the remuda north toward Alazan. The herds traveled separated by a couple of miles.

Traveling fifteen miles per day, it would take a good fifteen days to reach the Red River. The cattle would have some time to graze along the way and hopefully not lose a lot of weight. They would have water assured at the Neches, Angelina, Sabine and Sulphur Rivers and the many tributaries running into them. They would drop 300 head of branded young heifers along the Alazan Creek. They would take the rest to Bowie County.

Juan stayed with his crew branding more Longhorns while Donny protected them by having his crew outriding the area and circling the camp day and night. On several days, Donny's crew confronted strangers. Most were traveling alone. The largest group had only three riders. They were passing through and seemed to offer no threat.

When Billy showed up at the branding camp with his crew that had ridden south to the Big Thicket, he reported to Donny that they had not seen anyone or any tracks. When Jack showed up with his crew that traveled up the Trinity to Crockett he reported, "I followed the trail of nine riders who seemed in a hurry and knew where they were going. No idea of their destination, but they were going up the Trinity toward Dallas. I left their trail on the Trinity just past Crockett. I know every hoof print, and as soon as I get back that way, I'll make sure they kept going."

CHAPTER SEVENTEEN

Lost Pines

The ride to the lost pines was going well until Creed reached the Brazos River. He had heard many tales about the river's swift water and the crumbling sand banks. On the black gelding he rode the east bank of the river until he decided on his entry point into the river and his exit trail out, which was about three hundred yards downstream. The water was swifter than Creed anticipated, and he was swept past the intended exit trail about a mile.

After seeing another potential exit trail ahead, he released the pack horse hoping she would follow. After getting the gelding in position to exit the river, he leaned forward and kicked him in the flank. The horse lunged forward several yards onto dry land before sand started caving in around his feet. After a mighty struggle, he overcame the sand and reached the top. Creed had seen the pack horse being swept downstream behind him as he was reaching the top of the river's bank. Creed gave chase down the river until he was close enough to lasso her. He led her to the river's edge and pulled her up the riverbank freeing her from the crumbling sand she encountered.

Francisco Lazerine had told Creed that his sister, Mariana, had married Perez DeLeon. DeLeon and his brothers fought with Sam Houston at San Jacinto and had received the Republic of Texas bonus land grants. They owned most of the lost pine forest along the south side of the Colorado River and several thousand acres on the west side of the Brazos River.

The last time Francisco talked to Mariana was at a gathering the two clans held on the Brazos to discuss what to do about the potential secession from the Union. War was evident at that time. Both clans sided with Sam Houston and chose not to participate in the War on either side. Juan crossed paths with one of Mariana and Perez's sons a year ago. He told Juan they were living mostly off poke salad and catfish from the Colorado River. He said they had run out of tainted flour and cornmeal months before and were rationing the salt they had left. The pine timber land was not conducive to raising a garden for the lack of sunshine.

"They all will be glad to see you, Dakota," Francisco had said.

All were not glad. The first DeLeon clansmen that Creed found was ready to fight. Their leader was Pasqual DeLeon, grandson of Perez and Mariana. His first words were "You are surrounded, and you will be killed if you don't leave now." Creed knew he was not surrounded and had located everyone in the area before he rode in, keeping his hands away from his guns.

In Castilian Spanish, Creed spoke, "Francisco Lazerine told me I would be welcome here."

"You may or may not be. What do you want?"

After a short conversation Creed learned that Perez had died, but Mariana was holding the clan together. Creed told them of his relationship with the Lazerines and asked for and received an audience with Mariana and most of the clan. Creed learned that all the land had been bought on the courthouse steps by a group of carpetbaggers and the clan had been evicted. The new owners soon moved to Austin looking for better investments and the clan moved back in as squatters. No one in Texas had money to buy anything and the new owners felt that they had made a mistake in buying the timbered land and having no one to buy the land or the timber.

It was evident that Pasqual DeLeon was the dominant male in the clan. He was the one who stepped forward with questions and answers and was instrumental in helping form an agreement.

If Creed could buy the land from the carpetbaggers, he would give the DeLeons the same lifetime estate lease on the property as he gave the Lazerines. For the lifetime estate lease, Mariana would let her vaqueros work for the Empire Timber & Cattle Company. The younger and older DeLeons would stay behind and protect their leased estate. They furnished Creed with the name of the lawyer in Bastrop who handled the transaction for the carpetbaggers.

Creed crossed the Colorado on a wooden bridge to find the carpetbaggers' lawyer Phillip Stewart in Bastrop. The lawyer was sitting outside under his shingle waiting for anyone who might need a lawyer. Creed introduced himself and told him of his desire to buy the lost pines and the Brazos River property if the price was right and that he wanted to do it as soon as possible.

"The owners want a small profit, but they want to get their foot out of the trap worse," said the lawyer. "Do you have the money to buy it?"

"If Wells Fargo has any money, I do."

"Walk over to the telegraph office with me and I'll line this up with my carpet—uh, clients." Stewart said laughing.

After several wires, the attorney turned to Creed and showed him the price. "The greedy bunch wanted to make a profit on the transaction. I gave them a lowball figure you might pay which was less than what they paid for the land. They were glad when I told them I thought I could get their money back for them. If we leave within an hour we can get to Austin before dark. We can get the papers signed in the morning and we all can go to the Wells Fargo office there and you can get their money. I know you could get the money here at Wells Fargo, but I had rather not travel with that kind of money. I'll get my carriage ready to travel and you be back here within an hour."

Creed rushed back across the bridge and met with the DeLeon clan. "I can buy the land. Let's get ready to travel. Make a list of everything you will need to get to the Trinity River flats and a list of everything needed here for those who are going to stay. I'll travel with Stewart to Austin. We'll be leaving within the hour. I'll sign the papers in the morning and will be back here before tomorrow night.

"Pasqual, I've looked at your horses and they look great. We will need more for our remuda. I want each of you to have one of the new Henry rifles and a case of .44-caliber ammunition if you can find them. I'm going to give you money to pay for everything except the horses. I will pay for them when I return. Be sure and buy some candy for the kids and new dresses for the ladies. Take the women and children along to do the shopping."

Everything went well in Austin and, on the way back, Stewart expressed his pleasure at being rid of those greedy carpetbaggers. Creed and Stewart arrived back in Bastrop around 3 pm. On the trip back Creed hired Stewart as his attorney to handle his legal affairs west of the Brazos. Creed gave him a large sum of money for his escrow account with instruction to give Mariana money as she requested.

Creed rushed back across the bridge to find the clan.

Pasqual had found fifteen Henrys at four different stores and plenty of .44 ammunition. "Pasqual, we will spend the rest of the day packing and we will get a full night's sleep. I want to leave early in the morning. How are we doing with the remuda?"

"We all had at least one extra horse, some had two. I have located thirty but feel like we need at least thirty more than that."

"Do you think you can find thirty more horses?"

"I will find them."

Creed filled out the lifetime lease agreement for the DeLeon clan and signed it along with Marianna and Pasqual. The agreement gave the DeLeon clan a legal right to live on the property and gave Creed the Vaqueros he needed for his empire. If any of the DeLeon family needed money while their head of household was away, Marianna could get it for them.

Pasqual showed Creed the remuda and the amount that he needed to pay for them. Creed wrote a note to his attorney Philip Stewart to pay the bearer of the note the money listed for the horses. "Give the seller this."

"These are fine looking horses, Pasqual, but what are you doing with those two small ones?"

"I was afraid you were going to ask me that. That is "Sweet Pea" and "Apple Blossom." My sister raised them from birth. She is insisting on going with us." Before Creed could speak, Pasqual continued, "She is my little sister, Constantina. Our mother died giving birth to her and our clan raised her. She attended the Catholic school in Bastrop and after she finished the sixth grade the church hired her to teach math in the school. She also taught any parishioners who wanted to learn. One summer the church sent her to

Austin to help audit the parish books there. She's been riding her own horse since the age of two. She is sixteen years old and can ride and shoot as well as any boy. She grew up with the boys and they know they'd better not mess with her. She can herd with the best of them and doesn't mind riding drag. She said she would work for free if you would feed her."

"Pasqual, do you want her to go?"

"Yes, but I understand if you don't."

"It's okay with me. I'll pay her the same as the others if you think she can do the work."

"She can do the work. You will see."

Creed still had a little over forty thousand dollars deposited with Wells Fargo. His labor and food for all the employees and the horses come to around five thousand a month. He was not overly concerned but realized the necessity of cash flow to start coming in instead of all of it going out.

Creed estimated they could travel about thirty miles per day with the remuda. The distance was one hundred and eighty miles to the branding camp.

"Pasqual, what do you know about the ferry at Washington on the Brazos?"

"I know it's the only ferry for miles in either direction. It would probably take us all day to get the remuda across, but it could take us longer if things went wrong with us fording the river. It's a mighty dangerous river. We're talking about a six-day trip if everything goes well fording the river and seven days if we take the safe ferry."

"Which way do you want to take?"

"The safe way,"

"The ferry it will be," Creed said, ducking his head with

a hidden smile. Creed had Pasqual distribute the fifteen Henrys to the outriders. "The Henry is deadly accurate at one hundred yards. There are other rifles that have more power but there are none faster," Creed told them.

They pulled out after breakfast and goodbyes. There was giddiness in everyone's voices and actions during their departure. It took a few miles for the pace to stabilize.

Creed had not met all the vaqueros and was making a point to introduce himself to them all. He planned to ride beside each for several miles to get to know them better. After the third day they were getting close to Washington on the Brazos. Creed had not yet met Constantina. It seemed that each time he had seen her at a distance she would disappear. *Accidental or intentional?* Being smaller than the others had made it easier to pick her out.

The horses were easy to drive. Horses tend to like company and do not stray often. If one did, and she was near, Constantina would break away from the herd and drive them back in line.

It would take six trips and all day to get the vaqueros and remuda across the Brazos on the ferry. Creed and Pasqual went to the front and assisted loading the one-hundred and eleven horses. Eighteen or nineteen horses and five or six vaqueros were on each crossing.

Several times Creed got a glimpse of Constantina moving back toward the rear. When the fifth load had boarded the ferry, the last group moved forward. Constantina was at the back and on the far side away from Creed. He rode to the rear and she started moving forward on the far side. Creed followed her. There was no place for her to go but into the river.

She had her back to Creed. "You must be Constantina,"

he shouted, "I'm Dakota." Creed sat in the saddle with a slight smile on his face. He wanted to assure her that she was welcome and that he was glad to have her riding for the brand. He wanted to do away with any insecurities she might have. She was definitely a tomboy and might act tough if challenged. As she turned Creed was floored by what he saw. Her hat had shielded the olive tinted face until she looked up. Her black hair flowed to the back and Creed saw her slight smile and piercing dark green eyes darting with excitement and happiness. It made Creed happy to witness such happiness.

"Mr. Creed, I've seen you at a distance and was wanting to meet you. Every time I saw you, you were busy, and I did not want to disturb you."

"Constantina, I'm thrilled to have you riding for our brand. I want you to know we'll always take care of you and yours... and please call me Dakota."

"Dakota, you have already done more for my family than anyone ever has. I will repay you with hard work and loyalty to you and the brand."

"Thank you, Constantina."

On the seventh day after leaving the lost pines, Creed rode into the branding camp ahead of the horses and vaqueros. He pulled Donny aside.

"I need to tell you something. You know that in Texas if you do harm to a woman, someone will give you a ticket straight to the promised land, right?"

"Sure, I know that, Dakota. What's up?"

"What's up is that we have a young woman who will be joining us shortly and she would do the killing part herself. She is very pleasant to be around. Don't think that her being pleasant is a sign that she's smitten on y'all. She's a vaquero. She's smart, can ride, rope, herd, shoot, *and* doesn't mind riding drag. The only problem is that she is knock-down gorgeous. I'm not kidding about her killing someone who messes with her. It's quite possible. She also has thirty-six vaqueros riding with her who are either brothers, uncles, or cousins. She is also kin to all of Juan's and Jesús's crew and you can add me to the pile as being one who would kill anyone who messes with her."

"Dakota, sure glad you told me about this. I'll go and tell all the outriders. On second thought, I'll wake everyone and tell them.

"Juan, I don't know if you know Constantina DeLeon."

"Of course, I know her. Haven't seen her for several years. She is the pride of the clan. We all love Konstantina."

"She and thirty-six of the DeLeon vaqueros and a remuda of over a hundred horses are crossing the Trinity twenty miles upstream. Pasqual DeLeon is leading them. I want you to come with me and decide where everyone is needed."

"That's great news, Creed. I rode back down the same trail we rode before you left, and I think there are more Longhorns in the twenty-five miles than there were back then. I think the Big Thicket has so many Longhorn cattle in it that some are being crowded out. We have not seen one foreign brand on a Longhorn in the bunch yet."

When Juan and Creed neared the DeLeon vaqueros and remuda, they saw Constantina break from the group and race toward them. Pasqual held up his hand to stop the remuda and rode in behind Constantina. The smile on her face was radiant. She hugged Juan and asked about her great uncle Francisco. "I love him so," she said.

Creed thought of Kathy Ann and wondered if she had

uncles she cared for this much. If she did, they were not mentioned.

Juan and his crew had branded 5,400 Longhorns while Creed had been gone. He decided to break in three new branding crews and try to brand nine hundred mavericks a day for three days and put 8,100 on the trail north. He would put them in four herds and keep the herds a mile apart. The remuda would be held north of the camp and the branded stock strung out northwest of the river.

After the third day of branding by the new crew a storm was building to the southeast. Juan, Pasqual, and Creed decided it would be best to tighten up the herd of Longhorns and hold them closer to the river. They stopped branding and the remuda was moved farther from the river and closer to the camp. The Longhorns that had not been branded had been driven away from the camp and most had moved into the timber.

"Before the storm hits, let's have each vaquero mount his best horse from the remuda. Get the word out," Creed said.

As the thunder neared, the Longhorns became restless. They were bellowing as they tried to move around in the tight herd. The vaqueros were coming in and changing their mounts. Each grabbed a fast bite to eat and a quick cup of coffee. Constantina astride Sweet Pea arrived at the camp, held her reins, and jumped to the ground.

"We've got them as tight as we can, she said while gulping down a cup of coffee "They are mighty restless now and will bolt at the drop of a hat."

The sky lit up just south of them and Constantina threw the cup down, grabbed the saddle horn, and mounted Sweet Pea in one leap without putting her foot in the stirrup. She leaned forward in the saddle and raced forward as the thunder exploded in her ears. She knew one clap of thunder was all the cattle would need to start stampeding. Creed had mounted and gave chase as well. He saw that she had caught up with the herd and that the vaqueros were trying to push the herd toward the river while the Longhorns were trying to get away from it.

Creed could see a vaquero ahead of Constantina that was closer to the herd. A Longhorn behind the vaquero was forced out of the herd and clipped the hind legs of the vaquero's horse. The horse fell, sending its rider to the ground scrambling to get out of the way. Without hesitation, Constantina removed her left foot from her stirrup and slung her foot toward the back of the saddle and stood up on the right stirrup. She grabbed Sweet Pea's mane and laid the rein on the right side of the horse's neck. Sweet Pea responded with a dash left toward the running vaquero. When her horse was close enough, the vaquero jumped, grabbed the saddle horn, and slid his right foot into the stirrup that Constantina had opened for him. Sweet Pea carried him to safety and darted away chasing the herd.

Creed let the vaquero mount behind his saddle. He asked to be taken back to his fallen horse to retrieve his saddle and to check on the horse, which, unfortunately, was dead. "Take me back to the remuda," the vaquero said. "I need to get back in the chase."

After the storm passed, most of the exhausted herd was again pushed tight along the Trinity.

Creed checked on the vaqueros as they came in. No one was hurt and only the one horse was lost.

"I want to thank all of you for the job you did today," Creed said as he turned, catching Constantina's eye with a grin on his face. She ducked her smiling face.

CHAPTER EIGHTEEN

New Longhorn Contract

Pasqual appointed his right-hand man, Eldondo, to stay with half the crew and continue branding at the branding camp. The eight outriders would be armed with the Henry repeater rifles and the branding crew would have two Henrys close by and handy. They would not try to keep the branded Longhorns herded. When they were ready for another drive they would be herded up at that time. Donny, with thirteen of his outriders, rode out with 7500 head of tired Longhorns with Pasqual and his vaqueros with Constantina riding drag. They planned to divide into three herds the next morning.

"Donny, I need to talk to you. As you know I've hired a lot of hands and bought lots of land. I will not have any money coming in until we deliver the first thousand head of Longhorns, I will be close to running out of money.

"If push comes to shove on the money, do you think the outriders would go along with not being paid their money until we deliver the second thousand head of cattle?"

"We will work that out. We have trusted you with our lives, getting them to trust you with their money will be a cake walk."

"See you in Bowie County in three weeks or so, Donny. I'll have Bo Brailey looking for you there. He will lead you through Bowie County to the Red River." Creed could not resist catching a look into Constantina's eyes as she rode by after the herd. They were always filled with happiness. He was sure Kathy Ann's eyes would be filled with happiness, too, when he returned to take her away with him.

Creed was traveling light. He had his two saddle bags full of ammunition and food. His two bed rolls were behind his saddle, his Henrys were in their scabbards. His pack horse had no pack. He planned to travel thirty miles a day and trade out the horses at least every four hours.

Creed spent the first night on the hill leading down to the Neches River. He crossed early the next morning and was approaching Ralph Tillman's trading post in the Lufkin community around 9 a.m. In the distance he saw two riders, one wearing a Derby hat and the other riding a large bay horse. Creed stopped a few minutes and scoped the riders until they were out of sight, then rode in.

"Hello, Creed, I told the deputy you planned to stop by to see Mattingly when you had time," said Tillman.

"Who was that with the deputy?"

"You need to know this! They were asking about you. The other man goes by the name Pico de Mendoza. He is a dangerous wannabe bounty hunter. Everyone he captures is brought in dead. He always has the same story---that they tried to escape."

"What else can you tell me about him?"

"Rumor has it that Mendoza tried to ride with Quantrill's gorilla raiders toward the end of the war. Quantrill didn't trust him because he couldn't verify where he had been during the War. Mendoza killed a group of Union captives of Quantrill's trying to gain his favor. Granted, Quantrill would have killed them himself or had one of his people kill them since he's known for not taking prisoners.

"It's a fact Mendoza fought for the Union in Missouri before joining Quantrill's Confederate Raiders. It is said

Mendoza was not seen by anyone for two years after the War. Then he showed up in Texas soon after the carpetbaggers did away with the Texas Rangers.

"He held himself out as a bounty hunter who heroically fought for the Union. The likes of Mattingly welcomed him with open arms."

"Anything unusual about his looks or his horse?"

"Well, he *is* tall for a Latino. He wears large silver spurs. He looks at everything without turning his head and rides a large bay horse. I'd keep an eye out for him. You might want to go see Mattingly before this gets further out of hand."

"Do you think Mattingly has put a bounty on me?"

"Why else would he be asking questions about you?"

I'm not going to see Mattingly, but I am going to see Pico de Mendoza. Mattingly has put him on my trail, and I will get him off. He needs to find a different place to be.

"I sure don't have time to see Mattingly now. Pass that on to him when you get a chance."

"Sure will. They keep asking me what you looked like. I told them you weighed about two-hundred and fifty pounds, and you were about five-foot-four inches tall. I change it a little each time they ask. I have your weight up to around two hundred and eighty now. I told them you rode a paint horse that had a slightly swayed back."

"One of his deputies has been by here every day since your herd moved through here a week and half ago. This is the first time I've seen Mendoza with any of them. The deputy says Mattingly heard about the herd of cattle and went crazy to find you. The rumor is that his deputies rode up fast on your herd and turned and ran from the show of force that was exhibited by your outriders."

"Humph! Mattingly and his greenhorns don't know you don't ride up on a moving herd too fast without being challenged?"

"Probably not! Mattingly did stop by the day after the run-in with your crew and wanted to buy nine Henry repeating rifles. I told him I didn't have any. He told me he wanted the next ones I got. As far as he knows, I will never get any more. I have several. Do you want them?"

"I'll buy them but will have to pick them up later."

"That's fine, they'll be here."

"Thanks, for your description of me. I'm glad they didn't start a stampede or get anybody shot. He may get himself killed before I have time to get by to see him." Creed liked Tillman from the first time he saw him. *Tillman can think on his feet. I have a lot of respect for a man who can do that.*

"Listen, I know you're in a hurry and this is not the time but when you do get the time, I'd like for us to get better acquainted."

"I would like that, Tillman."

Creed picked up the cattle's trail west of the Lufkin community. The trail stayed on the west side of the Angelina River. He saw where the three hundred Longhorn heifers were driven toward Alazan as planned. The rest continued to be moved along the Angelina's west bank and never had to cross the river. They were approaching the Sabine River when Creed caught up with them just before dark. They would keep moving up the west side of the Sabine until they found a suitable low-water crossing.

Erskine filled Creed in on their conflict with Mattingly's deputies.

"They came riding in hard, but we saw 'em at a distance

and were ready for 'em. The ten of us raced toward them to keep them away from the herd. They were riding bunched up and we were spread out. We all had our Henrys in our right hands with the stock on our hips. They didn't have rifles. Just snub nose .38-caliber pistols pointed at us.

"When we got about seventy yards from them, we stopped and raised our rifles toward them. They knew they were well out of range with their .38s and panicked. They ran into each other and two of them fell off their horses. The rest rode away. The two who fell off their horses could not catch them. The more they chased the horses the farther they ran. They threw their guns on the ground and held up their hands.

"I tried to keep a straight face but just couldn't. After I gained my composure, I rode up to them and asked what the hell they were trying to do riding up toward us with their guns pulled. I didn't give them time to answer. I was too eager to let them have a piece of my mind. I told them they were lucky they didn't all get killed, anyone with half a brain wouldn't ride in toward a cattle herd like a bat out of hell. I assured them that when you're driving a herd of Longhorns, and someone attacks the herd, people are gonna die.

"Juan had asked them what was on their minds when they rode in that way. They told us they were looking for you. I asked why they were pulling their guns when they were just looking for Creed. They said they were scared. I told them you had left word that you would stop by to see Mattingly when you got time. I got off my horse and unloaded their .38s and handed them back to them. They turned, kicked the two of them in the rear and sent them running home."

"Thanks, Erskine. Y'all did a good job." Creed spent the night in camp, ate with the crew then left at the break of day loaded down with bacon and fresh hardtack. He stopped in Bowie County and left a note at Desmond Duke's office for Bo to meet and guide the herd over company land to the Red River.

In Fort Smith, Creed left his two horses at a stable with instructions for their care. He noticed a large bay horse in the next stall that startled him. A bay horse and a man who rides one had been on his mind. *Could this be Pico Mendoza's horse? What would he be doing here?* Creed unsaddled his horse and looked for a brand on the bay but didn't find one. He put his saddle and other gear in the tack room and went to the hotel.

After bathing and changing clothes, Creed went below to the café, ate, and found himself looking for Pico de Mendoza. His attractive waitress made Creed long to see Kathy Ann again. With the progress he was now making he would be ready to return to her in less than a year. The thought made him smile. He would want her to meet and maybe even become friends with Constantina.

"Do you know the man who rides the big bay horse that was here last night?", Creed asked the hostler at the stable the next morning.

"Don't know his real name but some call him Pico. He's here to collect a reward from Judge Parker."

"So, he's a bounty hunter?"

"Yeah, but Judge Parker doesn't trust him."

"Why not?"

"He doesn't hunt anyone other than those who can be brought in dead or alive and he only brings them in dead, almost always shot in the back. Judge Isaac Parker, the hangin' judge, wants them brought in alive so he can have a trial and then hang 'em."

It is natural curiosity that makes every westerner look at brands on horses. If it is a good looking or unusual horse, he normally takes a good look according to the cowboy's unwritten code. Creed was convinced that Pico de Mendoza would have looked at the brand on his horse and would be checking out who rode in on it.

Creed guessed that Mattingly had put a bounty on his head. Why else would a bounty hunter be at Tillman's Trading Post with one of Mattingly's deputies looking for him.? Creed knew he was on top of Mattingly's list, and he had not heard of anyone more out of favor with Mattingly than he. It would have been a private bounty because Creed had no charges brought against him. Creed had never hunted a man. Creed knew he had to bring an end to Mattingly and his deputies now that Mattingly was hiring gunmen and paying them a bounty to kill him. Unfortunately, he had to kill Mendoza before Mendoza killed him.

Creed took a lantern with him to retrieve his tack from the tack room. He hung the lantern on a post near the stall where he had seen the large bay horse. He backed one of his horses near the gate of the stall shielding the hostler's view. Creed removed the lantern and slipped into the stall behind his horse. The bay's hoof prints were one width of his spread hand wide and one-and-a-half hands long. The horse had often stood on three hooves with the tip of the left rear foot barely touching the ground and the right rear hoof print dug deep into the dirt.

Creed put his saddle on the black gelding and vigilantly rode to the west side of town. When he neared the federal building, he rode past Judge Parker's gallows. It could accommodate eight prisoners at one time and had one trap door for all with one linchpin. Creed said a silent prayer for the families of those who would hang there.

Ryan Maxwell, head of Indian Affairs for the Territory, heard Creed in his outer office. Ryan's heart sank. *Is he going to tell me he can't furnish the cattle?* He was in a bind for food for the Indians and not getting the Longhorns would bring about rebellion and Indians would be leaving the reservations. It would be embarrassing for U.S.Senator Phillip Maxwell that his nephew Ryan had failed in the job he went out on a limb for and had used political collateral to secure the position for him.

"Creed, where are the Longhorns?"

"They will be at the Red this weekend."

"How many are there?"

"I've got your thousand."

"How long will it take for you to get the next thousand?"

"I have 4,500 in two herds. You can have as many as you want."

"I want them all. The army is flooding the reservations with mouths to feed. They have the Indians on the run in Texas, New Mexico, Utah, and Arizona, and they are arriving in the Territory every day. We have plenty of land for them but not enough food. Do you have any more on the trail?"

"I have 7,500 head about two weeks behind them."

"May I have all of them?"

"Yes! Are you going to need more than that?"

"Creed, this is going to be a long-lasting affair. When they were hungry, they killed a buffalo. The white man has killed most of the buffalo now. They will have nothing to eat without the Longhorns. If there are no Longhorns, the Indians will go hungry, leave the reservation, and go back to Texas, New Mexico, Utah, or Arizona, killing and raiding to get food. If I had enough Longhorns, I'm thinking we might ship so many we might have more than they could eat. We could have a sustaining herd in the Indian territory in two or three years."

"Mr. Maxwell, hear me through. Correct me if you think I'm wrong. I'm thinking the 4500 head of longhorns you will be getting by the end of the week and the 7,500 head you will be getting two weeks later should hold you for three months."

"I agree, Creed."

"Good! I know I have the cattle. On October the first, or sooner, and every week for ten weeks, I could have 8,000 head at the Red waiting to cross. I would have to alter the route to ensure adequate grazing for each herd and increase my branding operation. Do you think the 80,000 head you will have in the next ten weeks will be enough to establish the sustained herd you're thinking about?"

"I think it would be a great start. My problem is not knowing how many Indians they are going to send me. Could we extend the delivery for several weeks if we need to?"

"Of course. The only problem I would have doing that is the growing season for grass is over. There is plenty of grass on the alternate routes now, but I think that I would have to buy hay if we increased delivery past the ten weeks."

"Don't worry about the cost of the hay. I will cover your cost on that. Can you commit to the numbers, Creed?"

"I will commit to the 80,000 head and the extension if

you will commit to me that you will not buy any Longhorn cattle from anyone but me. If I do not meet the requirements of the contract, you would be free to buy from anyone you wish. Of course, *force majeure* would be in effect. I want the contract held in confidence by you. If you accept this, I want to get paid for the whole 12,000 head when the first 4,500 head cross over the Red by the end of this week. I need the money to buy additional acreage to develop a sustainable herd and I will commit to you that you can timely have a hundred percent of the cattle I have that you want."

The *force majeure* clause not only covered an act of God. It covered any problem that occurred that was not of Creed's doing and was out of his control.

"I'm sticking my neck out on paying for the additional 7,500 head in advance. I trust you, Creed, and I desperately need them. I appreciate you working with me on this. I'll have the contract and payment voucher ready this weekend at the Red."

Creed knew he was sticking his neck out. His new plan was to start shipping the first 8,000 Longhorns on July 15th and follow it with another herd every seven days. He would need four crews driving the herds fifteen miles per day. That would take fourteen days and the return to the branding camp riding at 30 miles a day would take seven days. Twenty-one days for a round trip. Sixteen crews with six herders in each crew will be needed to meet the goal. He'd better get to work!

CHAPTER NINETEEN

Pico de Mendoza

When Creed left the federal building, he saw a large crowd gathered around Judge Parker's gallows. Eight shackled prisoners stood on the gallows, and a hangman's noose was being placed over their heads. Not wanting to see the hanging, Creed mounted his gelding and was riding past and away when he felt someone watching him. He turned and looked up into a second-floor window. He saw a stern-looking man looking directly down at him. Creed's body quivered as he looked away. He heard the lynchpin pulled and the trap door fall along with the murmur of the crowd. Creed looked up into the window and saw the man turning away from the window and then with a jerk of his head, he looked straight at Creed.

That had to be Federal Judge Isaac Parker. Creed was puzzled why his own body quivered at the sight of the man. He had faced death numerous times and that had never happened before. Creed said a quick prayer for the hung prisoners' families then rode straight to the blacksmith and ordered twenty sets of the Empire Timber & Cattle Company branding irons.

On Tuesday morning, Creed was well on his way to the Red River for his scheduled meeting with Ryan Maxwell on Saturday morning. Creed saw familiar hoof prints ahead of him enter the trail he was on. He slowed his horses and eased them to the side of the trail then stepped off in the grass and walked back on the trail and bent over the hoof prints. A horse had stopped here and rested his left leg by standing on the other three. The tip of the hoof he lifted made a small crease in the trail. He measured several hoof prints and they all matched Mendoza's bay horse... and they looked fresh.

Had Judge Parker put Mendoza on his trail? If not, why was Judge Parker looking at him? Why did his body quiver?

He needed answers. He was short on time, but he had to kill Mendoza now before Mendoza killed him. He would be alive and could face any consequences of the killing if they should come up.

Creed did not know how good a gunman Mendoza was but assumed he was probably one of those bushwhacking back-shooters. He also did not know if Mendoza had ever seen him or had a good description of him. *Was he looking for me in Fort Smith before? Was he* ahead *of me looking for a good place from which he could shoot me in the back?*

There were rocky foothills of the on the east side of the trail. Creed had learned early in life that the rocks gave good cover from oncoming bullets and sight advantage of things below. He also knew you should never try to fight from them. Ricocheting bullets from the rocks increased fire power from below and limited escape routes. A smart bushwhacker would never want to be pinned down in the rocky foothills.

Creed watered the horses in a creek off the trail and covered all evidence of being there. He found a thicket nearby where he could hide the horses. He removed their saddles and sprinkled a liberal amount of oats on the ground then built a rope corral around them in the thicket and prepared to continue on foot. He slipped on his moccasins and threw a canteen of water around his neck along with the telescope. The saddlebag he threw over his shoulder held jerked beef, hardtack and plenty ammunition for his Colts and Henry rifle. Creed started his walk on foot to the east to find the southern trail again. When in sight of the trail he saw the bay's, hoof prints. He had followed the prints for less than a mile when he saw that the rider had left the trail and gone north. *He' making a loop to go back to see if anyone has cut his trail.*

Creed backed off the trail and thought. *What will Mendoza do when he finds that I have found him? Will he follow my tracks?*

Creed jerked his head to see behind him when he had the thought.

Comanche Indians would pick the least likely spot to attack from. They never picked the highest spot or the spot that had the most foliage or most cover. They would come off the ground at your feet and often from a buffalo wallow with no cover at all.

Creed decided he would use the Comanche tactic and stay nearby where he was and turned to look back in the direction he had come. He would make Mendoza come to him and he would be ready.

He checked his Colts and moved downhill on a game trail for a hundred yards not trying to cover his tracks. He moved off the trail a couple of feet into the scrubby grass on his left. Creed eased to the ground and settled into a prone position facing uphill with the trail on his left. He placed his Bowie knife on the ground in front of him and the telescope close to his head. The Henry was on the ground near his arm. He silently cocked both .45s and placed them beside the Henry in easy reach. The canteen and a hardtack were near his mouth. There were small patches of brush some distance in front of him. Some twenty feet behind him was an abundance of thick, tall brush. There would be shade on the entire area for the rest of the day.

Creed constantly checked his surroundings. It had been three hours from the time he had settled in, but he was a patient man. He never forgot the words that his father said: *the first man who moves is dead.* Creed was determined not to be that man. Even though he was barely 19 years old, he had been in this situation several times before and had never been the first man to move.

What was that? Creed eased his eye to the scope and in seconds he could see it well. He moved his eyes away. Creed had seen a small portion of a silver spur that had caught a ray of sun. He estimated the spur to be a little over a hundred yards away but in sight of the game trail he was on. He moved the Henry closer to his head and in the right direction. Again, he saw part of the silver spur. Creed moved the scope to where a leg should be but saw nothing. He saw a limb move but could see nothing behind it. He moved the scope away then moved it back to get a fresh look. Creed determined that the spur was not attached to a boot, but the spur did move, and the wind did not cause it to move because there was no wind.

Creed was convinced Mendoza would not leave without his spur and when he reached for it, he would pay the ultimate price—his life. As nighttime approached, no one had reached for the silver spur. Creed was not worried but had to think this through. *Does Mendoza know that I'm near the trail? Does he think that I will try to escape when dark comes? Should I try to make it across the trail and go back where I first found Pico's horse tracks and attack him from the rear?*

He came to the same conclusion as before: he would be the last man to move. Darkness fell and light fog was creeping in around him. Creed felt he had the advantage. Mendoza was a bounty hunter. He now was the hunted one and it had to be a new experience for him. To escape, Mendoza had to move. Creed would be ready.

Two more hours of darkness. Fog hugged the ground. The moon peeked out of the clouds. No movement. Wait!

He had heard a whisper of sound that had drifted down the trail and lingered on top of the fog before being extinguished.

Creed stayed alert. He knew Mendoza was on his way. All the trees cast their dim shadows on the ground when the moonlight penetrated the fog. Several minutes later Creed felt someone's presence. He knew no one could see him unless they were directly over him; even then it would be hard to see him through the dense fog. A shadow covered him when moonlight penetrated through the fog. It was Mendoza's shadow. He was standing about five feet to Creed's left on the trail and in front of him. He was peering into the darker brush behind Creed.

Creed could have shot him but was sure Pico could get off a shot before he died, meaning he would also be killed or wounded. With the Bowie in his left hand and one of the cocked Colt .45s in his right, Creed waited. Pico moved forward and stopped. He was standing beside Creed's prone body and was still looking into the darker brush behind Creed.

Creed reached out with his Bowie and swung it with all his strength with intentions of cutting through Pico's boot and the Achilles tendon. A terrifying scream rushed from Pico's mouth as he was falling toward Creed and lowering his right gun hand to break his fall. Creed dropped the Bowie and grabbed Mendoza's right hand and pulled it aside as he shot upward into the body until the six bullets were gone.

The acrid smell of the gun smoke mixed with Mendoza's blood, seemed to linger in the fog. It brought back terrifying memories of battles that Creed had often prayed would be wiped from his mind. He scrambled from beneath Pico Mendoza's body.

Creed was covered from head to toe with Mendozas blood. He recovered his Bowie and Colt, then found his other possessions and ran up the foothill to escape the odors and memories.

There was enough water in his canteen to wash his hands and face. He entered a nearby creek with his clothes on and washed until most of the blood was gone. He took off his clothes and rung out as much water as possible and put the clothes back on. Cold and wet, he searched out his two horses, moved them about two hundred yards from Pico's body, and pulled them close together. By snuggling between them he was able to draw heat from their bodies and finally, stop shivering. In the distance he heard sounds of fighting animals. When it was light enough to see, Creed saddled his gelding and rode to Mendoza's body.

Creed had his lasso ready. The Bowie had cut Pico's moccasin-clad foot totally off at the ankle. Creed found the foot and stuffed it behind the dead man's belt. He left Pico's knife in the scabbard. I one of the pockets, he found a thousand dollars that he presumed was bounty money Pico had received from Judge Parker. Another pocket contained several greenbacks and a fresh wanted poster. *I don't want to explain this to anyone, especially Judge Parker. I'll make sure this body is never found.*

Creed found the gun Pico had probably held in his right hand because a Colt was still in his left holster. Apparently, Mendoza had dropped the gun while falling or reaching for his foot.

Creed lassoed the body and dragged it into the foothills. He had no shovel so would bury him under several hundred pounds of rock. As Creed pushed the body in position to cover it with stones, he pitched Pico's gun down beside him. It was then Creed realized the foot was missing *I'll find it on my way out of the foothills.* When Creed finished the burial, he paused and said a prayer for Pico de Mendoza's family.

While he finished covering all signs on and around the trail, he looked around but didn't find the foot. He found the bay horse, saddle, boots and spurs. Creed wanted nothing that could tie him to Mendoza. He found a place he could bury the saddle, boots and spurs under a landslide he created in the stony foothills. He led the Bay away from the area for several miles and untied her. He scattered a hat full of oats for her and rode away. He was pressed for time and had to find a creek where he could bathe and change clothes. He did not like the idea of having lost the foot and leaving it, but at least there was no way to trace its identity.

At the Red River crossing, both Creed and Ryan signed the contract and Ryan handed a government demand voucher to Creed for $480,000 in payment for 12,000 Texas Longhorns. The 4,500 Longhorns were counted as they entered the river driven by the vaqueros and were met halfway by the Indians. Ryan was pleased with the condition of the herd. Creed was incredibly pleased and relieved, with the demand voucher for the $480,000.

"Mr. Maxwell, I won't be here when the 8000 Longhorns

come in each week. Here are my deposit numbers with Wells Fargo. Would you mind just depositing my demand voucher with them each week?"

"I don't mind at all, Creed. I know how busy you will be."

"You're right! I'm going to be mighty busy." *I will head to Nacogdoches and stay mighty busy until I kill Mattingly and his crew.*

"Jesús, you and Erskine take these additional branding irons and get back to the Trinity and start branding. I want you and Juan to scatter some branded stock all the way to Crocket and leave two branding crews there. Erskine, figure out a way to give them protection."

CHAPTER TWENTY

Trigger Fingers

Creed rode to Wells Fargo in Texarkana and deposited the government voucher. With the receipt in his pocket, He fought a strong desire to head north to see Kathy Ann. She had told him she would wait for him to return, and he still had so much to do. He headed to Boston to find his attorney Desmond Duke and Bo Brailey.

Creed found Duke first. "How is Hitch doing, Desmond?

"I don't want to know too much, but I do know he has everything under control."

"That's good, Desmond. I want to talk to you about working for the Empire Timber & Cattle Company full time. Are you interested?"

"Absolutely! I have only one reservation."

"What's that?"

"I know you know how to spend money, but do you know how to make money? All I've seen is money going out and none ever coming in. That can't last forever."

Creed pulled out the deposit receipt from Wells Fargo and flashed it before Desmond's eyes and returned it to his pocket.

"Oh my! That answers my question."

"Do you think you can work with a young Yankee lawyer."

"I could even work for a woman if you told me to."

"That may just happen."

"I don't care! I just want in!

They agreed on a salary and set forth a plan. Creed gave him a copy of the cattle contract and emphasized the confidentiality of the document. Creed transferred a large sum of money into his escrow account with Duke. Creed gave him Glad Mathews' and Philip Stewart names and addresses in Nacogdoches and Bastrop. "Contact them and set up a meeting. When y'all decide on a date let me know and I will be there."

Creed contacted Bo. "How is Hitch doing with your problem, Bo?"

A grin came on Bo's face as he said, "The Carpetbaggers in this county would rather fight a swarm of mad hornets than mess with Hitch.

Creed and Bo rode southwest to find Pasqual, Donny and the herd of 7,500 head of cattle owned by the federal government's Indian Affairs. He found them a few miles farther north than he expected. Pasqual and Donny were just stopping to set up camp and Creed introduced them.

"Bo will lead you in on Empire Timber & Cattle Company land all the way to the Red River. I'm going to look over the herd and see how they're doing. I'll be back before dark."

Creed kept looking for Constantina. He didn't want to ask about her for fear some might question his reason for doing so. He had his woman, Kathy Ann. He just enjoyed being around Constantina. She was a happy person and her good nature made him happy. *Kathy Ann will love her.*

Creed decided to go to the end of the herd that was stretched out for about a mile to look for the vaquera. When he was in sight of the tail end of the herd, he saw two vaqueros riding drag. He asked where Constantina was.

"She was riding flank on the left side of the herd and her horse stepped in a gopher hole and hurt its leg. She asked us to cover her flank and told us she'd catch up."

Creed rode back down the trail trotting his horse. He had traveled less than a mile before he saw her. She was on her knees holding Sweet Pea's head in her arms and was talking to her. She looked up when she heard Creed.

"She has a broken leg. Would you give me a few more minutes with her before I put her down?"

"Take all the time you need. I'll take care of her for you, Constantina if you'd prefer."

"No, that's my job, Dakota. I just want to be alone with her another few minutes."

Creed turned and rode off. About five minutes later he heard the shot.

Constantina had taken her saddle and bridle from the horse and was still petting her when he rode back.

"Come on, jump up behind me and I'll get several of the boys to come back and bury her."

"That would be fine, Dakota. They could pull her body off the trail and bury her next to those two big pines."

Creed and Constantina rode into camp a little after dark and told everyone what had happened. The men packed some picks and shovels, lit torches and went back to bury the body of Constantina's beloved horse.

Creed met privately with Pasqual and Donny and told them of the new contract without going into details. He explained how the 8,000 Longhorns would be broken into smaller herds and kept about a mile apart. "Mention the contract to no one. After this herd is delivered, Pasqual, I want you to hire all the vaqueros you can find. Donny, I want you to hire all the outriders and guards that are out there. There certainly should be some Texas Rangers out there looking for work. Let's get the word out to them that we would like to talk to them. Also try to hire family members and friends of the family. Make sure they will be loyal to you and the brand."

Pasqual spoke up, "Constantina and I plan to drop by Alazan on the way back and say hello to Uncle Francisco. He should be able to recommend several friends outside the family."

At breakfast, before Creed moved out, he spotted Constantina and spoke to her. "Constantina, I know you can't replace Sweet Pea in your heart, but I saw a small horse several weeks ago and when I saw her, I thought of you. If it's what you'd like, I am going to see if I can buy her for you."

"That would be great. Apple Blossom will appreciate that. In the meantime, I saw a horse in the remuda that is a little smaller than the rest and I will try her out soon."

"Pasqual, let's you and I ride into Boston and meet Desmond Duke before I head back to Nacogdoches. You'll have no problem catching back up with the herd."

Constantina had just saddled Apple Blossom and overheard the conversation and asked to join them. "I've got to buy some personals," she said, smiling.

Creed introduced Pasqual and Constantina to Desmond.

"Boys, I have some shopping to do; I'll be at the mercantile store. Pick me up on the way out."

Creed discussed the increased demand for the Longhorns with Pasqual and Desmond and sought their opinions of possible problems the demand could create.

After the meeting Creed went with Pasqual to the

mercantile store to wish Constantina farewell. She was in the middle of trying on a dress.

"I *am* a girl, in case you haven't noticed," Constantina snapped, throwing her nose in the air and laughing.

"We know," laughed Dakota. He was in awe of the way Constantina bounced back from her loss of Sweet Pea.

Dakota sat in his saddle and watched Pasqual and Constantina ride off from the mercantile store to catch up with the herd. As he paused a moment thinking how beautiful this cowgirl had looked in a dress, he felt someone watching him. Dakota turned in time to see two men rush into the store. These two had their short-barrel guns slung on their left hip. The thought ran through his mind that they could be using their left hands because they had lost their trigger fingers somehow.

Dakota had promised two men with their trigger finger cut off that he would kill them if he ever saw them again. *Whoever they were they did not want me to see them.* Creed decided to let it slide. He rode south, crossed the Sulphur River, and rode till dark. He decided to do without a fire and would eat jerked beef.

Creed had only gone about a mile from where he spent the night. He winced when a bullet entered his left arm. The bullet would not have unseated him from his saddle, but he threw himself from the saddle as if fatally shot. Two shots had been fired but only one hit him. Creed pulled the Colt on his right hip from the holster before hitting the ground. He also had his left hand on the other Colt.

Creed slipped his bandana from around his neck and tied it around his upper left arm using his teeth and right hand. The bullet had not hit a bone and he still had good feeling in his hand and fingers. *I knew it was those two I promised to kill. This is what I get for not killing them in Boston.*

Creed could not see them but heard them laughing and congratulating themselves. *I will join in on this celebration.*

Creed needed to know if he could use his left hand to fire his Colt. He removed the cylinder from the Colt in his left hand and pulled the trigger with ease. He replaced the cylinder and immediately jumped to his feet ready for action. He caught them completely by surprise by rushing in firing both Colts. He had one bullet left in each when he holstered his guns and pulled the Bowie knife. The two had not fired another shot. When they received their first wound, they were busy trying to keep blood from escaping from their bodies. They were now feebly trying to get to their guns. Creed moved in closer with his Bowie knife and made sure they wouldn't bother him again.

"Give the Buzzards a few meals, fellas. They need to eat too!"

Creed found their horses and released them. He went through their saddle bags and found an unopened bottle of whiskey and a sewing kit with several sizes of curved needles. He opened the whiskey bottle and poured some over his wound entry point and tried to splash some of it on the exit wound. He thought of sewing up the wound in front but could not reach the exit wound and decided to leave them both open. He kept the sewing kit, never knowing when he might need it, and the whiskey, as well.

Creed was vigilant riding into Nacogdoches. His left arm was swollen but there seemed to be no fever. He made it to Glad's office without incident and the attorney shook Creed's hand and slapped him on the shoulder. Creed flinched away in pain.

"Sorry! What's wrong with your arm?

"It's just a scratch," replied Creed.

"If you haven't seen a doctor about that scratch, you need to! Creed, Mattingly and his deputies went wild when he heard the number of cattle in the last drive and the size of the trail they created. They want to see you."

"Didn't you tell them I would stop by when I had time?"

"Sure did! They said they had heard that before, but you haven't shown up."

"Don't worry about it. I've been putting it off on purpose because I don't want any trouble out of them."

"Were you able to buy the spring and the fifty thousand acres around it?"

"No! I had to buy eighty thousand acres around it and now we need some money in the new bank I bought yesterday,"

"Wow! That's great news about the bank and land." Creed said happily. Mathews explained.

Creed gave him a copy of the contract for the Longhorns and transferred a hundred thousand dollars into the Empire Timber & Cattle Company Bank account.

"Can you find me a builder who can build a home with logs? I want you to buy all the land between the Neches and the Trinity Rivers all the way southeast, including all the Big Thicket, and as far northwest as Crockett. I will cut the hardwood timber from the south side of the Neches to build the home. I'm going to be away for a week or two. There is something I've got to take care of. I'll contact you when I get back."

CHAPTER TWENTY-ONE

Attoyac Bayou

Creed had no plan. He would play it as he went. He supplied up on ammunition, food, and oats. He saddled his black gelding and loaded the pack horse with the supplies for a long trip. He said a silent prayer saying he had to do what he had to do and asked the Lord for forgiveness if needed. He mounted up and left Nacogdoches. This time he didn't care who saw him. He headed southeast straight to his 80 thousand acres and the spring.

When he arrived, Creed rode around the outside of the crest of the large hill, looking away from the spring. He then rode over the crest and around the top of the hill looking down at the spring. It was more beautiful than he remembered. *I can't wait to show this spot to Kathy Ann.*

Creed went to the spring and let the horses have their fill. He too had his fill then poured out the water in his canteens and refilled them with water from the spring. He rode back over the crest of the hill and made camp where he could see a great distance in all directions. Creed hobbled his horses on the spring side of the hill and let them graze. He ate some jerked beef, checked his weapons, and went to sleep next to a large pine with both Henrys by his side.

Early the next morning, Creed moved away from the tree down the ridge of the hill to the southwest carrying his food sack. He built a small fire, cooked and ate, then spent all day looking for signs of tracks and found only his. He attended to the horses and went back to the large pine for another night. With Mattingly, his eight deputies, and the possibility of other hired guns hunting him, no one had to tell him to be careful and patient.

On the fourth morning, a horse nickering got Creed's attention. At the northeast, he spotted two riders coming into view. Creed slowly rolled up off the ground and sat up leaning his back against the tree. With his scope, he was able to determine that one of the riders was a woman. The other was a slick-looking fool probably trying to look tough for the girl. The incoming rider's hat was pulled low over his eyes. He had two tied-down Colt .45s with a leather strap tying down the hammers on each gun and a rifle in his saddle scabbard. *If he tried to use the Colts it would take him a second or two to get the straps off the gun hammer, but the rider still rode with a confident swagger.*

When the two saw Creed, he was sitting quietly by the tree with one of the Henrys in his lap. Creed startled them.

"Who are you?" The man shouted.

"Who wants to know?"

"I'm Swifty McCord. I'm working for Sheriff Mattingly, and this is Sheriff Mattingly's daughter Orchid. I'll ask one more time and you had better answer. Who are you?"

"My name is Oscar Wheat, why do you want to know?"

"I'm looking for the man who bought this property several days ago. His name is Dakota Creed. Do you know him?"

"I might. Why are you looking for him?"

"That's none of your business," Swifty said.

"Well, then I don't know him."

"What are you doing here?"

"That's none of your business, Swifty. You're no gunman. Don't let this good-lookin' girl overload your brain or you're lookin' to get yourself killed."

Swifty went for iron, then realized he had the hammers tied down. Creed hadn't moved but did have his eyes on Orchid and Swifty. She pulled her horse out of harm's way.

Swifty lunged to the ground and went for his rifle in the scabbard. He injected a shell into the chamber and was raising the rifle to fire. Creed had calmly raised his Henry, pointed at his target, and pulled the trigger. Swifty's head snapped backward, and his body melted to the ground after the bullet struck him in the head.

"I'm sorry ma'am. I tried to talk him out of drawing, and he had plenty of time to defend himself. I had to fire or be killed myself."

"I know that Mr. Wheat. Dad is going to be terribly upset. Not at you, but at Swifty! Swifty had told him how tough he was. Dad has been trying to catch this Creed fellow for quite some time now. My father realized that New York detectives do not have the knowledge or daring that is in the blood of most Texans. He hired Pico de Mendoza to find Creed. He accepted the job, but Mendoza had some job he had to finish first. So, that's when Swifty showed up and convinced Dad that he could get the job done before Pico returned. Dad was in a hurry and gave Swifty the job."

"What is that job, Miss Mattingly?"

"Dad had tried to get this guy Creed to come in and talk to him. You see Creed bought some land that my dad was supposed to buy. Creed's company started buying up land everywhere in the county, including this piece of property. Dad wanted to buy this property too. This guy Creed has driven two herds of cattle with thousands of head in each herd across the county and Dad thinks the only way he can stop him is to kill him."

"It makes no difference to me, ma'am, but doesn't your father know that Texas is open range?"

"He does, but he wants Creed killed anyway and Swifty was supposed to do it."

"Did your father agree to pay Mendoza money to kill this Creed feller?"

"Yes! I heard him offer Mendoza a thousand-dollars if he would kill him."

I suspected that Mattingly put Mendoza on my trail with a bounty. Now I know for certain!

"What were you doing with Swifty?"

"I was showing him the property Creed had just bought. Dad thought Creed would show up here sooner or later to look at the property and asked me to show it to."

"Miss Orchid… that is such a beautiful name. May I call you Orchid?"

"Of course! That's a lot better than 'ma'am.'"

"Great! Orchid, do you think your dad would give me the job?"

"I'm sure he would. Swifty was also supposed to teach Dad's deputies how to draw and shoot a .45 from his hip and shoot a rifle. I know you can shoot a rifle, but can you shoot guns from your hip?"

"Orchid, everyone can shoot from the hip. Not everyone can hit everything they want to hit that way." Creed turned, drew one of his Colts and shot a pinecone from a limb. Before the cone hit the ground, he had shot and hit the cone four more times before it scattered to the ground. Creed replaced the five spent shells.

"Orchid, I would like to escort you back to your home and see if your father will hire me. Do you think that would be permissible?"

"I'm sure father would want you to escort me home and I'm sure he will want to hire you after I talk to him, Mr. Wheat."

"Please call me Oscar."

Creed retrieved his two horses and loaded and tied Swifty on his horse. Yankees paid little attention to brands, and he wondered if folks would notice that both of Creed's horses carried the Empire Timber & Cattle Company brand. He had his story ready in case he was asked about it.

Orchid led Creed eastward with Swifty's horse and his pack horse in tow.

"Our home is on the Attoyac Bayou. Dad thought if it were ever attacked it would have to be from the west. He thought the Attoyac would give us all the protection we would need from the east."

"That's good thinking on his part, Orchid. That bayou is crawling with water moccasins and alligators. Your father must be very smart, Orchid."

"Oh, he is Oscar. If you give him and his deputies a little training on western ways, they could wipe out the Empire Timber & Cattle Company themselves."

Creed ducked his head trying to cover the grin on his face with his hat. He hoped her dad was as naive as Orchid.

"Will your mother be at home when we get there, Orchid?"

"Oh no! She still lives in New York. She said she was not coming here until Texas was more civilized."

When they arrived, Orchid jumped from her horse and greeted her father and deputies who had arrived several minutes before them. Mattingly and his deputies had just unsaddled their horses and put them in the barn.

"Dad, this is Oscar Wheat. I think he's the man you need

to hire to kill Creed. Swifty tried to draw on Oscar with both pistols and rifle. Oscar shot him between his eyes with his rifle. Swifty never got off a shot."

"Where did you get your horses?", the Sheriff asked.

"You can't be particular where you get a horse if you don't have one and you are in a hurry." No sooner had the words left Creed's mouth than he heard the desired response.

"That's a likely story, Boss," one of the deputies said as he reached for his .38. A bullet from Creed's .45 blew the deputy's head apart. Creed had the bullet replaced as the deputy hit the ground. The others froze in place. The draw and shot were so fast that their brains had not had time to register what had just happened. "That's something you guys had better learn. If you call a Texan a liar you had better be ready to kill him because he will reach for his iron," Creed warned.

"I told you, Dad! Oscar is the one you need," affirmed Orchid.

"Settle down and listen to me," Mattingly said. "Johnson, you and Martin get one of the pirogues and take Swifty's and Crawford's bodies deep into the bayou and feed them to the 'gators. Orchid, would you and Oscar please come into the house with me.

"Wheat, after what my daughter told me and what I just saw, I definitely want you to work for me."

"What all do you have in mind?" asked Creed.

"First, I want you to find this guy Creed and kill him. If you cut the head off the snake the Empire Timber & Cattle Company will crumble, and I will pick up the pieces."

"That's smart thinking Mattingly. Do you think the same would happen when you get killed?"

Before he could answer Creed had killed Mattingly with a bullet in the head. Orchid raced toward the door screaming. She was killed by fire from the trigger-happy deputies as she opened the door.

Through the window Creed saw Johnson and Martin about fifty yards out in the bayou, out of pistol range. They were turning, trying to get back to shore. He located the other five deputies and determined the order in which he would kill them. He killed the first two from the window then ran to the door, planning to kill the other three. The three were running toward the woods and firing back over their shoulders.

Creed's left leg felt as if it had been hit with a hammer. His forward motion slowed, but his mind and two Colt .45s didn't. The three men crashed to the ground and were thrashing around. Creed could see the three deputies had dropped their .38s. Creed holstered his .45 in his left hand and reached down and stroked his upper left thigh. There was numbness where he had placed his hand and a little blood. Johnson and Martin changed their minds about trying to get back ashore and turned and were headed deeper into the bayou.

First things first. From his horse, Creed retrieved one of his Henrys and with two shots killed Johnson and Martin. Two more shots sunk the pirogue, sending Johnson, Martin, Swifty, and Crawford to the bottom of the bayou. It was not necessary to check to see if Mattingly and his deputies were dead. He was sure of that, but he did check Orchid to make sure she was dead.

Now to the leg. Creed cut his pants away from his wound. The bullet had entered near the center of the upper thigh and was headed out toward the side of the thigh. He could feel the bullet under his skin less than an inch deep and two inches from the entry point. The entry hole was larger than a .38 would normally make, telling Creed that the bullet had ricocheted off something before it hit him.

Creed had a lot of work to do here and decided to bandage the wound and worry about it when he was through. He cut off his shirt tail and placed it over the wound. He took two belts from the bodies and pulled them tight against the bandage on his thigh. He wrapped Orchid's body in a blanket. After emptying the pockets of the seven lawmen for their money, Creed placed four of the bodies—one of which was Mattingly's—in the other pirogue He rowed deep into the bayou, dumped them overboard and returned and loaded the other three bodies. When he was near the area where he had dumped the first four, he saw that the alligators were having a feast.

As he returned to the shore after dumping the bodies he saw a ragged shirt that Johnson had worn. The wooden pirogue's front half had floated to the top with the shirt on it. The water there was muddier than in the rest of the bayou but was now calm evidence that the alligators had found the bodies.

Creed retrieved the ragged shirt from the pirogue with his paddle. He didn't want others finding the shirt and go looking for what might be left of the bodies. He would bury the torn shirt with Orchid. When he got to shore, he removed the saddles and bridles from the barn and turned the horses loose. He loaded his pirogue with five of the saddles and paddled out to the half-submerged pirogue and tied the saddles and bridles in the front and waited until it sank to the bottom.

He returned to shore and filled his pirogue with the other

six saddles and used a long pole to push the pirogue out into deep water. The pirogue sank to the bottom shortly after the second shot from the Henry hit it.

Creed found a shovel in the tool shed and carried Orchid's body into the woods, dug a deep grave, pushed her in and threw Johnson's ragged shirt in after her. He filled the grave, then said a prayer over her, and covered the grave with dead leaves and dead limbs. He returned to the house, clearing all tracks. Bayou water washed blood from the floor and porch and dirt from the shovel. He covered all the tracks to and from the house, barn, and tool shed and left the shovel there. Creed had taken two bottles of whiskey from the house and two sets of pliers from the tool shed and put them in his saddle bag. He also added oats to his stash for his horses.

Creed hated that the deputies killed Orchid, but he was pleased that he had killed those who planned to kill him.

CHAPTER TWENTY-TWO

Scrapping Valley

Creed wanted to get as far away from the Attoyac Bayou as he safely could and hide out until his leg healed. He covered his horses' hooves with burlap and rode southeast skirting the bayou. After a mile, he opened one of the bottles and poured whiskey over the belted-down bandage then rode until near dark and made a fireless camp. He removed the bandage from his leg and washed it with water from his canteen. The wound was red, puffy and bruised. He felt the bullet between two fingers but let go of it immediately. The pain created by touching it was more than he wanted to deal with, and he decided he would try to find a doctor to remove it. Creed poured more whisky on the wound and rebandaged it.

Creed had heard of a ferry at River Bend on the Sabine River. He thought he might go there and head into Louisiana and find a doctor. The bullet was in an awkward place for him to reach. But he knew it had to come out. The next morning Creed poured more whiskey on his bandage and took off for River Bend. Jerked beef, hardtack, and the thought of being rid of Mattingly kept his spirits high until he looked through his scope at the River Bend Ferry. At least fifteen men were there, including seven in army uniforms. The seven were checking out people wanting to ride the ferry. *Are they after me? How could they know so quickly that I'm here?*

After he watched them for a few moments, he realized that they were not actually looking for him, but if he were stopped at the ferry, he would have some difficult questions to answer.

Creed eased back in the woods and headed southwest knowing he would have to remove the bullet by himself. Creed rode until dark and again had a fireless camp. He needed to get farther away from the army troopers and find a hideout the next morning and remove the bullet. Creed had heard of a place called Scrapping Valley and he thought that might be a good place to stop.

Scrapping Valley was described as a beautiful but desolate place. Desolate because in early 1800, over two hundred settlers had been killed by a Coushatta Indian tribe. The tribe was wiped out a short time thereafter. The rumors of it being haunted discouraged most people from going there.

Before noon the next day, Creed knew he had found Scrapping Valley. Spring-fed creeks were abundant and with magnolia trees were growing randomly. There were sandy hills with seeping water in all directions. Abundant game animals confirmed to Creed that not many people had been there over the last fifty years.

About halfway up a dry hillside he built a lean-to under a thick cluster of magnolias looking south over the valley. The trees and hillside provided a natural windbreak from the north. Creed unsaddled the horses and spread a liberal portion of oats for them, ensuring that they would not wander far. He spread his bedrolls in the lean-to and placed his weapons, jerked beef, scope and water nearby. He gathered dry wood to build his fires, trying to bring in a two-week supply. The dry wood would put off little smoke and trees would disperse the smoke that was created. Creed suspected that he had a fever building up and had to hurry.

The bullet was in an awkward position, but it had to come out. Creed made several large bandages and laid them aside in the lean-to along with small limbs from a nearby sweet gum tree that he cut to length and de-barked. He cleaned the swollen wound around the bullet and wiped his Arkansas toothpick repeatedly. He bit down on the stick and slid the thin knife under the skin and pushed the bullet up in the direction that it had entered. Blood and puss exploded from the wound.

Creed had seen many wounds of this kind in the War, but now the pain was his. The stick he held between his teeth broke when he bit down harder, and he replaced it with another. Abruptly the bullet quit moving. It was lodged. In pain and weakening, Creed made a difficult decision. He turned the knife blade upward leaving the entry channel and ripped a new hole to the surface, then viciously gouged the bullet out with his fingers.

Creed grabbed the thin knife and cut the entry hole all the way to the surface. When he caught his breath, he cleaned out the infected hole with one of the bandages and saturated the hole with the whiskey. He applied another bandage over the wound and tied it on with the belts.

Creed reached for his Colts. He had no idea what time it was; he just knew it was dark, and something woke him. He remembered nothing after he tightened the belts over the bandages, and that was two hours before dark. Several minutes later what he heard brought a smile to his face. His stomach was growling. He reached for the jerked beef and canteen of water. After satisfying his hunger, he reached for his pocket watch. He stopped midway in retrieving the watch and pushed it back into his pocket. *I have no light and I'm not about to light a Lucifer.*

Stiff, throbbing, and sore all over from tensing his muscles that had fought the pain, he unbuckled the belts over the wound. It relieved some of the throbbing. He would have to wait until daylight to look at the wound and he had no clue how long that would be.

Creed thought of Kathy Ann but wanted to think of the things that happened back at the Attoyac. *Kathy Ann would understand if she were here, wouldn't she?*

It was hard for them to defend themselves running away. I was unlucky to have been shot with a ricochet bullet. I'm not going to moan and groan about that. They are the ones dead and I'll never have to worry about Sheriff Mattingly again. Creed's thoughts drifted back to Kathy Ann, the Empire Timber & Cattle Company and Constantina. A smile crossed his face.

When it was light enough to see the wound, he could see that the infection had spread, and muscle tissue was rotting.

Pushing through the pain he built a small fire an arm's length away. Creed placed one end of the lightest and longest piece of wood he had in the fire and the other end easily in his reach. He made sure he had several small, peeled, sticks to bite down on ready. He took two of his bullets and removed the lead from them with the plicrs he had taken from the tool shed on the Attoyac. He placed one of the small sticks in his mouth and bit down.

With a fresh bandage he wiped the wound dry removing all the rotting flesh that he could and poured whiskey into the gaping wound. He dried it with a clean bandage then sprinkled the gunpowder from both bullets over the wound. He touched the long flaming stick to the gunpowder. His loud grunt was muffled by biting harder on the stick as the acrid odor of the fired gun powder and burnt flesh filled the lean-to. He laid a loose bandage over the wound.

It was several hours later when he looked at the wound again. He would wait a couple of days before he would lace the gaping wound closed using the sewing kit, he had taken from the two without their trigger fingers. He had his weapons, food, and water nearby and his two horses were leisurely searching out oats. He felt secure where he was and knew it would take time to heal. He did not try to get up until the next morning and when he did, he realized it was time to lace the wound closed.

The pain was not near as bad as cutting and gouging the bullet out. After a few days Creed felt he was out of the woods with the wound. He was getting his strength back and started riding his horse without much discomfort.

He marveled at the beauty of Scrapping Valley. he had not seen a single ghost… and it was a good place to recover more fully.

CHAPTER TWENTY-THREE

Nueces Strip Rustlers

Two weeks later, it was early in the morning when Creed neared Tillman's trading post. He had scoped it out and watched the last customer leave, then rode in slowly.

"Come on in, Creed, and have some coffee," greeted Tillman.

Creed was relaxed and his leg was much improved. Casual questions flowed both ways. He learned that Tillman's father had been in the logging business before the War and that Ralph had helped his father from an early age. During the War, their local timber business had been destroyed and they had no way to ship the timber or lumber to the big markets that were coming back. Most of the markets were along the gulf coast.

"Tillman, I have an idea. In about four weeks, could you spare a few days and go with me? I have something I want to show you."

"Sure, I could use a few days away from here. By the way, the sheriff nor any of his deputies have been in here during the last two weeks or so. That's pretty unusual."

"When they do show up, tell them that I am about ready to come by and see them," Creed said, grinning.

Creed rode to the branding camp. Jesús and Erskine had returned from their first drive with their crew four days earlier and were now gathering the cattle that Eldondo's group had branded.

"Eldondo, tell Jesús and Erskine to start moving the herd

north when they have 8,000 or more head. Have them send someone ahead when they are within three days of Boston to find Bo Brailey and send him to Fort Smith to give Maxwell an early estimated time of arrival."

Creed picked a Flying Dust mare from the remuda and rode the big black gelding. He headed to the Big Thicket. Creed elected to ride southeast and in sight of the Trinity River. It seemed that everywhere he looked he saw Texas Longhorns.

Creed stopped and made camp after about 30 miles riding. He had seen signs of Billy and his small crew where they had ridden back and forth to the Thicket, but he had not seen a living soul along the entire journey.

Creed hobbled his two horses, made coffee, cooked bacon on a green stick, and ate hardtack. Plenty of daylight remained so he read Devereaux's French book for the third time. It had been much easier than he had thought. Many of the French words were like English and Castilian Spanish, making the effort to learn a lot easier than it might have otherwise been.

Creed paused in his thoughts. His head turned in different directions. *What was that I just heard?* It took him several minutes, then it dawned on him. It was not something he just heard; it was what he was not hearing. He was not hearing many of the sounds normally heard in the forest. He heard no birds chirping, squirrels barking, or frogs croaking.

He slowly stood with his back to a large pine tree. With his hands cupped behind his ears, he slowly turned his head from far left to center, then to the right. Stopping, he turned slightly back to his left and stopped. He heard a faint repetitive heavy sound that was not rhythmic. Creed was sure that the sound was from several horses being ridden through the woods. He quickly buried the fire, making sure he made no sound and checked his weapons.

After he pulled off his boots and slipped on his moccasins, he left his horses hobbled and stalked away from camp. He carried his canteen, Colts, one of the Henry rifles, his Bowie and the telescope. He wanted to distance himself from the buried fire and smells he had created cooking and the horses. *These are not my men*! The number of horses he heard would be at least eight. Creed had to know what they were up to. His needs to catch up to the horses were not overridden by the knowledge that being seen could bring sudden death.

Another 30 minutes passed, getting darker. Creed caught a glimmer of movement back toward the Trinity and his right hand fell to his Colt. The movement he had seen was that of a cautious man. Creed was careful not to look directly at him. His eyes squinted and followed the man as he came closer.

Creed's next glance produced no vision of the man. He continued standing with no movement but his eyes. He still could not locate the man and the light was disappearing fast from the forest floor, but then he saw a hand ease out from behind a tree and wave. He peeked around the tree and recognized Billy.

"Where's your crew, Billy?" Creed whispered.

"They are on the trail of nine horses with riders we picked up early this morning."

"What do you know about them?"

"Well, we picked up the trail about ten miles north of the Thicket. We know they didn't come out of the Thicket. They knew we were on their trail and they have been trying to throw us off all day. They seem to know where they wanted to go. They seem to not want to attack us, but they didn't want us to catch up with them either."

"Do you want my help?"

"I found out at the branding camp that you were down this way and when we discovered the nine on our way back to the Thicket, I wanted to let you know and make sure you didn't bump into them unexpectedly. We're outnumbered but the Henry rifles are a great equalizer. I doubt they have anything as fast. I'd better get back; I may be needed."

Creed visited with Billy for several more minutes.

"I better go, Creed."

No sooner had the words left his mouth, they heard multiple rifle shots northwest of them. They quickly determined that there were more rifles being fired than the four of Billy's crew and the nine that they had been following combined. Many more! *Where were they coming from?*

Billy retrieved his horse and carried Creed back to his two horses. A war was going on northwest of them making enough noise to cover anyone's approach.

They rode as fast as they dared in the dark. When they got close enough to see the flashes of fire coming from the rifles they stopped and dismounted. A large campfire was giving off a flickering, shadowy light.

"My men were trailing. I'm assuming the gunfire coming from that direction is our men. The ones who were following must have met up with the others."

"Billy let's tie our horses here and we'll circle around and attack them from the northwest. Try to stay about ten yards back but don't lose sight of me in the dark. We may be here awhile so let's each carry a saddlebag full of ammunition, a canteen, and a pocket of jerked beef My thinking is they will be looking at our men and we'll be at their backs. Shoot the closest one to you so the ones in front of them will not see them fall. Our crew will figure it out because they will see the fire from our guns and see the ones in front of us fall. Shoot them as fast as you can because when they figure out what's happening, we will have a battle on our hands. Let's go!"

There was still enough noise to mask any sound the two of them would be making getting in position. Creed stopped and quickly counted seventeen shooters and eight bodies on the ground. They were all facing toward the southeast shooting from cover of the large pine trees.

Creed and Billy were fifty yards behind them and had an elevation advantage of about ten feet. Creed killed the one closest to him and Billy took the shooter next to him. Creed and Billy fired three more shots each before the nine left in the gang realized what was happening. All nine turned and scrambled to the other side of the trees to shoot at Creed and Billy and exposed their backs to Billy's four men. All nine were shot in the back by Billy's crew. The gunfire ended.

The heavy acrid smoke from all the gunfire brought bad memories and nausea to Creed. It took him several minutes before he could speak.

"Creed, here! Everyone stay where you are and don't move. That goes for everyone. I'm coming out." There were moans of several wounded that were bleeding out. Creed stood and counted twenty-five bodies. Now only two showed any signs of life. Creed walked to each body making sure they were dead while staying in position to face any he had not checked. When he got to the first wounded, he removed all his weapons.

"What's your name?"

No answer. Creed rushed to the second wounded man to get information only to see him die as he approached.

Creed ran to his four crew members who had been pinned down. All four stood and only one had been wounded. "Julian, what happened to you?"

"Boss, I got bark-shot. When the shooting started, I grabbed the biggest pine tree I could find and got as close to it as I could. I know now how a squirrel must feel when it's bark-shot. After I got a face full of bark, I got even closer to the tree."

"Are you going to be okay?"

"I just need someone to pick all the bark out of my face."

"I'll volunteer Kirby for that job. Tyner, tell Billy and me what happened here."

"Boss, the ones we were following knew we were on their trail. They didn't care much, they slowed us down a couple of times but never really tried to lose us. We thought they were looking for a good place to bushwhack us. We grew extremely cautious."

"The nine we were following found the ones they were looking for. They're all over there on the ground, dead, alongside the rest of them. When the groups found each other, they had a big celebration. After several bottles of whiskey had been downed, we decided to move in and act like we were part of them. The big gang didn't know the other nine we were following and none of the nine knew any of the big gang. We acted like the other drunks, but we listened."

"What did you hear, Tyner?"

"We found out that two of the sixteen they met up with were part of Sam Bass's gang. Seaborn Barnes and Thomas Spotswood had hired on. Sam wanted nothing to do with cattle rustling but he agreed they could hire on to help wipe us out, and then they would return to Sam's gang. Sam had a big heist planned for the bank in Round Rock and he needed them for that.

"Gleeson Hallbeck, the one over there next to that rotting stump, had planned the whole thing and was their leader. The nine we were following came up from the Nueces Strip in South Texas. They rode with King Fisher there and learned the cattle rustling business from one of the best. They were the vaqueros that would drive the herd. Hallbeck's crew was supposed to wipe us out and would protect them all the way to the buyer of the herd in Paris. This was all Hallbeck's doing from the get-go. He had scouted us out earlier. Preston was with Jake when they followed Hallbeck on the Trinity through Crockett heading to Dallas."

"I'm sure it was Hallbeck," Preston said. "They planned to kill us all and not worry about our brand being on the cattle. Their plan, after killing us, was to drive every Longhorn they could keep together to Paris. The buyer there had tipped Hallbeck off as to where our cattle were. He was plannin' to sell them to Indian Affairs."

"We decided to slip out of the party one at a time. Kirby went first and took a defensive position a hundred yards out. Julian then followed and separated from Kirby farther west. Tyner took a position in between them. I was the last to move out and with those three covering me I started slipping out. Somebody in the crowd hollered out to me and asked me where in the hell I was going. I told him I was just going to take a leak. He bellowed out to me that I didn't have to go that far to take a leak as he rushed toward me.

"A lot of attention was directed toward me, but when

Tyner, Kirby and Julian started firing, the attention shifted to them. The distraction gave me an opening to slip away. They were all drunk and they had eight dead with the open volley of fire coming from Kirby, Julian and Tyner. We had figured them not knowing our number made them want to sit tight and fire from cover and possibly wait for daylight. That's about all I know, Creed."

"Do any of you have anything to add to Tyner's and Preston's information?"

"Yes! I did hear Hallbeck say the buyer's name was Melrose, but he called himself the Kid. Hallbeck said the Kid told him he could borrow money from ol' man White if he needed more. I don't know who ol' man White is, but he might not be hard to find. There was a lot of loose talk going on, and Hallbeck said he wanted to make sure Melrose had the money to pay for the cattle and he checked out ol' man White. Hallbeck said he was certain the Kid could get the money from ol' man White, regardless of the number of Longhorns he delivered."

"Thanks, Kirby, that is important information. Billy, your crew did a great job here. When you get back to the branding camp, report what happened here to Donny, but I don't want anybody else to know.

I can see that there are some good rifles and .45s among the dead. Let's use their horses and haul the weapons and ammunition back to camp. Destroy any weapon that is not of good quality. Any horse that's not branded, brand them and turn them into the remuda. Swim the branded ones across the Trinity and turn them loose.

"Billy, you search their pockets and take all their money. Split it amongst yourselves. I think it best that you and the crew pull all the bodies deep into the Big Thicket. Do everything you can to ensure they're not going to be found.

"Get word to Tillman at the trading post that I will have to postpone our get-together. Also go to Marion's Ferry and look up Perry Hoffman. He has a place on the right before you get to the ferry. He has a horse that looks like Constantina's Sweet Pea. Buy the horse regardless of the cost. She is a fine-looking horse and I saw her work helping load cattle on the Ferry. Bring her back and give her to Constantina.

"Billy, while you're gathering the weapons, see what food supplies they have. I need enough for at least two weeks. Pick out one of their unbranded horses I can use as a pack horse. Gather any oats they may have, and I'll take them along. I'm going to Paris, Texas, and find someone who wants to buy some Longhorns."

CHAPTER TWENTY-FOUR

Paris, Texas

Five and a half days after leaving the Trinity flats near the Big Thicket, Creed scouted out the terrain for a defendable site to pitch camp. He was less than ten miles to Paris. He had crossed the Southern Fork of the Sulphur River several miles back and knew he was getting close. There was no high land around, so Creed settled on a small creek that led back to the river for his camp spot. He had good line-of-sight but little cover. There was a low area that would conceal his horses and campfire as well as dry wood and thick mesquite to disperse any smoke.

The intended buyer of the Longhorns, the Kid, was a threat and Creed would kill him. He prayed no others would be hurt.

Early the next morning, Creed washed and brushed the black gelding, making him shine. Creed loved the big horse whose strength showed in every muscle even when he was only walking. He saddled and hid the brand with one of the Henry scabbards. He cleaned his Bowie, two Henry rifles, his two nine-inch Colt .45s and wiped his saddle clean. After he bathed in the creek and changed into clean clothes, he tied two hemp pigging ropes around his waist and chose the black shirt to go with his low-crowned black hat. He cleaned his boots and dusted his hat. After tying the Colts low on his hips, he loosened them and his Bowie in their holsters. *It might make me look like a gunfighter but I'm okay with that. I'm ready to be a gunfighter if I need to be.*

Creed rode into Paris with the sun at his back. Only a small, lonely dust devil darted out in front of him. It picked up dust and led him into town and slowly faded away, dropping its dust. Every head he passed had turned to look at him. The sound of his horse was the only sound in town until he heard someone running ahead. Creed saw the runner look back at him before entering a building. He guessed that he would get his boss to have a good look at the stranger. Creed planned to get a good look also.

The runner appeared at the front door standing next to a young, tall man. He had a Colt belted high on his hip. *That Colt would be hard to get out of the holster. Is the tall man the Kid? Probably!* Creed looked him in the eye and acknowledged him with a slight nod and a tip of his hat as he passed.

Two doors down he pulled up across the street in front of a saloon. He tied his horse and lifted his two .45s and then replaced them loosely back in their holsters. Creed lowered his hat and peeked across the street. The two men were no longer there. While Creed had been riding past the building all his attention had been on the runner and his boss and not the building. The door was nearly blocked with sacks of flour and cornmeal, stacked four high, under the covered porch of the building. He raised his head and looked at the sign above the store. It read, *White's Mercantile and Feed. Ol' man White!*

Creed closed his eyes and slightly opened them as he walked toward the swinging doors of the saloon with his right hand resting on his Colt. Creed entered and took a quick step to the left side of the door, stood still, and then fully opened his eyes. Cigarette smoke was hanging from the high ceiling and an exit door was located near the end of the bar. Three poker players at a table and a bartender all looked at Creed for a moment then the activity at hand. Creed went to the far end of the bar, turned his back to the latched exit door, and faced the swinging door. The three poker players took turns glancing at Creed while he waited for the tall man to come in.

The bartender brought Creed a coffee. *What was taking the tall man so long?* The bartender looked up when the tall man entered. "Sit down Kid. I'll get you your regular."

Creed ignored him and was looking toward the three poker players but was able to see every move the Kid made. The Kid drank the shot, picked up the bottle and slammed it down on the bar and spoke loudly. "Damn, that's good stuff!" He paused and looked at Creed, who showed no reaction. "You're new in town, aren't you?"

"Might be," replied Creed. "Why do you ask?"

"I'm looking for a good man to hire," said the Kid.

"To do what?" Creed asked.

"Let's sit at that table next to the wall where we will have some privacy and we'll finish this bottle. I'll tell you about it."

"I'll sit at the table with you, but I want none of your bottle; I'll just have my coffee."

"How long you plan to be in town, stranger?"

"Depends," said Creed.

"On what?" Asked the Kid.

"On how much you are going to pay me."

I'm Melrose White. My friends call me the Kid. What's your name, Stranger?"

"Wheat," said Creed. "Oscar Wheat."

"Mr. Wheat, I can tell I'm talking to someone I want to hire. I knew it the moment I first saw you. When you acknowledged the most powerful man in this part of Texas with that slight nod and tip of your hat. I knew you were smart since you had never seen me before."

"I don't do business with people who are not powerful or smart or those who don't have money," said Creed.

"Let's go to my office across the street and have some serious conversation," White replied.

Creed untied his horse, looked at footprints on the ground around his horse, and walked across the street with Melrose and tied his horse there.

"What's with all the flour and cornmeal?"

"That belongs to my grandfather. He has a contract with Indian Affairs at Fort Smith to furnish all the flour and cornmeal to the Eastern Division of the Indian Territory."

"That sounds like a big deal."

"Not near as big a deal as the one I'm going to tell you about."

Creed followed Melrose into the building. The building was dark inside and had the pleasant odor of cattle feed. The slight odor of two coal oil lamps struggling to light the entire big room spoiled the pleasant odor of the feed in places. The Kid's office was in the back corner of the building. Creed cautiously followed him into the office with his hand on one of the Colts.

"Oscar, let's cut to the chase and talk about each other before we get down to business. I've got some questions and I'm sure you do also, okay?"

"Fine with me, Kid. Lead out."

"You and I know you hire out your gun."

"How do you know that, Melrose?"

"You denyin' it? Melrose asked.

"Nah! I'll do anything if the money is right. Get on with it. What do you want me to do?

"We're a lot alike, Oscar. I too will do anything for money.

I only have two questions. How good are you with your weapons? Or are they just for show?

"Melrose, I know my weapons well enough to know you removed my two Henrys from their scabbards outside the saloon before you came in and that I will not use them until I check them out to make sure the ammunition is still in them. I can assure you nothing I do is for show. I do things for money. I only have two questions. What do you want me to do and how much do you plan to pay me?"

"I'm impressed, Oscar. I did remove the shells. Thought it could give me an advantage if things didn't work out. I now know that it will work out. I want to make you a deal you can't turn down."

"How about answering my questions first?"

"They will be answered in the deal I'm gonna present to you.

"Oscar, hear me out before you make a decision. I'm layin' all my cards on the table. This is going to be the biggest deal you ever heard of and I and have it all planned. You are the missing link to getting it done."

"George White owns this Mercantile. George is my grandfather. My mother and father worked themselves to death building this business. They both died of consumption a few years back. I feel that the business should be mine. There is no telling how much money George has. He was smart enough to have all his wealth in gold before the War started, hidden in vaults. I know where three of the vaults are hidden. He has vast land holdings and has paid all the back taxes and reconstruction fees to the government. I've borrowed money from him in the past and had to work for him to pay back the debt. I am his only heir."

"Several months ago, I went to the Indian Affairs office in Fort Smith, Arkansas, with George. He tried to sell the Indian Affairs head man, a man named Maxwell, some Longhorn cattle for the Territory. Maxwell told him of a deal he had on Texas Longhorn cattle and that he couldn't buy from anyone else unless the provider failed in fulfilling his end of the bargain. Only then would he buy from George. George fished around until he was told who the provider was and where the cattle were coming from."

"George was not going to do anything more than stay in touch with Maxwell and hope that the provider of the cattle would fail on a delivery. I arranged on my own initiative to have the provider and his whole crew killed. There should be a herd of somewhere between five to eight thousand Texas Longhorns on the way here as we speak.

"Now this is where you come in, Oscar. George will not loan me the money to pay the rustlers. The money George has is rightfully mine. Your job is to kill George for me so I can take his money. My plan is to pay the rustlers' gang leader, a man named Hallbeck, for the cattle. Then before he can pay his gang, you will kill Hallbeck and take the money back from him. With that money, you will pay the gang the money they have coming and become their leader. You will have them work over the brand and I will go to Indian Affairs and get a procurement order for the cattle. You and I will split the money that's left, then you will go back to where the Longhorns were being originally gathered and bring back herd after herd and we'll continue to split 50/50.

What do you think?"

"Melrose, I love the plan. I'm ready to kill George right now. I don't know why we shouldn't with the herd on the way, do you?"

"I've been ready," the Kid said.

"Melrose get him in here then."

"I'd rather that you kill him in his office instead of mine."

"Okay. Take me to his office and let me do all the talking. I like to let anyone that I kill know why they deserve to die."

Melrose knocked on the door of George's windowless office. "George, I want you to meet a friend of mine."

"Melrose, I don't think I want to meet any friend of yours," said George.

"Mr. White, please give me a few minutes and hear me out. Melrose has a plan that will interest you," said Creed.

Unnoticed by Melrose or White, Creed had both Colt .45s drawn. "I don't want anyone getting shot here, so I'm going to take your guns."

Giving Melrose a slight wink, Creed disarmed him first.

"Mr. White, Melrose here tells me he thinks all the money you have belongs to him."

"That dirty scum-bag!"

"Whoa! Whoa! Whoa! Hear me out. He says he is your only heir and since he will get everything when you die, he has hired me to kill you. He needs the money now for a big deal."

"That ..."

"Hush! Hear me out. I know more about this than Melrose does." Creed said.

Melrose was turning white around the gills.

"Melrose thinks he has a herd of rustled Longhorn cattle of mine headed this way. He doesn't. He thinks the outlaw Gosnell Hallbeck, who he hired without the money to pay him, is leading the herd here. He's not, because he's dead and so are all his gang—which numbered twenty-five."

Creed slapped Melrose against his head with his pistol when Melrose reacted to his statement. "Shut up, Melrose, or I'll kill you now."

"So, you see Mr. White, Melrose does not need your money and neither do I, Dakota Creed."

Melrose started shaking and sobbing and Creed slapped him. "Shut up, Melrose!"

"Now, Mr. White, I want you to know that Melrose White, your grandson, is about to die. I have every right to kill him for the attack on my vaqueros and attempting to rustle my cattle. I feel *you* have every right to kill him as well, for hiring me to kill you and him planning to take all your money. You know if we kill him with a knife, we won't attract anyone's attention here. In fact, there's no place any better than your office and no time like the present.

"I want to do it! Melrose has been on the teat way too long. I've always thought that he was never from my son's seed."

He turned to his sobbing grandson. "Melrose, I hate you for what you have done in your life and the stain you put on the family name."

Melrose tried to run but there was no place to go. Creed grabbed his neck with one hand and crammed his bandana into his mouth then pushed him to his knees. He tied the bandana in place with a hemp pigging rope and used another to tie the Kid's hands behind his back. Creed jerked

Melrose's head back and placed a wastebasket under his head. He handed his Bowie knife to George White who looked into Melrose's terrified eyes. "You deserve much worse than this, Melrose."

Melrose's eyes widened as the knife neared his throat. "Hold still, Melrose! I don't want your sorry blood all over my office."

The knife glided across the Kid's neck.

"I'll help you get rid of the body Mr. White, if you wish."

"You've done enough. I'm very indebted to you for what you've done for me. I have a barrel of slop out back on a wagon backed up to the loading dock. I'll pour the blood in it. I feel responsible for him and his doings. I can move the body with a dolly to the wagon. I have a good place in mind where I can dispose of him. No one of importance will ever miss him."

"If I were you Mr. White, I would make sure he could never be found."

"I can assure you when the hogs get through with him, he will never be found."

"Let's walk back to the front of the building and be seen together before you leave," suggested George.

"Mr. White, if I can ever be of help to you, don't hesitate to holler.

CHAPTER TWENTY-FIVE

The Big Thicket

Creed left Paris and rode south ten miles to pick up his other horses, then headed east in hopes of running into Jesús and Erskine driving their herd north near Boston. He saw a heavy fresh trail of Longhorns heading north and correctly guessed they were ahead of their schedule. He decided to head south in hope of finding Pasqual's herd. When he ran into the herd he turned and rode back north with them until dark just to have a meal with Pasqual and Constantina. That girl always made Creed think of Kathy Ann.

When Constantina first saw Dakota, she raced to him on her new horse. "Dakota, Billy brought the horse to me. I love her. She reminds me so much of Sweet Pea that I changed her name to Sweet Pea. Thank you so much for her. It is so sweet of you."

"I'm glad you like her. I thought you would." Creed loved the excitement in her eyes and the smile on her face. He looked forward to seeing the same in Kathy Ann's when they could be together.

On the way back to the branding camp, Creed thought of the house he would build on the hill above the spring for Kathy Ann. He might get Constantina to look at the area and give him a woman's perceptive view as to where the home should be built. This thought brought on other realizations that would keep him awake all night. He didn't really want to sleep, he wanted to plan.

He was aware that Constantina was being greatly underutilized. She was intelligent, and people were drawn to her. It wasn't just her beauty but her understanding and compassionate nature.

Donny and Erskine looked after their crews and the brand as if it were theirs. Juan, Jesús, Pasqual and Eldondo did the same. Creed was excited about his plans. First, he was going to increase the Vaqueros' and guards' wages to 40 dollars a month. That was more than anyone in Texas earned unless they were gunmen. He would give Donny, Erskine, Juan, Jesús, Pasqual, and Eldondo a raise and come up with a profit-sharing plan for each of them. He hoped everyone in Texas would want to work for the Empire Timber & Cattle Company.

Creed remembered Constantina trying on the dress in Boston. He knew she loved being a vaquera, but she would love wearing dresses and doing lady things, too. She would also make a lot more money. Women did not work in banks, but most women were not vaqueras either. *She would be great at running the Empire Timber & Cattle Company Bank and I need her there. I'll make this work.*

He had been near the Big Thicket before, but Creed would see it today for the first time. He needed the tranquility of the Thicket to think his plan through.

The Big Thicket was as beautiful as he had been told by those who had seen it. The wide, shallow, sandy-bottom creeks were his favorite part. He saw wildflowers and trees that bore fruit and nuts. Wildlife was abundant.

Creed rode back northwest hugging the Neches River, then turned south back to the branding camp.

At a meeting with Donny and Pasqual who had just

returned from delivering another herd to the Red, he told them of the raises and the profit-sharing plan he was developing for them. Both were incredibly pleased. Creed asked Pasqual to stay for a few minutes as Donny was returning to his duties.

"Pasqual, when we saw Constantina trying on the dress in Boston, it got me thinking. I know she loves being a vaquera, but I think she would also love being a young lady. Keep an open mind on this, Pasqual. I have never seen a woman banker, but I had never seen a woman vaquera either. I need a banker. Given the chance, she could be a great banker. She is smart enough to learn. If you would give me your permission to talk to her, would you please be present?"

"Creed, I know being a vaquero is a young man's job. I have worried about Constantina for some time now. She is as good as the boys, but she needs to learn something else. When do you want to talk to her?"

"I would like to do it now, if you have time and can find someone to relieve her of what she's doing."

"Come with me, Creed. We'll find her."

"There she is," Pasqual said. He waved at her to come to them. The slight smile on her face changed to a big smile when she realized Dakota was with him.

"Good to see you again, Dakota."

"Constantina, I need your help. You are the only one riding for the brand who can help me."

"I'll be glad to help if I can, Dakota."

"You had better hear what I want you to do before you commit to it."

"Dakota, I don't care what you need me to do. I will do it. As much as you have done for all of us I will gladly do it.

What do you need?"

"Constantina, we have a lot going on. We have all the land, cattle, and timber. There is a lot of money coming in and going out. It all needs to be counted, recorded and protected. I'm hoping you will help me do this. We bought a bank in Nacogdoches. We have changed the name to Empire Timber & Cattle Company Bank. We will spend time with Glad Mathews, our attorney, for guidance, but you and I must run the bank. I don't want outsiders counting our money and knowing too much about our business. Will you help me with this?"

"Of course, I will help you. When can I start?"

"Constantina, we are looking for two Texas Rangers to Guard the bank around the clock..."

"I can guard it in the day."

"I know you could Constantina, but you won't be able to wear your .45 with a dress on."

"Dress? I'm going to wear dresses?"

"I am leaving for New Orleans in the morning. I need your sizes. I will be buying you a whole wardrobe of dresses and shoes for you.

I want you to pick out a room in Miss Milo's boarding house in Nacogdoches. It's near the bank. Pasqual can introduce you to Glad. I will give you a letter with instructions for him to give you anything you want to see and anything he thinks you should see. Here is two hundred dollars. Get your room and buy anything you might need while I'm gone."

"I know I will do a good job. I am good with numbers and keeping records," said Constantina with an excited smile and gleam in her eyes.

"You may not know this, Constantina, but you have a

way about you that makes people want to be around you. You will make a great banker."

"Banker? Yes, I will! Thank you, Dakota."

Creed was preparing to leave the branding camp for New Orleans. Juan, Jesús, Eldondo, Pasqual, Donny and Erskine had diligently been gathering hands. The word was out and the forty dollars a month made every cowboy who heard of it want the job. Of course, each cowboy had to pass muster on their loyalty to the brand.

Caution was taken not to alienate any of the many who were rejected. One was so belligerent that Pasqual thought that it might be necessary that he had to be eliminated permanently or he would surely cause trouble down the road.

Creed was walking by and glanced at the belligerent cowboy. Creed reached for both his .45s but did not draw them. He rested his hands on their butts and searched the area with his eyes but held his head steady. He had recognized the man instantly and was searching for his kin. After inbreeding for over sixty years, a Wallander had his family features chiseled into their face from birth. Creed saw none of his kin but knew others might be nearby somewhere.

"Pasqual, this man looks to me like someone we need. He looks as if he has been in a fight or two and we need fighters. We haven't hired enough men of his character."

Pasqual looked at Creed in astonishment. He had no idea what was going on until after Creed spoke again.

"Pasqual, you don't know a good man when you see one."

Pasqual knew Creed was up to something. He would shut up and let Creed play it out.

"I want to hire you. Do you know of anyone else around of your caliber we could hire?"

"Sure do. I've got twelve cousins who are all as tough as boar hogs."

"Where are they now?" Creed asked.

"They're close by, I could go get 'em."

"How long would it take?"

"I could be back with 'em in a coupla hours."

"Do they want a job?"

"They would want this job."

"Go get them, I want them all," said Creed.

As the man rushed off Creed said, "Pasqual, that man is a Wallander. He's part of a clan of thieves and murders. As soon as he is out of sight get all the outriders in here and any of your men who know how to fight, and hurry! We are in danger! Have them bring their weapons and plenty of ammunition. We are going to have a fight on our hands. They will try to steal the herd by stampeding them. They like to shoot first and we must turn the table on that. We *must* kill them all. He said he had twelve cousins, expect twenty-four or more. I want them killed away from the camp. Hurry!"

Within minutes twenty-six of Creed's men were there and some stragglers were on their way.

"Listen up! I will track the man who just rode off to the north. Donny, you barely keep me in sight and Pasqual you keep Donny in sight. When I catch up with them, they will be on their way here. I will try to get a count and signal it to Donny. Donny, you get back to Pasqual as fast as you can and set up an ambush. I will get out of the way before the shooting starts so don't be afraid of shooting me. I must go. Everyone, just follow Donny and Pasqual's orders."

Creed picked up the Wallanders' tracks with ease. Creed figured he was about twenty minutes behind him. The tracks were basically in a straight line and Creed moved twenty yards away from the trail and checked often to make sure the trail was still going in the same direction. After trailing the tracks for an hour, Creed turned toward Donny and signaled him to come to him.

"Donny, hurry back and get the rest of the men. Set up the ambush here. Make it wide enough and bowed enough to prevent escape from the rear."

Creed rode west a half mile then turned back north and rode slowly. After twenty minutes, Creed heard them. He was closer than he wanted to be. He dismounted and led his horse west until he found a cluster of brush and tied the horse off. With his loaded Henry and saddlebag full of ammunition, he lay prone hugging the ground and dared not look up. They were only about fifty yards east of him. He lay still with his finger on the trigger of his Henry. He felt revenge creep over him. He had plenty of ammunition for the Henry and would like to use it all killing Wallanders.

When they passed and had their backs to him, Creed's horse snorted from the cluster of brush. Creed shifted his eyes from the ground up to the backs of the riders. Only one turned and looked back toward him. Creed closed his eyes and a few seconds later peeked with one eye. The lone rider again turned looking toward him and Creed closed the one eye.

Creed waited until they should be out of sight. He stood, then started chasing them on foot. In less than twenty minutes chaos broke loose.

He soon saw three Wallanders in retreat heading toward him. Their horses were running full out. The riders were looking back over their shoulders firing. They never saw Creed standing on the ground off to their left as he pulled the trigger three times. They were blown from their saddles. Behind them, four more were holding onto their saddle horns. They were shot to ribbons trying to escape. Creed jumped in front of them to finish them off. He knocked two from their saddles with his Henry as the other two horses turned and raced back toward their ambushers. Their action brought a thunderous reply of rifle fire that made Creed dive for cover.

Now there were occasional shots fired from .45s, killing the wounded. Creed raised himself from the ground and sought out the five he had shot and cut each of their throats. A quick check proved that none who rode for the brand were killed or wounded. An opinion from each was that all the Wallenders who were there had been killed.

Creed said no prayer for the Wallanders' parents, but he did pray that all the Wallanders who were there were indeed dead. He had been told previously of their number and knew there were others that were not there.

He had his crew bury all thirty-nine Wallanders that were killed.

"Listen up! We dodged a bullet today. If any of you see anyone who looks like any of these thirty-nine, we buried today, stay cool and alert. I know you are all brave but don't do anything on your own. If you see one, there will be others nearby. Alert everyone you can find who rides for the brand and make plans to wipe them out like we did today. Y'all did a great job today protecting the brand," said Creed.

CHAPTER TWENTY-SIX

Captain Drake and Quick Tender

"Donny, I want you to personally deliver this message to Glad. I want you to select fifteen of your best men and take them with you everywhere you go. Be ready to ride with me on a minute's notice."

Creed ate with the crew leaders at breakfast and made sure all the crews were organized and the new members were mixed in with the established crews. Creed had confidence in his foremen and crews to handle any situation that arose while he was gone.

Creed had sent and received several letters to his friend Lance Devereaux who he had met in Jefferson. They had made plans to meet in New Orleans.

Hugging the Trinity River to the southeast, he rode one of his Flying Dust mares and had another on a lead rope. The two had both the Flying Dust and the ETCC brands. He was behind schedule one full day and was traveling light, carrying only oats for the horses and jerked beef, hardtack, and coffee. The two Henrys were in their scabbards. He had his saddle bag full of ammunition and Lance Devereaux's French book, along with the sewing kit. His brass telescope was hanging on his saddle horn. His plan was to run his horses in all the flats to make up time and switch horses every hour.

The farther Creed rode southeast he saw more maverick Longhorns and the lack of graze became more apparent. He realized his taking the Longhorns out of the area would prevent further over-grazing of the land that was happening during and since the Civil War when ranchers sometimes failed to round up their free-range cattle, causing massive die-outs of Longhorns and lesser breeds of cattle.

Lance had sent Creed a schedule of a three-mast schooner that traveled from New Orleans to Corpus Christi then back to New Orleans. There were stops in Sabine Pass, Galveston and Port Lavaca. According to the schedule, the schooner would be leaving the port of Sabine Pass in three days and heading for New Orleans. Creed had allocated himself four days to get there, now he had to get there in three. Sabine Pass is on the west shore of the Sabine River where it enters the Gulf of Mexico. Louisiana is across the river on the east shore. The schooner would be leaving the port just after dawn.

The schooner carried passengers, their horses and carriages as well as freight. Creed loaded his horses the evening before departure and their brand caught the attention of the ship caption, Dag Drake, who knew of the famous Flying Dust Ranch. His interest in the horses induced him to invite Creed to join him and his grandson, Quick Tender, for dinner. Creed had never been as impressed with anyone as he was with these two. Ideas exploded in Creed's mind with Captain Drake's mention of railroads, banks, and geography. They talked into the night.

"If you ever need help with a railroad, wire me," said the Captain.

Late the next evening, the schooner pulled into the port of New Orleans. Once he left the boat, Creed followed Lance's instructions and found his destination nearby. Creed greeted Lance in French and the two carried on a conversation for several minutes. Creed returned the book

Lance had loaned him.

"I'm very impressed with your knowledge of the French language."

"Thanks! But, of course, I'm not very good with pronunciation. That's hard to get from a book. Lance, do you know of barges other than the log ones that are tied together with rope?"

This question created a three-hour conversation. It ended with the decision that the Empire Timber & Cattle Company Bank would lend Lance the money to build three large barges and a tugboat. The barges—each with a loading crane, side and end walls—would carry timber down a river. A large two-handle sump pump would be in place at the rear of the barge to pump out any unwanted water. The tugboat would have a steam engine fueled by firewood. Lance would receive a contract from Empire Timber & Cattle Company to haul timber down the Trinity River to the Texas gulf coast.

"Dakota, I have a customer who ships various kinds of freight. He wanted to ship mining timbers to Matamoros, Mexico. He suggested I could go all the way in the intercoastal canals. The InterCoastal Canal was too close to the high winds of the Gulf of Mexico and they would drive the ship ashore. I had to turn him down."

"Can I talk to this customer?"

"Sure! He's around all the time."

"Let's find him. If he has a way to contact his client in Matamoros, we should be able to make a deal."

When Devereaux and Creed found Doyle Skillman, they asked him questions on many subjects, including mining timbers and the Shorthorn breed of cattle call the Durham, which were raised for beef in Britain. .

Each made a contract with Skillman to ship mining timbers to Matamoros. Then Skillman said something to Creed that made his heart beat faster. He didn't know if it was because it could place him closer to Kathy Ann or that it was a tremendous opportunity for his Empire. Skillman mentioned the fact that most of Europe was out of timber. The forests that were left belonged to royalty and the penalty for cutting one of their trees was death. There was no timber to build more furniture or replace windows and door frames that were built three or four hundred years before. Creed thought of the four hundred thousand acres of the finest timber he had ever seen and that was the timber just north of the camp where he had worked as a slave.

"Mr. Skillman, I know where to find furniture-grade white oak, black walnut and white ash timber. It is northern grown. Most of the timber does not have a knot showing for the first forty feet up the tree. I have taken core samples from white ash trees whose circumference was so large, the hearts of the trees were less than ten percent of the total wood. It is top quality. What could you pay for timber such as that delivered to New Orleans on a long-term basis?

After a few moments of scribbling down some figures and muttering to himself, Skillman answered the question. "On furniture grade I could pay $200 dollars per thousand board feet on a sixteen-foot log figuring it on a Doyle scale."

"I will be back with you in less than two months, Mr. Skillman," said Creed, as he reached to shake his hand.

"Lance, you might need a larger tugboat and larger barges with larger water pumps on board to handle the Mississippi. I'll loan you the money. Give me a rate from St Louis to New Orleans. I have an idea I can put this together. I'll let you know in about four weeks. Get started on the barges for the Trinity and I'll start gathering the timber."

Creed arrived in Nacogdoches with three bundles tied to his pack horse. He went straight to the bank. As he walked in the door, Constantina rushed to meet him.

"Dakota, I could hardly wait until you returned. I started to come and get you. I've signed up every business in town and fifty-six individuals to bank with us. I convinced them our bank was safer than a buried fruit jar." She reached out and grasped his forearm, looked in his eyes and said, "Thank *you* for having faith in *me*."

He placed his hand on hers and looked down at her. "Thank you, for having faith in me."

"Come out and help me in with these packages." Creed was as excited as she. They untied the packages and took them to her office. One package excited her more than the others. "I didn't know you were going to buy me hats and a parasol," she exclaimed.

Glad entered the office. "I've got to see you alone, Creed!" His voice betrayed a note of concern.

"Okay Glad. May we go to your office. I don't want anyone raining on Constantina's joy."

"That will be fine. I'm afraid all hell is about to break loose. Sheriff Mattingly, his daughter and his eight deputies have disappeared off the face of the earth. The locals started missing them about three or four weeks ago but said nothing except among themselves and three weeks ago, some carpetbaggers stopped by to see the Sheriff and left a note for him to get in touch with them. After the Sheriff did not get in touch, they went to the State Police in Austin and now State Police are all over town asking questions. Some have gone to Mattingly's home on the Attoyac Bayou and have not returned.

"What's that got to do with us? I think it would take a full crew to make that many people disappear from the face of the earth and we've been as busy as a one-armed paperhanger. All our men and I can be accounted for. None of us have gunshot wounds that surely would have occurred if we had been in any kind of a fight with them. I'm sure you can sell that good of a story to them. We should not be bothered with their disappearance."

"You've got me sold, Creed. I'm sure you didn't have anything to do with it."

"Just remember, Glad, they did enough to others to make a lot of people want them to disappear. I wanted to let you know that I'll be gone a few weeks. After that I will be spending a lot of time here. Have you closed on all the land between the Trinity and the Neches from the Big Thicket all the way to Crockett?"

"We've got it all, Creed."

"Any progress on the message Donny brought to you."

"Yes, I will have it done by the time you get back."

"Please tell Donny to get ready for my return. He will know what that means."

"Will do, Creed."

"Have you found the home builder?"

"Sure have! He's ready when you are."

"Line me up a surveyor and I'll lay it out as soon as I get back."

Creed rushed back to the bank. Constantina was still trying on hats. It was the first woman's hat that she had ever owned.

"Constantina, I need for you to fill me in on the cattle drives. Come and have something to eat with me." During the meal there were a lot of giggles and smiles from Constantina. She seemed incredibly happy. She always seemed happy, but this seemed special.

"Constantina, I need to leave again. I'm going to St. Louis, then to Fort Smith to see Maxwell. I'd love to see you in one of your new dresses and with your hat on when you enter the bank. I won't leave until I see that. You could be married and gone by the time I get back," he said with a smile.

"How long are you going to be gone?" She asked.

"Not over five weeks."

"Oh! That's okay. It will take a little longer than that for me to get married. With these new clothes I'm going to be mighty picky," grinned Constantina.

"I hope you will be anyway," Creed said with a little hidden sadness in his heart. He was lonely for Kathy Ann and Rascal.

"When I get back, I want your input on the house. Glad has found me a home builder. I would like for you to draw a floor plan for the house, barn, stables, and two detached guest houses. As soon as I return, I will take you to the site on the 80,000 acres southeast of here and we will stake out the spot that you think would be best. I think a lady's opinion on those matters are superior to that of a man's. Once we stake it, Glad will send out a surveyor."

"Dakota, I will love doing this. I've always dreamed of building a house I would love to live in."

Creed arrived early at the bank the next morning. When Constantina walked in, she filled his sail with wind. "Wow!"

Creed had seen women in New Orleans dressed as she was but not one who looked any better and more at ease. He was so happy for her.

Creed was already packed and ready to ride when he left the bank. He nodded at the four riders passing by and hoped that they wouldn't follow him. All four wore a star. He rode slowly out of Nacogdoches and this time didn't bother to cover his trail.

CHAPTER TWENTY-SEVEN

State Police Visit

"We want to see Miss DeLeon right now!" One of them barked.

When Constantina heard the commotion outside her office, she immediately opened her desk drawer on her right and placed her hand on her Colt .45. She knew it was ready to fire but checked it to be sure. She did the same with the one in the left drawer. She heard Billy McBride confront the intruders. She determined they were lawmen and thought it best to have them shown into her office.

"Billy, show them in."

"Are you sure, ma'am?"

"Show them in and close the door. You stay in the lobby."

Constantina stayed seated at her desk. "I'll apologize for Billy. Texans are having a hard time accepting the rudeness of some people. Whether they are lawmen or not. Now, what can I do for you?

"You probably saved Billy's life. We are tired of all the run-around we've been getting in our effort to find Dakota Creed. You will need more than Billy to fight your battle because you are going to tell us where we can find Creed."

"I fight my own battles and I'm ready to fight when you are ready."

The four lawmen were speechless as Constantina stood with a Colt in each hand. One of the lawmen reached for his weapon and as it cleared leather it exploded in his hand.

"The next one of you who draws a weapon on me will be killed. Now each of you remove your guns and put them here on my desk, one at a time and be careful. We don't want any accidents happening now, do we?"

"Billy, come in here. Gather these weapons and take these gentlemen to the lobby. I will work one of them into my schedule as soon as possible. Let it be their choice witch one.

Forty-five minutes later Constantina opened the door. "I will see one of you now. If anyone else wants to see me, make an appointment for tomorrow."

"Miss DeLeon, I'm Caption Livingston Tarver of the State Police. We've tried to locate Dakota Creed for the last week and all we get is the run-around from everyone we've talked to. We've heard several references to you."

"Mr. Tarver, I'm the only person in this county who knows where Mr. Creed is, and I have never been asked."

"Why are you the only one who knows?"

"Because Mr. Creed wants it that way. Will you tell me why you want to know where he is?"

"We think he might know what's happened to Sheriff Mattingly, his daughter, and his deputies," Tarver said.

"Why do you think Mr. Creed would know?"

"It's well known that the Sheriff had been looking for him for weeks and Creed hid from him."

"Humph, that's funny. Mr. Creed doesn't hide from anyone. He is a busy man and I sent word to Sheriff Mattingly that he would be by to see him as soon as he had time. Mr. Tarver, Sheriff Mattingly never told anyone why he was looking for Mr. Creed. I was told Mattingly was angry at Mr. Creed for legally buying land that Mattingly was in line to buy. Mr. Tarver, Mr. Creed will be gone for several or about five weeks. When he comes back, I will ask him to stop by and see you."

"Where is he?"

"He is headed to St. Louis then to Fort Smith."

"What is he going to do there?"

"That's none of your business, Mr. Tarver."

"Look, you're lucky I didn't arrest you for shooting the gun out of one of my men's hand."

"Mr. Tarver, you're lucky Billy or I didn't kill all four of you. This is a bank. You rush in here raising hell. Y'all have law badges on, but they can be bought anywhere. I had no way of knowing you weren't bank robbers."

"If you thought we could be bank robbers, why would you let us in your office alone?"

"There were only four of you and I knew I could handle that few of you and I wanted none of my customers or clerks involved."

Her response left Tarver speechless, and a frown crossed his forehead. "Hopefully, we will find Mattingly and his daughter and deputies safe."

"I hope you find them, Mr. Tarver," said Constantina as she led him to the door.

"Billy, give them back their weapons and escort them out of the building."

The lawmen left meekly. They were embarrassed that a woman was able to get an upper hand on them. *Women weren't supposed to work in banks and should not be able to shoot a gun*, thought Tarver. It went without saying that none of the four would ever say a word to anyone about what happened at the bank that day.

"Billy, come into my office, please."

Constantina closed the door. "Billy, don't mention this to

anyone. I don't want what happened here today getting back to Dakota. He has enough on his plate, and I don't want him worrying about us."

"Miss Constantina, you did a great job. I was worried that I was going to have to kill them, and I know how much trouble that would have caused."

"I will talk to the clerks and then we will never mention this again. "

Creed rode hard to catch up with one of his herds four days out and spent the night with Juan and his crew. There was no problem with the graze. A Longhorn would eat anything that was green including leaves and small branches.

All the new hands wanted to make a good showing and competed for attention with their skills in riding and roping. They wanted to keep this job. That was for sure.

Creed found two Flying Dust mares in the remuda and switched them out with his. After riding about thirty miles a day after leaving Nacogdoches, he arrived in St. Louis on the eighteenth day. There was enough time before dark to catch the ferry across the Mississippi over to East St. Louis, Illinois. He rode to Cahokia, which was a short distance south of the ferry crossing.

Carlyle lay a little over fifty miles east and he wanted to travel a few of them before dark. He did take time to look at possible loading sites for timber at Cahokia.

Creed arrived in Carlyle at mid-afternoon the next day. He located Mr. Simon and talked with him but never gave him a clue that he wanted to buy his land. Creed just asked questions. Mr. Simon told him the timber was worthless because there was no way to deliver it to the market.

"The land would be worth more if it did not have a stick of timber on it. Then it could be planted in corn. The corn could be moved out with side-boarded wagons or it could be used to raise hogs nearby. I had the land sold several months ago but the buyer killed himself in an accident. I had been trying to sell it all during the War and after but couldn't find a buyer."

Creed bought all 400,000 acres of Mr. Simon's land for fifty cents per acre. He would build a narrow-gauge railroad track starting at the high bluff in Cahokia that overlooked the Mississippi River and St. Louis. The track would run east and curve south before reaching Carlyle and then run south all the way to the clear-cut near Mound City.

The timber would be lowered from the bluff in Cahokia to Lance Devereaux's barges below. Creed would have a railroad crew start at the northwest end of the property near Cahokia and build the mainline in the middle of the property all the way to the north property line of the slave timber camp. Spurs would be built out from there. They would use gum and hickory trees for the railroad ties. The train would have a wood-fired steam engine and use red oak and hackberry to fire the boilers. The timberjacks would also furnish all the firewood for the steam engine in Lance's tugboats.

Many of the stumps could be pulled from the ground using the strength of the train engine. Others would be burnt in place using treetops and limbs as fuel.

There were low areas throughout the property that Mr. Simon called lagoons. They consisted mostly of fifty-to-one-hundred-acre tracts. They would be left untouched for the animals and future growth.

After harvesting the timber, Creed would prepare the

land to grow corn. His plan was to harvest the corn and use it locally to raise hogs and bale the stalks and ship it by rail to Cahokia. He could sell it up and down the Mississippi or Ohio Rivers for cattle feed; or Lance could take it all the way to Jefferson on barges and wagons where it could be shipped anywhere it was needed by the Empire Timber & Cattle Company.

When Creed crossed back over the Mississippi on the ferry, he telegraphed Doyle Skillman and Lance Devereaux.

I have purchased 400,000 acres of hardwood timber land. You will have a steady supply of timber starting in less than a year and it should last your lifetime.

The one to Lance Devereaux added:

Start building your Mississippi barges.

Creed also telegraphed Captain Drake for advice and recommendations on building his railroad. Within an hour, he received a telegraph from a railroad construction company. After several telegrams, Creed had a crew headed his way. The surveyors were the first to arrive. The timberjacks were next. They were to cut cross ties when needed and harvest the furniture-grade timber. The crews to lay rails arrived next with enough rail and spikes to do the job.

Another wire went out to Doyle Skillman:

Change that to six months or less.

Creed made a contract with the railroad construction

company to furnish a rail crew on a fulltime basis. They would have the knowledge and equipment to move the spurs when needed and load the timber onto rail cars and haul it to the dock at Cahokia.

After meeting with the surveyors, the timberjacks and railroad crew, Creed was confident everyone was on board and left. He would find someone to ride for the brand who knew how to raise corn and hogs.

CHAPTER TWENTY-EIGHT

Memories

Being so close, Creed was again tempted to go to The Flying Dust to see Kathy Ann. But he dared not. He had so much to do with so little time to do it. He would not want to leave without taking Kathy Ann and Rascal with him and that would take more time than he had.

He checked the steamships heading south and found he was in luck. The *Mississippi Rose* was in port and would be leaving within the hour. Creed booked passage for himself and his two horses to Wickliffe, Kentucky.

Creed paid close attention when they neared Cairo. He gazed at the timber camp where he had been held as a slave laborer. The buildings at the camp had been torn down. Creed shook his head as if to shake off the sad memories. The *Rose* did not stop for wood for the boilers, there was none. The dock was gone, and no one was in sight.

The *Rose* headed toward the entrance of the Ohio River that flowed into the Mississippi. The boat groaned fighting the current of the Ohio pushing it westward toward the middle of the Mississippi. Creed saw where he had left the river and shuddered thinking how cold he had been. Even the memory of the cold could not block out the smile that appeared on his face when he remembered the happiness he had felt that day; being free for the first time in five years.

As the boat neared Wickliffe, Creed again thought of Kathy Ann and Rascal. He would be only a half day away from The Flying Dust when he left the boat to catch the ferry into Missouri. He knew Kathy Ann was a happy person, but she was also fragile. She was beautiful and wanted things her way. He smiled and thought it would be fun making her happy. If he left after seeing her for only one day, she would not be happy. He would just go on back to Texas regardless of how much he wanted to see her.

Creed left for Texas by way of Fort Smith. The first herd of Texas Longhorns bought by the new contract should be there when he arrived. If it were, it would be a month and a half early.

He met with Maxwell at the Indian Affairs office. "Creed, the Indian Reservations in the western sector of the Territory are full of Indians. They can't take any more. That means I've got to feed all the new Indians being brought in."

"I'm told Jesse Chisholm is having to gather his herds as far south as the Rio Grande. Goodnight and Loving have contracts for every Longhorn they can get to Denver. Chisolm is in the same situation with him taking his to Abilene, Kansas. They completely bailed out of taking any Indian Affairs contracts."

"A lot of newcomers are trying to move in on the Longhorn business. A few said they could get the Longhorns if I gave them a purchase order. Don't know how successful they would be. Some looked believable but most looked shady. They have talked to me about my source. I told them I was taking all the Longhorns you had. I'm telling you now, I will take every Longhorn you can bring me." Maxwell said.

"You have my word that you will get every Longhorn that I sell, Mr. Maxwell, and I have a lot to sell." Creed asked Maxwell not to discuss his agreement with anyone.

"Mr. Maxwell, I have a problem I need to discuss with

you. I may need your help."

"What kind of help do you need, Creed?"

"It concerns the State Police in Texas. I bought acreage I needed in fulfilling my contract with you. It happened that the sheriff in Nacogdoches had intended to foreclose on the property the next day and he was to buy it on the courthouse steps that day. It was his "turn", whatever that means. I never talked to him, but I was told he was angry about me buying the property."

"I went to the courthouse the day I bought the property and paid all back taxes and reconstruction fees on the property. I had things to do and left town after paying the taxes and fees. When I got back to Nacogdoches, I had several people tell me the sheriff was looking for me. I was going to try and see him the next day. I was too busy that day and told everyone who saw him to tell him I would drop by as soon as I could," Creed explained.

"I was told that his eight deputies rode in on the second herd you received. The deputies were riding hard with .38s drawn. My crew rode to meet them to keep them from stampeding the herd. My men gave them harsh words about their actions and the possible danger they might create and asked why they had their guns drawn. They were told by the deputies they were going to arrest me for not turning myself in to Sheriff Mattingly."

"I was out of town when I heard this. I rode back to Nacogdoches to talk to Sheriff Mattingly and was told no one had seen him or his deputies for three days. I could not wait around and when I got back three weeks later, I was told the Sheriff, his eight deputies, and his daughter had disappeared and that four members of the Texas Police wanted to talk to me about it. I can account for myself and my men every day, I assure you."

"I've got Longhorns to brand and drive. We don't have time to spend waiting for the State Police. Can you help me?"

"Creed, I wish you had told me about this sooner. I don't want you worried about anything but getting my Longhorns to the Red. I will take care of this. Someone close to me is a friend of President Andrew Johnson who appointed governors of all the southern states during reconstruction. He appointed Andrew Jackson Hamilton as the provisional governor of Texas. Just recently an election was held and Hamilton's recommended candidate, James Throckmorton won the election, and as you know, is now the governor. I will give you a letter to show to anyone wanting to talk to you or any of your men. I will instruct them to telegraph Governor Throckmorton first, then I'll go through the channels to get word from President Andrew Johnson to Governor Throckmorton of your importance to Indian Affairs."

Creed received his letter and headed to Texas. The thing he heard that concerned him most was that newcomers were moving in. He was glad that he had Juan send the four vaqueros south to the Big Thicket area to brand mavericks. He needed to increase branding before a newcomer slapped a brand on them. Now that he owned the land, he could fence off the easy crossings of the Trinity and put up "no trespassing" signs on the fence.

Creed eased into Nacogdoches at midnight and went to Glad's boarding house. He knew the rules of the house were that no one could have visitors past 9 pm and they could only visit in the parlor. He knew where Glad's room was located on the third floor. Not wanting to wake the owner or other guests he would slip in and go straight to Glad's room. The room door was locked, and Creed had never learned to pick a lock, so he took his Bowie and whittled the door lock from the facing and slowly entered the room. He placed his hand over Glad's mouth and held him steady with the other. Glad struggled until he realized it was Creed.

"Hate to disturb your sleep but I'm just passing through and I must talk to you. Have you finished the deal south of Marshall?"

"Yes, all 150,000 acres."

"Good! Where is Donny?"

"After I gave him your last message, he moved to Alazan with fifteen of his men. He told me to tell you they would be there and ready."

"Glad, we will be gone two or three weeks. Pass that on to Constantina. Here is a twenty-dollar gold piece; get your lock fixed!"

Creed waited for daylight before he rode into Alazan. He was led to where Donny and his crew were camped.

"Are you ready to ride, Donny?"

"Been ready, Dakota."

"Donny let's have breakfast and then have a meeting. We're going to have a hard ten to twelve days of work. I want everyone to know what we are walking into and I want everyone committed to the task. Those who can't be committed should not go with us."

Everyone ate a big breakfast but ate it quickly. They all knew something big was coming down and were anxious to hear about it.

"Men, Donny selected each of you to join me in a venture some might think is a personal vendetta. Once you know the details you may not want to join me. There will be no glory or bragging about what I plan to do. Along the way you might want to leave the group. There would be no hard feelings from me if you make that decision. I would like for you to come to me and tell me. It would not affect your job of continuing to ride for the brand. The only thing I want to tell each of you is that this is a totally secret mission.

"Eight years ago, my family was attacked by the Wallander Clan, the same people who tried to infiltrate our company on the Trinity. You were all there. I have information that there are twenty or twenty-five of them hanging out south of Marshall licking their wounds and looking for an opportunity to attack us again. I would like to kill them all myself. You all are now part of my family and I want to get this over with. I promised my father it would be done. "That day, eight years ago, they rode in shooting, and killed my mother and sister."

"I bought 150,000 acres of land south of Marshall. Here is a map for each of you. Study it until you know every trail, nook and turn. This is where they are supposed to be. I plan to bushwhack them without warning. I don't want to drive them from our land, I want to kill them all. Even if I thought for one minute that they would never attack us again, I would still wake the sleeping dog. I don't know if they really know who Dakota Creed is, but I can assure you, they know Quin.

"It would make no difference to them if they did. The local law is afraid of them and the State Police will do nothing. There should be no complaints coming from anyone. I bought the land because my mother and sister are buried there. I would like to kill all of them by myself, but there are too many of them. If you get a chance to shoot one of them in the back, take it because they would shoot you in the back. Anyone want out?"

"Creed, I know my men and I can speak for them. We're in!" shouted Donny.

All the men shouted their agreement.

Marshall, Texas, is 90 miles from Alazan. When Creed and his men reached the southern boundary of the 150,000 acres, Creed handed out a wanted poster of a generic Wallander. "If you see someone who looks like that, kill them and bury them deep."

Creed's informant was not the most reputable person in the country, but Creed put a lot of faith in what he was told. The reason being was that the snitch was smitten with one of the Wallander girls and got caught. He was able to escape, but he too wanted all the Wallander boys killed because they were hunting him to kill. The informant told him that the Wallanders often visited the spring in the hollow. He planned to look there first.

Creed saw a dim curl of smoke coming from the hollow. He stopped and put on his moccasins. "Spread out and tag along behind me." When Creed got within fifty feet of the hollow, he signaled for the crew to hold up. Creed eased to the ground and crawled to the rim of the hollow. He counted ten men. He had to restrain himself from standing and rushing into the hollow when he determined that all ten there were Wallanders.

Creed killed three on the first three shots fired. He rolled five yards to his left, peeked over the rim and killed two more. He ducked below the rim and ran fifteen yards to his right. He peeked over the rim again and saw one turning back toward him. Creed rushed his shot and wounded him. He didn't know if his victim was mortally wounded, but knew he was in no condition to fight back. He saw him crawling into a hole.

Creed gave up on that position and moved back left to his original position. By that time, he saw one trying to get over the north rim. Before he got off his shot, the man threw up his arms and fell back into the hollow. Donny had shot him. The other four were killed by others in in the crew.

"Hold up! Don't shoot the one in the hole. I want to talk to him," barked Creed.

"Donny, post five of your men around the top of the ridge. All the shooting might bring attention. The rest of you help me make sure all of these are dead except the one in the hole. I'll keep my eye on him and the rest of you keep your eyes on the others. Some of them may be playing possum. If they are, go ahead and shoot 'em."

"Okay! You, in the hole. You're not hit that hard. Roll out of there and let me see your hands. They had better be empty," Creed bellowed.

"Help me, I'm losing a lot of blood," the man pleaded.

"Okay I'll help you but if you give me any trouble, I'll just go ahead and kill you. You understand?"

"I won't give you any trouble, just stop the bleeding!" He begged.

Creed checked with Donny. "Are the rest of them dead?"

"They're all dead."

Creed bent over the man and asked. "What's your name?"

"I'm Woodrow McKinsey."

"Okay Woodrow let me stop this bleeding for you."

Creed cut his shirt away and bandaged the wound.

"You should be okay now, where is the rest of your kin?"

"I don't have any kin. They were all killed in the War."

"Are you kin to any of these dead men on the ground?"

"No, I just met them last night."

"Donny, have your men pull all the bodies over here and put them in a row." Donny did as Creed told him, and they laid the bodies next to one another. Creed didn't even have to glance before he spoke,

"Interesting, Woodrow! Look at that. You all look like the same pea in a pod."

"Well, they're not my kin!"

"Woodrow, let's cut to the chase. How many Wallander boys are left?

"I'm not going to tell you."

"Well, Woodrow, I could snatch this bandage off you and let you bleed out slowly until you die, but I won't do that. I'll just gut-shoot you and rub salt in the wound and let you die in three or four days if you're lucky."

Creed backed up about ten feet and pulled out his .45.

"Donny, go get some salt." When Donny returned, Creed spoke. "I'm going to gut-shoot Woodrow. Have the salt ready and rub it in the wound. I want to make sure I don't hit his spinal cord and I know you don't want any of his stinking guts on you. So, back up a little for now."

Creed and Donny stepped back a couple of feet more and Donny spoke. "Let's pull the bodies away from him. I don't want the men having to handle the bodies with Woodrow's guts all over them."

Creed had been looking at Woodrow the whole time Donny was talking. Woodrow did not like hearing about his guts being splatter all over the bodies.

Creed took aim then stopped.

"Woodrow, turn your body just a little this way."

"Wait a minute! What do you want to know?" asked

Woodrow.

"I have several questions. If you hesitate on giving me an answer I will just go ahead, and gut-shoot you," Creed said.

"Okay! Okay! I'll tell you everything you ask me if I know the answer. Just give me time to answer."

"The first question Woodrow, how many Wallander boys are still alive?

Woodrow started counting on his fingers. "Twelve!"

"Do you know where they are?

"No! Most of 'em hang out here some, but I don't know where they are now."

"Where else do you think they might be?"

Woodrow hesitated and Creed started reaching for his Colt, "Three of 'em are headed to Elysian Fields to fetch some 'shine," Woodrow quickly answered.

"Donny, you guys drag all the bodies out of the hollow and search all their pockets. You know the routine. Then we'll bury them. I want to get out of the hollow. I don't want to be trapped in here," Creed said.

After a quick burial Creed led Donny with the crew and Woodrow to the hideout where his mother and sister were buried. "Donny, choose two of the men and send them towards Elysian Fields. It's on the map. Woodrow here told me three of his kin were headed there to buy 'shine. Have them do what they need to do and have them bring the 'shine back here. Woodrow might need a drink to kill some of the pain in his shoulder."

"Rotate eight of the men to outride the hollow and our hideout here. Woodrow told me some of his kin hang out at the hollow. If any of you run into something you can't take care of yourself, report it back here. Don't take any chances. I'm going to clean my mother's and sister's graves."

Two days later, the two men sent to Elysian Fields showed up with the 'shine. Creed gave Woodrow all the 'shine he wanted. No other Wallander had shown up at the hollow. Creed was now on Woodrow's good side. The drunken Woodrow was in hog heaven. He was alive and felt no pain. Creed complained to Woodrow about none of his kin showing up to drink with him. The drunk Woodrow slurred out. "You got to send them the signal."

"What signal, Woodrow?"

"The signal that we got 'shine."

"What is that signal.?

"Don't you wish you knew?"

Creed slowly drew his Colt and pointed it at Woodrow's gut.

Woodrow sobered and hollered "Whoa, wait a minute! I was just kiddin'. Build a big fire in the hollow and put a green cedar over it and send up three puffs of smoke about every three minutes for fifteen minutes. If they are within twenty miles they will show up."

Creed did not want to scare any of the Wallanders away with gunfire and hoped this signal might lure them closer.

"Woodrow, are you sure about the number of your kin?"

Woodrow put the bottle of 'shine down and started counting on his fingers. He didn't remember the number he told Creed. "How many did I tell you before?"

"You tell me, Woodrow," Creed said as he eased his .45 from the holster.

"Wait a minute! I need to count again to make sure."

Woodrow was having a problem getting past ten because he ran out of fingers.

After three attempts and Creed abruptly pointing the .45 at his gut, Woodrow screamed out, "twelve!"

Woodrow gulped down all the 'shine left in the bottle and reached for another as Creed gathered Donny and the crew for a pow-wow.

"I will start the fire and give the signal at four this evening. There are only three entrances into the hollow and according to Woodrow there are only twelve of his kin left. We know three have been taken out near Elysian Fields and that leaves nine. Donny, put five of your men on each of the three entrances. Send one of the five out on the trail that leads to the entrance they are guarding. If more than five arrive together we will go ahead and shoot 'em. If less than five of 'em, try to lariat them to the ground and send them to the promised land. Don't take any chances. I'll stay at the bottom of the hollow with Woodrow and start and work with the fire. I'll stay close to the hole and crawl in it if there is gunfire into the hollow."

Creed started the fire on schedule and had the green cedar branches ready. Within an hour Creed heard three horses racing toward the hollow from the north. The hollow seemed to trap the sound and swirl it around. It was getting louder as the horses drew nearer. The rhythm of the hooves ceased, and other sounds filled the hollow. There were sounds of men screaming and horses whinnying. In less than a minute, a hand rose above the rim at the north entrance with three fingers held up.

Donny cleaned up the north entrance and waited for the six others. Creed felt good about the possibility the remaining members of the clan would all show. Wallanders loved their 'shine.

Near dark Creed heard many more horses approaching from the north. There was no doubt there were more than four. The ones guarding the east and south entrances abandoned there post and rushed north to the entrance.

The crew was well hidden and the Wallanders rode straight into the ambush. If the Wallanders got off a shot, they had hit nothing of importance.

After the count, Donny reported to Creed. "That should be all of them."

"Give me a minute and you can take Woodrow with you," Creed said.

"Woodrow, snap to!"

Woodrow opened his eyes with a drunken smile on his face.

"Can you hear me, Woodrow?" Creed asked.

"Yeah! I can hear you."

"Because you helped me, I'm not going to gut shoot you.

The smile on Woodrow's face brightened. "You are the last Wallander, Woodrow. The one I've been looking for." In a flash, Creed cut Woodrow's throat, ear to ear. "It's done, Father!"

CHAPTER TWENTY-NINE

Return to Nacogdoches

Creed knew the letter from Maxwell had not circulated back to the State Police. Those types of things take a lot of time.

Billy McBride was on night guard duty and let Creed into the bank.

"You haven't seen me Billy, understand?"

Creed used his key to let himself into Constantina's office and left her a letter stating he would be back in ten or twenty days and would need to see her.

Creed left the bank and forded the Angelina River in the dark. At daybreak, Creed scoped Tillman's Trading Post. Seeing nothing unusual, he rode in.

"Mr. Tillman, do you have time to ride with me for about four days? I have a business proposition I want to run by you."

"I'll take time. The State Police are driving away all my trade. They question everyone they see about your whereabouts. They want to know what they have heard about the Mattingly's disappearance. They're keeping a close eye on the Post in hopes they'll find you here."

"I can account for myself and the crew's whereabouts. I don't mind talking to them, but I don't really have time right now."

"I advise you to stay clear of them. They think you and some of your crew had something to do with it."

"I guess I'll go see them when we get back. I'll come by

at daybreak tomorrow. I'll bring a pack horse with vittles for us both."

"It might be best for us to meet south of the Neches. Like I said before, they are keeping a close eye on the Post. I know the trail like the back of my hand, and I will leave well before daylight and meet up with you on the hill south of the river."

"Sounds good to me. I'll hold up near there and get some rest."

Creed was sitting off the trail halfway up the hill that was south of the river at daylight. Shortly thereafter he saw Tillman moving up the hill toward him. Creed sat tight until he was sure Tillman was not being followed. After seeing no one, he moved back to the trail. The branding camp was a day-and-a-half away. Creed and Tillman turned a little westward in hopes of seeing one of the cattle drives. They saw Longhorns in all directions. Toward the end of the day, they turned back southeast toward the branding camp.

They spent the night on the trail and Creed told Tillman his plan. He explained that he would like to make a contract with him to cut all the ripe and defective pine trees all the way from the Big Thicket to Crockett. They would be cut into mining timbers and stacked with spacers on the high bluffs along the Trinity River. "You can continue to cut timber in the rainy season in the spring, but you can't do it close to the river because of flooding. I also want a barbed wire fence built on the north side of the Trinity River in every low water crossing area with a "no trespassing" sign. We'll take it down before the flood season starts and put it back up in May."

"Do you own all this property?"

"Yes, I do, Ralph."

The next day they reached the branding camp. They were in time to have a plate of beans, with chopped peppers and beef for lunch.

Juan and his crew were in camp. Creed pulled Juan aside to have a private conversation with him. "Juan, help me get the word out that anyone working for the brand can have enough land to build their own home and have garden space. Some might want to move their families here. If we have enough takers, we will lay out a town and help build each other's homes. Let me know how many are interested."

"Will do, Boss-man."

"How are the cattle drives going, Juan?"

"We're way ahead of schedule. We're making some drives in seventeen days. That's an average of fourteen miles a day. The days getting longer helped. We've had a lot of onlookers along the way. A show of force by our outriders convinced all of them they would only be onlookers."

"Indian Affairs wants as many Longhorns as they can get for as long as we can supply them. Goodnight and Loving are shipping their herds to Denver and Jesse Chisholm is driving his to Abilene, Kansas. We are the only supplier to the Indian Territory. Maxwell told me some newcomers were looking for mavericks. So we will need to be on the look-out for them They could cause us a lot of trouble."

"I want you to get with Jesús, Pasqual, and Eldondo and come up with four new crews of the best vaquero herders, ropers, heelers and branders we have, and have them doing nothing but branding. Make sure the branding crews have at least two Henrys and give them one outrider each with a Henry. The crew that brands the most stock will be paid an extra ten dollars that day.

"This is our land, but a maverick is a maverick and as you know anyone has a right to slap a brand on any maverick other than one suckling a branded mother. The only other way is to fence the mavericks in, and we don't have time to do that. We will try to discourage them with a fence in the low water crossing areas. When you herd the cattle, leave all the young, branded heifers here. Make a special effort to brand all heifers you can find."

"Creed, why don't we keep the four new crews together and start at the edge of the Big Thicket. There are so many maverick Longhorns there, they won't have to go looking for one to brand. They could camp and eat together. We could use two of the outriders to drive the branded stock northwest each day. It would give the crews more protection."

"That's okay with me, Creed said. "When they start back, I want those that they branded scattered out on the way back here, especially the young heifers."

"How long do you want to do this?"

"As long as we can without getting behind on delivery. I think with the added ten-dollar bonus for the crew that brands the most cattle at the Big Thicket, we should do the same for the branding crews at the branding camp. The vaqueros will be fighting to stay behind and do nothing but brand even though it is one of the most unpleasant jobs. Let's do that and see how that works out."

Creed and Tillman rode over the timber lands for two days. "Tillman, the last thing I ever want to do would be to overcut this timber. If we do, we will have nothing but a forest of brush. Just cut the ripe and defective trees and let the rest grow tall.

"You're right about that, Creed. It will take me two days

to come up with a proposal for the fence and cutting the mining timbers to size. I will have no trouble finding the timberjacks. A lot of hands don't like handling barbed wire. There has not been much of it used in East Texas, and those that strung it have given it a bad reputation as far as getting caught by the barbs We can get it done because a lot of people are looking for work. Most of them know nothing about cattle or horses—but could learn to make fences quickly."

Creed and Tillman headed back to Lufkin.

Creed scoped the area of Tillman's Trading Post then handed the scope to Tillman. "Look at the two horses, Tillman."

"They belong to the State Policemen."

"I don't have time to talk to them now. I'll leave you here and head to Nacogdoches. When you get your figures together, come to my bank there and ask for Constantina. Tell her anything she asks concerning our business. She will know where I am."

Creed avoided the ferry at Marion and crossed the Angelina River on horseback. He felt the ferry would be under watch by the State Police and he wanted to see Constantina as soon as possible. She would be looking for him to arrive today. He wanted to be brought up to date on the deliveries of the 8,000 Longhorns each week. Each delivery should bring in $320,000. He had to trust that Maxwell was actually making the deposits since there was no telegraph in Nacogdoches.

Creed was cautious entering Nacogdoches. He listened at the side door of Constantina's office. Hearing nothing, he tapped lightly on the door. It brought a quiet response,

"Who is it?

"It's me, Dakota. Open up, we need to talk."

"Hurry! Get in! Dakota, the State Police must know you're in town. They have not been by for five days and they have been by three times this morning. They plan to arrest you because you have not come by to talk to them."

"I'm sure they know I've been off with Ralph Tillman for several days; and now that Tillman is back, they probably think I'm back also."

"You've told me about Tillman. You don't think he told them anything, do you?"

"Absolutely not. He could have turned me in many times with Mattingly. He and I are on the same page. He will be by here in the next two days to close a deal on cutting the timber on the Trinity. When he shows up here, I want you to bring him to Alazan. The Lazerines there will know where to find me. Do you know the names of the four Texas Policemen?"

"I know that the Captain's name is Livingston Tarver and the Sergeant's name is Linwood Langford. I don't know the two corporals' names."

Constantina had not lost eye contact with Dakota the whole time he talked with her. *Dakota is such a special person. But I worry about him sometimes.*

Each time Creed saw Constantina, her happiness and smiles made him think of Kathy Ann and his love for her.

Creed was wondering what was making Constantina so happy. *She must have someone she is looking forward to seeing as I* do.

"Dakota, I've stuck my neck out and given money to Manual and Jesús to buy hay. The graze is getting thin in some areas. We're okay on all the herds traveling now but all the future herds will need hay."

"Constantina, you can stick your neck out anytime you want. I can't be everywhere I need to be.

I asked Desmond, Glad, and Philip to line up a meeting and to set a date and I will be there. Have you heard from them?"

"I received a letter two days ago. The meeting is set for Wednesday of next week. I was expecting you today to tell you,"

"Constantina, in a short time the Empire Timber & Cattle Company will be a true Empire. I plan to appoint Desmond Duke to be over our business in Bowie County, the Indian Territory, and the Carlyle timber deal. Philip Stuart will handle everything around Bastrop and all the land and cattle west of the Brazos. Glad Mathews will handle the rest of the land and cattle in East Texas. Constantina you will handle all the money, and they will report to you and you will report to me."

"Dakota, I..."

"Constantina, this is the way it must be. I don't have time to keep up with them, but I can keep up with you and I'll make sure you know where I'll be. I want to spend most of my time here, New Orleans and St. Louis. It will be a lot easier to communicate when we get the Telegraph."

"Dakota, I can do the job, but I don't know if they will want to work for a woman."

"Constantina, they will work for you. Don't forget you hold the purse strings."

"We will make this the biggest Empire in all of Texas." She said as she reached out and squeezed his arm.

These were the kinds of things he liked to hear. He wanted all his employees hitched to the brand and especially wanted Constantina to feel loyalty and passion for the

Empire brand.

Creed continued. "Constantina you get with Glad and go to work buying all the land we can from Nacogdoches to the Sabine River and from there to the Sulphur River. We need a ten-mile-wide stretch to drive cattle and raise hay. We need this property. I plan to fence the 48,000 acres we own at Alazan. It will be our controlled breeding ranch. We have three-hundred Longhorn heifers there and I have twenty-five Shorthorn bulls on the way from England. Others will be fencing their property also and we can't afford to be fenced out getting to the Red."

In the short time Constantina had been in charge at the bank, it was obvious to Creed that she was in complete control of the bank and all the male employees. With the new organization in place, Creed knew the company would move faster and smoother toward the Empire he was working to create.

CHAPTER THIRTY

Division of the Empire.

Constantina was concerned for Dakota's safety. The State Police were still looking for him and knew he was back in the area. She moved the Wednesday meeting with Dakota, Desmond, Glad, and Philip to Alazan in her Uncle Francisco's home where security would be easier to control.

Creed laid out his plan for management of the Empire's holdings. There was not a sign of resentment or negativity on anyone's part. They all wanted to be in a leadership role in building the Empire Timber & Cattle Company into the greatest Empire in Texas. Desmond and Philip were as impressed with Constantina as Glad had become. Creed laid out his plans for the company.

Creed and Constantina met with each of them alone and expressed things that they wanted each to do. Creed gave the Carlyle timber contracts to Duke. "Desmond, I need you to find and hire three hands who will ride for the brand for our Carlyle venture. One who is an expert on raising corn and one who is an expert on raising hogs. I want the best there is and pay them accordingly. Figure out a profit-sharing deal for them. The third man needs to be a coordinator who can work with the railroad contractor, timberjacks, Lance, and the two men you hire to raise the corn and hogs. He will report directly to you. We'll pay what it takes to get the best. You will control all the Indian Affairs contracts and the Bowie County dealings."

Philip was instructed to buy the land to make the property along the Brazos contiguous to the Lost Pine Forest.

Ralph Tillman joined in for Glad's meeting. The four of them went over his proposal on cutting the timber and fencing off the low-river crossings. Creed, Constantina and Glad were impressed with the proposal and confident that Tillman could do the job.

A horse with the ETCC brand was tied to the hitching rail outside the State Police office in Nacogdoches. It was the break of day. Dakota Creed was sitting in the lone chair outside the door. His boot was resting against one of the columns that held up the roof of the porch. He saw a horseman enter the main street two blocks away. A glimpse of a reflection from the sun left no doubt that the rider was wearing a tin star. Creed didn't know what to expect but was ready for almost anything.

The reaction of the approaching rider as he noticed seeing the Empire brand of the horse tied to the hitching rail in front of his office was foretelling to Creed. The rider stopped and stiffened in his saddle, then started to dismount but stopped. He fumbled with his gun. Where Creed was sitting would be out of range of the .38 carried by the officer. The rider seemed to be unsure what to do.

"Settle down officer, everything's okay. My name is Dakota Creed, I…"

The officer reached for his gun. Before he could clear leather, he was looking down the barrel of one of Creed's .45s. Creed was still seated and kept his boot propped up against the post. The officer had not seen Creed draw the gun. The officer pushed his gun back in place and Creed put his Colt back in the holster. If the officer decided to pull his revolver again, Creed knew he could outdraw him.

"I heard you wanted to talk to me, and I've just now had time to do that. Why did you pull a gun on me?"

"Uh! You're Dakota Creed, uh…"

"Yes! I'm Dakota Creed. I told you that. What does that have to do with you drawing a gun on me?"

"Mr. Creed, Sheriff Mattingly, his daughter, and his eight deputies have disappeared."

"What does that have to do with me?"

"We understand the sheriff wanted to talk to you about some land you bought and two herds of cattle you drove through the county.

"Let me cut to the chase. I have here a letter from Indian Affairs you need to read. I didn't have time to talk to the sheriff and I don't have time to talk to you. Read this letter and do as it tells you to do."

Creed handed him the letter. When the officer finished reading, he took a note pad from his pocket and scribbled a note and handed the letter back.

"I'm going to hold you here in jail until I hear from the Governor. I've got to ride to Crockett where they have a telegraph. I figure it will take about five days. If the Governor doesn't tell me to let you go, then I'll know where you arc."

"That's not what the letter tells you to do. What charges do you have on me to hold me in jail for anything?"

"Well, you did drive two herds of cattle through the county, didn't you?"

"Yes, but is that against the law?"

"Well, it depends on where you got them."

"Officer, there was but one brand on them all and that

was the Empire Timber & Cattle Company brand."

"That doesn't tell me where you got them."

"I got them from my own land between the Neches and Trinity Rivers. Officer, I'm leaving. You check with the Governor. If he doesn't want you to release me, leave word with Miss Constantina DeLeon at my bank. I will turn myself in as soon as I get the message.

Creed stood and started toward his horse. The officer started to move toward him and began to speak. He stopped when he saw Creed freeze and look him straight in the eye. The officer looked away and Creed mounted his horse and rode off.

Creed caught up with Constantina before she left the boarding house.

"Constantina, please go back in and change into your riding clothes. Bring your house plans. We're going to start building a house. Ask Miss Milo to fix us enough food for lunch. I have plenty of jerked beef if we are late getting back. I have a bundle of wooden stakes and a hammer to mark the locations. We'll let Billy know that you'll be gone for a few days."

Once again Constantina's excitement made Creed happy. He hoped Kathy Ann would be as excited when she sees the house.

They left Nacogdoches at a trot. Creed did not see any of the State Police nor did he want to. After five miles of trotting the horses, they stopped on a high ridge and scoped back along their trail. Nothing. They continued to the spring-fed creek area.

"Oh, my! Dakota, this is the most beautiful place I've ever seen."

"Where do you think we should put the house?"

"I think it should be on top of the ridge. That way you could have a great view on each side of the crest. The first thing we need to do is to get a water witcher who will dowse the area to see if a successful water well can be located on the ridge. Let's select the best site and set the stakes for the houses, barn and stables. Then the witcher could work around the area before we survey the exact location."

Creed was surprised at Constantina's depth of knowledge on things that needed to be done before the start of building a house. She apparently had more schooling than most young women. Evidently the school had more books than the normal school and she had enough curiosity in her to want to know about many different things. Curiosity was a driving force for his own knowledge. He smiled when he realized that they were alike in so many ways.

They picked out the perfect place for the house, assuming water could be found there. Constantina took out her drawings from her saddlebag and they stepped off distances and drove stakes. The location of the stables would be lower off the crest of the hill on the southwest side of the house. This location would protect the animals from the north winds and give a good view of the barn from the house. A berm would be built to catch all the runoff from the barn and would divert the runoff away from the spring and creek below.

"Dakota, let's have lunch close to the spring. I love hearing the water flowing down the creek."

"You stole my thoughts, Constantina."

"Dakota, I was just sharing what I thought you might like."

It was such a caring touch of words. Someday, someone is going to get a great wife. I certainly hope we don't lose her when that happens. I must hurry and get back to Kathy Ann. Being around Constantina makes me know what I'm missing by not being with her.

"I spoke with Ralph Tillman and he's building a bridge over the Neches River to haul the logs for the house here. He will use the ferry at Marion to cross the Angelina. He's pretty sure the bridge he's building on the Neches will wash away in any big flood but will rebuild it if it does. As soon as the bridge is finished, he will have several wagons of logs ready to cross. Once we start on the house, I'm going to appoint Billy McBride to be your escort to bring you out here if I'm not available.

"I like Billy. I'm not afraid to come alone but it will be nice to have someone to ride along with me."

It was October and the weather was turning cold, and leaves were turning colors. It seemed that Creed's and Constantina's excitement fed off each other. The witcher found water just inside the ridge on the entire south side. The well was dug by hand and the well digger had to scramble up a rope as the water rushed into the hole.

The surveyors staked the buildings and marked the foundation footing locations. The larger circumference pine trees were harvested. All the sap wood was removed leaving the pitch pine heart wood to be used as footings. The pitch from the heart pine would prevent rotting and infestation from termites and other insects looking for a meal.

The white oak logs started arriving. Craftsmen of the building trade started shaping each log and fitting them onto the footings.

The construction crew camped out on the location and made a cook shed and a lean-to structure to keep workers and horses out of the rain. The first buildings completed were the barns and stables. Constantina was there each weekend and other days she was not needed at the bank.

Both Bastrop and Texarkana now had a telegraph. Phillip and Desmond sent a progress report each Friday to Crockett and Constantina hired a courier to deliver it to her each Monday. If there were things that Dakota needed to know in a hurry, she would take it to him and might stay a night or two in the camp discussing other business.

By now Creed felt he had his Empire in place and the house far enough along that he could leave and go for his bride-to-be. He was enjoying building the ranch house with Constantina and in a way hated leaving but was also excited about going for Kathy Ann.

"Constantina, I will be gone for about a month."

"The houses should be completed by then," said Constantina. "Don't you want to be here? A lot of decisions must be made about colors and furniture and you will be gone during Christmas."

"I was hoping you would make any decisions that need to be made. I hate not being here for Christmas, but I will celebrate Christmas with you and the others. when I return."

"I can do that, but it would be better if you were here with me. What if you don't like what I pick out?"

"I know I will love everything you choose. I must go. I hope I'm not too late."

"Too late for what, Dakota?"

"You will know when I return. You can wire me in Texarkana or Little Rock if you need me. I will check there on the way through."

"Be careful and hurry back, Dakota."

She smiled and waved as he rode away. *Constantina has such a great smile.*

CHAPTER THIRTY-ONE

Return to The Flying Dust

Creed made sure he had two of the Flying Dust branded mares when he left. He bypassed Nacogdoches on his way north. He had not heard back from the State Police. If they were looking for him, he would not be contacted for their fear he might run. They did not know Dakota Creed.

He rode hard getting in as many miles as he could in the shortening daylight. The farther north he rode the colder it got. The next time he stopped to change mounts, Creed dug out his sheep skin-lined coat and fur-lined gloves. The gloves fit loosely which would enable him to discard them if needed. A trigger finger encased in a glove that you could not get off easily would get you killed.

Every river had its share of river rats and for that reason he purposely avoided stopping or camping on the rivers. Not that he was afraid, but he would avoid any trouble if it did not interfere with his plans. It was going to be extremely cold by nightfall and Creed would need a fire and shelter for his horses throughout the night. He was three miles from the Sabine River but would stop near Rabbit Creek, which emptied into the Sabine River in Gregg County. He built a windbreak lean-to and gathered enough driftwood for a large fire that should last all night.

Creed had put his horses in the lean-to, and they stayed there without hobbling or tying them. The horses knew a good thing when they had it. He had checked all his weapons and ate several yards away from the fire in the dark. Creed was close enough to catch heat from the fire and was finishing his coffee.

"Hello, the camp!"

Creed did not have to look for his weapons. He had one of the Colts in his hand, and in just a second, had set the coffee aside and had the other Colt ready.

"What are your intentions?" Creed asked as he rolled away to his left after he spoke.

"It's cold and we want to share your fire and camp."

"How many in your party?" Creed rolled again as they were answering.

"Uh, two."

"Step forward into the light so I can see you two and go ahead and bring the other two people in with you."

Creed could hear them discussing the situation. He took this opportunity to change his position ten feet farther back into the darkness.

"We're just cold and hungry, mister. You're not going to turn us away just because there are four of us, are you?"

"No, but I might turn you away for lying to me. Come on in toward the fire so I can get a look at you. There are four of you and only one of me."

After further discussion and more silent movement from Creed, they answered, "Okay, we are coming in."

The four looked cold, hungry and dirty. Creed would give them every opportunity to survive. He had had times in his life when it didn't matter to him if he lived or died. It was different now and he would take no chances. He was on his way to claim Kathy Ann and he was not about to be killed now.

Each of the four had a revolver on his hip and a knife on

the other. They each had a heavy beard with tobacco stains masking their face. Creed could not determine if they were shaking from the cold, fear or for the want of liquor.

He was comfortable with his ability to handle the four. He laid his Colts on some leaves and removed his gloves. Picking up the Colts, he loosely eased the Colts into their holsters, eased them out, eased them back in, and walked out in front of the four.

"Why are you men out on a night like this?"

"We got lost," said their leader.

"You boys hungry?"

"We need to warm up first. Got any whiskey?" One of them asked.

"You are going to have to warm up by the fire here. I don't have any whiskey."

"That's a fine-looking coat he has there, don't you think, Scorpion?", Mike, their leader, asked.

"Yep, and I bet it's mighty warm."

"You would win that bet," said Creed.

"Boys, look at these fine-looking horses this kid has. Bet a man could get a hundred dollars each for 'em," Mike said.

"You boys are smart. You would win that bet too."

"Boys, I don't have any liquor and I don't have any food to spare. I need to get some sleep and am asking that you move on or we might have some trouble."

"I'll tell you what kid, you give me that coat and I'll move on without giving you any trouble. I don't speak for the others," Mike said.

"Scorpion and I will settle for the horses, said Calhoun, "What do you want, Pete?"

"I want those two Colt .45s."

"Okay! If I give you my coat, horses, and Colts, you'll

leave me alone?"

"Yeah! That's what we said," Mike confirmed.

"I would like for you to just ride out and leave me be."

"We will after you give us your coat, horses and Colts."

"That's your final answer?"

"Yeah! That's our final answer," Mike said as he moved his hand toward his Colt.

Their mouths opened and their eyes bugged out as two repetitive shots from each of his Colt raced toward a spot between their eyes. Their hands had not yet reached their guns.

Creed replaced his spent shells and slipped on his gloves. He pulled them away from the fire so they would freeze. He found the horses they had tied to a tree, removed the saddles and bridles and moved them closer to the fire. The horses were of poor quality but deserved to be treated humanely.

Creed had refilled his coffeepot and put it on the fire to have coffee ready when he got up the next morning. In the morning he buried the bodies, saddles, and bridles. He returned and cooked bacon and drank more coffee, while thinking of Kathy Ann.

She told me she would wait for me and that she would be there. That was good enough for me. I like her father and mother, Paul and Maude. If they want to be close to Kathy Ann, I've built a beautiful guest house for them. It is bigger than the house they now live in. There is plenty of room for all the horses they would want to stable, and there is plenty of space to build a racetrack.

Creed erased all signs of his presence there, then left a bit of oats for the four extra horses—not wanting them to follow.

The four river rats needed to be killed and Creed did not

have time or the desire to explain that to anyone. His conscience was clear.

He had holed up in Little Rock and Charleston, so the horses could recover from the frigid weather. He checked with Western Union in both towns for possible wires from Constantina and was a little disappointed that there were none. He stayed clear of the café in Charleston, not wanting to run into Clair, the waitress.

As Creed approached the Wickliffe ferry, he saw a line of people waiting to board. He knew he was too far down the line to board the next trip over. The ferry was unloading passengers who were heading west. To his pleasant surprise he saw Bob Randle getting off the ferry.

"Randle!" Hollered Creed.

Bob recognized Creed and stopped and visited.

"Where you headed, Bob?"

"I'm headin' to Texas."

"Are you still working for the Flying Dust?"

"No! I quit yesterday."

"Mind telling me why?"

"Not at all.! You probably need to know. A couple of months ago a guy by the name of Monty Creager showed up. I was never introduced to him. He was staying in the guest room of the Fairchild's house. He hung out around the stables a lot and started telling me how I should be training the horses. He demanded that I do some things he wanted done. That's when I told him to go to hell and that I worked for Paul Fairchild and not him. He ran and told Fairchild. Fairchild came to the stable with Creager and tried to get things smoothed out between us. Creager demanded that I be fired. Fairchild was having a hard time deciding and I helped him out by quitting."

"Well, unless you have something else to do, I.ve been planning to get into the thoroughbred horse business at some point. I'll pay you more than you made at the Flying Dust and will give you free rein on that part of the business. You will answer to only one person. That person is Constantina DeLeon. She is boss of the Empire Timber & Cattle Company."

"I've heard of your company. The Empire Timber & Cattle Company is the talk of this part of the country for buying 400,000 acres of hardwood timber land. You have a woman running your company?"

"Yes! You will understand when you meet her. She is a vaquera and is smart as any man I've ever met. She has a way about her that makes you want to hear every word she says. She has a slight smile that is always present and makes you enjoy being around her and she doesn't mind riding her share of drag."

"She sounds like my kind of woman. I believe I'll just take that job."

"Bob, I don't know how you are fixed for money, but you now work for the Empire Timber & Cattle Company. Here's a hundred dollars in gold coin to pay your way to Nacogdoches, Texas. Tell Constantina that the weather has delayed me, but I hope to be back in about three weeks."

Creed was a little concerned about this Monty Creager guy. His main concern was him sleeping in the guest room for such a long period of time. *I shouldn't worry at all since Kathy Ann promised she would be waiting for me and I am returning four months early.*

Creed had planned to get to The Flying Dust before dark. His room being occupied by Monty Creager might create a

241

problem he would prefer to face in the daylight.

It was going to be a cold night on the road to The Flying Dust. Creed decided to find a good shelter and build a large fire well before dark. He would then have only a few miles ride to The Flying Dust in the morning.

Creed shook off the light snow that had fallen during the night and got on the trail.

The sun had been up for two hours when he spotted the ranch. He had to fight back his desire to rush in to see Kathy Ann and Rascal. He took out his telescope and scoped the area. A curl of smoke was rising from both chimneys, but no one was in sight. Creed was excited but rode in slowly.

When he got within about fifty yards of the house, Rascal raced out toward him. The dog recognized him and was as delighted to see him as he was to see the noisy little mutt. Creed dismounted and prepared for Rascal's friendly attack. He jumped into Creed's outstretched arms, then jumped down and rolled around in the snow at his feet. Creed bent over and was scratching Rascal's belly when he heard a shout.

"Quit coddling that damn worthless dog!" Yelled a man Creed didn't know. He raised up about the same time that the man kicked Rascal in the side. Creed reached out and pushed the foot that had kicked Rascal higher in the air until the foot was over the man's head. This jerked the man's other foot off the ground, and he landed on his head and shoulders. Creed unleashed his own kick into the side of Monty Creager. He did not know who he had kicked until he heard Kathy Ann yell.

"What have you done to Monty?", she screamed.

Before Creed could answer, he heard her say. "Monty, are you okay? Please say something." Monty could not speak. He was out cold from the blow he took on his head when he fell. "I'll never forgive you for this, Dakota. You have no right coming in here and attacking Monty like this."

Before Creed could say anything, Paul Fairchild rushed out and called Kathy Ann down. "Kathy Ann, Dakota was greeting Rascal when Monty rushed up and kicked Ras…"

"Shut up, Father. This is none of your business. I'm sick and tired of you bad-mouthing Monty. At least he didn't run off and leave me like Dakota did."

Kathy Ann was crouched over Monty trying to bring him around and Dakota had gone to Rascal's side. Rascal had escaped serious injury and only had the wind knocked out of him. Fairchild saddled his horse and motioned Dakota to follow him, then rode off toward the tree that they had gone to when Dakota expressed his interest in Kathy Ann. Dakota and Rascal caught up with him. When they arrived, they built a fire near the log they would sit on.

"Dear God, Dakota, I'm so glad you've come back. This Monty Creager jerk came in here and has seemed to have swept Kathy Ann off her feet. He talks big and acts as if he is an authority on everything. He claims to be wealthy. My first realization that I did not like him was because he hates Rascal. I'm sure that now you are here you will be able to bring Kathy Ann to her senses and win her back."

"Mr. Fairchild, Kathy Ann and I had an agreement. I would be back within a year and we would pick up where we left off. It doesn't seem that she waited, and I might not want to win her back."

"Dakota, she is still the beautiful girl you left."

"Mr. Fairchild, beauty is skin-deep and ugly is to the bone. She was ugly to you and me today."

"With Monty out of the way she could wipe away all the

ugliness."

"When I've tried to wipe something away, I always see and remember those marks. I feel this was not fair to me. For me to try to win her back, and with me always seeing or remembering the marks would not be fair to Kathy Ann. For that reason alone, I think I must pass. She might be happy with Monty and his money."

"I don't know about his money. He has been sponging off me since he's been here. He says he is the one who bought the 400,000 acres of hardwood timber land across the river and that he is now a little short of cash because of that purchase."

"That's interesting. I thought Empire Timber & Cattle Company bought that timber land."

"They did. He says he owns Empire Timber & Cattle Company."

"This is getting to be a small world, Mr. Fairchild. I don't know how I should approach this. I know Kathy Ann won't be happy with all his money because he doesn't own the Empire Timber & Cattle Company or anything else if I had to guess. In fact, the real owner of the Empire Timber & Cattle Company would feel justified in killing him."

"How do you know this?"

"Mr. Fairchild, as I said I don't know how to approach this. Maybe you can help. This is a very strange coincidence that I had nothing to do with other than having been in love with Kathy Ann. I have proof in my saddle bag that what I am about to tell you is the truth."

"Dakota, I have never doubted the truth from you and never will. I remember that you most likely saved my daughter's life and I am indebted to you."

"Okay, Mr. Fairchild, hear me through. I own the Empire

Timber & Cattle Company."

"Oh, my!"

"You and I need to think this through together before we take any action. I will not tolerate anyone claiming ownership of the Empire Timber & Cattle Company for any reason. My first response is that I should kill him. My second thought would be to beat him so badly he would hope that I would kill him. Then I think of Kathy Ann. I don't want to destroy someone she might truly love. I care what she thinks of me even though I am now convinced that we could not have a happy marriage. What do you want me to do, Mr. Fairchild?"

"I want Creager off my property. I don't want you involved in me throwing him off. I would like the proof you offered in case I need it to convince Kathy Ann.

After reading the letter furnished by the Bureau of Indian Affairs, Mr. Fairchild's shoulders dropped.

"When I get back, I need to discuss this with Maude. She knows how I feel about Creager. This will be the crowning blow. We have asked ourselves: What if she leaves with Creager?

"Mr. Fairchild, I think I know Creager's character. He might not want to leave. He knows you have a lot of wealth, and he will try to get it any way he can."

"Over my dead body!"

"It might be. Keep that in mind. In your discussion with Creager, let him know he is going to have to deal with me when he leaves the ranch. Point out to Creager that it will be over his claim of ownership of the Empire Timber & Cattle Company and not Kathy Ann. It worries me thinking that Rascal gets kicked around. No animal deserves that. Would you see to it that no one holds Rascal back when I leave?

Rascal will follow me, and I will take good care of him."

"I sure will, Dakota. I know how much you love that mutt. It has been a constant battle protecting him from Creager ever since he showed up here. Dakota, I'm sorry how things have turned out. I must take care of this business. You may not get a chance to take care of Creager. I won't take any lip from him and will be prepared to kill him if necessary."

"Don't turn your back on him."

"Don't worry, I won't."

"I will stick around out of sight until you get through with Creager. I will need to get my letter back."

Fairchild turned off toward his house and Creed rode off toward the entrance of The Flying Dust and out of sight. Rascal was on his heels. He selected an area where he could hobble his two horses out of sight, and the horses could graze by kicking the snow off the grass. He selected a nook that was out of the wind but in the sun. Any movement by Rascal would be shielded by a cover of low brush in the area. From the location, Creed could move into enough shade to cover the end of the telescope to keep it from reflecting the sun. With the telescope, he would have a close view of all the buildings.

Paul Fairchild tied his horse to the rail in front of the house. Maude met him at the front door. "Creager is threatening to kill Dakota and Rascal. Kathy Ann is begging him to take her away from here."

"Where is she now?"

"She's in the guest room with him."

Paul reached in his pocket and pulled out the letter Dakota had given him. "You should read this." Maude read the letter and turned pale.

"Just as you thought. What do you think we should do?"

"I'm running him off, Maude. If Kathy Ann goes with him after she reads this, there is nothing we can do about it."

"I agree. I just wish Dakota had never left."

"He had a prior obligation, Maude, and Kathy Ann broke her agreement, not Dakota. Now, you stay here!"

The guest room door was open. Paul could hear Kathy Ann crying and Creager screaming at her.

"I'm going to talk to Kathy Ann for a few minutes alone. When I'm through I will talk to you." Paul grabbed Kathy Ann by the arm and led her away before either could protest. He led her to his bedroom and shut the door.

"Shut up and listen to me, Kathy Ann. I want you to read this letter." After she read it, she spoke in defiance.

"This is a lie. Dakota wrote this letter to try and get me back and try to get Monty in trouble."

"Kathy Ann, Dakota doesn't want you back. You broke your commitment to him. I am going to kick that poor excuse for a man off my ranch. You can go with him if you wish. I want you to know that Dakota Creed has a score to settle with Creager. It's not about you, it's about Monty claiming he owns the Empire Timber & Cattle Company."

"If he lays a hand on Monty, I will tell the law about him killing the two guys here on the ranch."

"If you do, I will confess killing them myself for what they were trying to do to you."

"Why would you do that? You don't owe Dakota anything and he will never be your kin?"

"He probably saved your life and because it's the right thing to do. Give me back the letter. I told Dakota that I'd tell Creager he would have to deal with him for claiming he owned the Empire Timber & Cattle Company before he got away from here,"

"Well, that's not going to happen. Besides, when I leave with Monty, I want half the value of the ranch."

"If you leave with him, you will get nothing."

"I've already told him I would get half for us."

"If he's so rich, why does he need half my money."

"Monty told me that half your money belongs to me and that we needed to take it if you didn't give it to us."

"I'm kicking you both out. Soon enough, that crook will have the opportunity to take all my money."

Fairchild loosened his Colt in the holster and rushed out the door.

"Watch out Monty! Daddy's coming with a gun!" Kathy Ann screamed.

Paul had to change his plan. He darted for the front door and grabbed Maude on the way out. They ran and dove headfirst into the open barn door as a bullet whistled over their heads. Paul returned a shot forcing Creager back inside. Creager was firing bullets from a window. The rancher could not return fire for fear of hitting Kathy Ann.

Creed, having seen what had just happened, unhobbled his riding horse and headed east. He was staying out of sight and would work his way to the back of the house. Rascal was on Creed's heels. Creed had his mind made up. He would kill Creager. It was enough to know that Creager was trying to kill Paul and Maude Fairchild and he was claiming he owned the Empire Timber & Cattle Company.

Kathy Ann saw that Creager was trying to kill her parents and tried to get him to stop. He finally turned and hit her with his closed fist and knocked her unconscious.

Creed tied his horse in the woods behind the house and signaled Rascal to stay with the horse. He eased into the house and located Creager looking out the front window. He eased up behind him and disarmed him. "Well, hello Creager, my name is Dakota Creed and I'm going to kill you for trying to kill the Fairchilds, for kicking Rascal and for saying that you own the Empire Timber & Cattle Company. It just so happens that I own the Empire Timber & Cattle Company. Now if you want to say a prayer, say it now for I am going to blow your head off." A bug-eyed stare came from Creager's face but he didn't say a word. Creed pulled the trigger and said a prayer for this con man's family.

Creed followed a blood trail that led him to Kathy Ann. Blood covered her face and clothes. The different thoughts he had brought a mournful reaction: Had the only girl he ever loved been shot? Had she been shot by a stray bullet fired by her father? Or had Creager killed her?

Creed called out to Fairchild. "Come to the house alone!"

Creed bent over Kathy Ann and realized that she had not been shot but had been knocked unconscious. All the blood was coming from her broken nose. Paul Fairchild rushed in. "What happened?"

"I killed Creager. Looks as if he hit Kathy Ann and broke her nose."

"Let's set her up, stop the bleeding and clean her up a bit before I let Maude know that she's hurt."

Creed moved from Kathy Ann to Monty and examined Creager's hands. "He did hit her. There is blood and torn skin all over his right knuckles."

"Dakota, Kathy Ann is breathing good through her mouth and I've stopped the bleeding. She should be coming around shortly. I don't want her to know you killed Creager. I know you had every right to do so but it would be easier on everyone involved if it was one of my bullets that brought him down. My justification would be that he attacked Kathy Ann."

"Mr. Fairchild, I still have feelings for Kathy Ann. Do what you think is best for her. I don't want her to think I killed Creager because of her relationship with him."

"That will be exactly what she will think if she knows you killed him."

"Okay! Let me slip out the back door and I'll ride off, circle around, and will come back into the ranch from the front entrance. You get Mrs. Fairchild and tell her what is going on and get Kathy Ann back on her feet. Throw a sheet over Monty and give me a signal when you want me to return, and I'll take care of burying him."

By the time Creed received Fairchild's signal, an hour had passed. "She is conscious and in her room with Maude, said Fairchild. "She said she tried to get Monty to stop shooting at us and that he turned and hit her before she could run. She is glad that I shot and killed him. She wants to talk to you."

"I don't know what to say to her, but I will listen. Let me bury Creager first. I'm sure you and Mrs. Fairchild will want to spend a lot of time alone with her and I'll leave after hearing her out and be out of your way."

"Dakota, you said you still had feelings for her."

"Well, yes, you can't just stop having feelings for someone you once loved, and I'll never forget you and Mrs. Fairchild's kindness toward me."

Creed and Fairchild wrapped Creager's body in a sheet and put him on a pack horse. "I will bury him deep and wipe out all signs of a burial. Only I will know where, and he will not be dug up by any animal," Creed said.

Three hours later, Creed rode back to the ranch by

coming through the front entrance. He was met at the front door. "Kathy Ann is in the sitting parlor. Let me know when you and she are through talking."

"I am such a fool, Dakota. I was looking for you to ride in every day since you left. When I saw Monty ride in the front gate, I thought it was you. I ran to meet him. When I realized it was not you, I broke down and cried. I was so lonesome, and I wanted it to be you so much. Monty put his arms around me and comforted me. It felt good. I listened to every word he said, and it sounded so good. I thought it would be words that you would say if you were here. I asked myself why wait for words that I wanted to hear from you someday when I could have them from Monty right now."

"Kathy Ann, there is nothing I can say. Time has a way of healing a lot of scars. I want you, your mother, and father to always think well of me as I shall of all three of you. If Rascal follows me away from here, may I keep him?"

"It would be best, Dakota. I failed to protect him from Monty as I should have."

Paul and Maude Fairchild returned the letter. "Thank you, Dakota. Don't forget, the door is always open to you at The Flying Dust. We will never forget you. You got our daughter back for us, again."

Creed rode away and wiped away a tear from one eye then another, caused by the dust that flew into his eyes.

CHAPTER THIRTY-TWO

Broken-Hearted

Creed did not want to think of anything but getting back to warmer weather. He had thought of Kathy Ann every day for nearly a year. Now the pain of having lost her was such that he shook his head and tried to think about the warmer weather. Anything was better than dwelling on what had just happened.

Rascal was a double-edged sword. He loved Rascal, but his thoughts of Rascal brought back conflicting feelings. He was not about to give Rascal up though; he would learn to block out the disturbing thoughts. When the little mutt got tired, he would make a running jump into Dakota's arms. Creed would place him on the saddle in front of him. Rascal would ride several miles and jump off the horse if he saw something of interest to chase or inspect. Creed would always raise a leg after Rascal jumped back on to help him stay on the saddle until he could get settled in. At night, he would snuggle up to Dakota to keep warm. Rascal would bring up rabbits he caught for Dakota to cook. Rascal could sense the man's loneliness and nuzzled him for his attention. He would scratch the dog's belly and pull on his ears until they both drifted off to sleep.

Creed started thinking of the ranch house he had been building for Kathy Ann. He was anxious to see it in its finished state. He would live in the house alone. He felt he would be happy sitting on the front porch with Rascal at his feet. He would watch the squirrels and deer with Rascal trying to sneak up on them. He would hire a cook and a housekeeper and would need a few hands to handle the horses and keep everything spruced up. But, for now, he was still five hundred miles from home. He would have it all figured out by the time he got there.

The next morning, Creed started thinking about the Empire Timber & Cattle Company. He would not be able to sit on the front porch and relax if he lost Constantina, too. He knew she was happy but wondered if it was a man that was making her so happy. *I need to find out, but how?*

Dakota had checked with Western Union for a wire in Charleston and Little Rock and was again disappointed. By the time he got to Texarkana, he had left the snow behind. He stopped at Wells Fargo and checked his bank balance. It was mind boggling. *It's amazing how fast money will grow when you deliver 8,000 head of Texas Longhorns and a barge of timber every few days.*

He stopped and checked with Western Union Telegraph while in Texarkana. He had a telegraph from Constantina wishing him a Merry Christmas. Her pleasant wishes made him smile. He needed to smile. It was his first one in a long time. Constantina had a way about her that always made him smile. He would not stop and look for Desmond or Bo in Bowie County. He wanted to get home to his ranch.

Creed had no assurance the State Police had talked with the Governor, but he was going to his bank to see Constantina even if it was risky. When he arrived, he tapped on the side door and it was opened immediately by a man who had his hand on his gun. The man was Bob Randle. "Creed, great to see you!"

Constantina rushed to the door. "Come on in, Dakota.

Bob just told me he was going to teach me how to be a jockey and will let me ride one of our thoroughbreds in a race." A broad smile covered her face.

"That's great, Constantina. I see you made it here okay, Bob."

"Yes, after you told me how great Constantina was, I could hardly wait to meet her."

"Bob, I just got here and need to talk to Constantina. Would you mind excusing us?"

"Sure thing, Creed."

"Constantina, can you change into your riding clothes and go to the ranch with me. We have a lot of things to go over."

"Oh yes, Dakota, I'm so glad you are back. I'm impressed with Bob. He is a great find for us."

"I thought you would like him." Dakota suspected some kind of connection between the two of them and felt a little envious.

Dakota introduced Constantina to Rascal who had been resting at the feet of the horses. He wagged his tail and pranced around as her hand went down to pet him.

On the way to the ranch house, Dakota and Constantina talked about the progress being made with all aspects of the Empire Timber & Cattle Company. Rascal wanted in on the attention that Dakota was giving Constantina and ran and jumped into Dakota's saddle, nuzzling him and wagging his tail. Rascal soon jumped off to chase a rabbit. When he returned Constantina motioned to Rascal and patted her saddle. Without hesitation, Rascal jumped into her lap.

"I'm jealous!" Dakota responded. They both laughed.

When they arrived at the homesite, Dakota was in awe. The main house had a porch that wrapped around the house and had two breezeways, known as dog trots in Texas. The dog trots had a double sliding door on the back side that could be closed in bad weather.

The ranch house had a fireplace, in each of the ten rooms. All ten chimneys had a column of smoke curling out of it. The curtains were drawn open on all the windows. The dog trot doors were also open. Rocking chairs and small tables beside them adorned the porches.

Workers were laying stones in the meandering creek from the artesian well to the barn and then to the berm. The flow of water over and around the rocks created a soothing rhythmic sound. Reaching out and putting his hand on her shoulder, Dakota said, "Constantina, this is perfect. I am so pleased."

"I was hoping you would be. I took the liberty to hire you a cook and a staff of housekeepers. If you don't like them, you can replace them. Let's sit on the front porch and I'll introduce them to you. They came with the highest recommendations."

"I'm so glad you took the liberty. I had thought of that myself but didn't know where to start." *I wonder what Kathy Ann would have thought of her new home.* Sadness filled his heart as his thoughts shifted to what was not to be.

"Dakota, are you okay?"

"Yes, Constantina, I just thought of something that used to be especially important to me and now it's not. I had promised myself to never think of it again and I was shocked that I had done just that."

"Would you like to talk about it?"

"No, but thanks, Constantina. It's no longer important."

Introductions were made, and a staff member brought out a pitcher of tea made from the cold artesian water. Another brought out a plate of roast beef with freshly made bread and another brought out a brass hand bell. The staff disappeared.

Constantina and Dakota ate with Rascal at their feet waiting for a morsel and hoping for a bone. When they finished, Constantina rang the bell, and a staff member came to take away the plates.

Rascal left the porch with a big bone in his mouth and headed toward the base of a magnolia tree. He abandoned the bone and stalked a squirrel until the squirrel climbed a tree trunk part way and turned back to bark at Rascal. They exchanged barks until Rascal decided he'd rather chew on his bone.

"I am so proud of what you have done here. I could not have done this without you, Constantina. You are also a key to the success of Empire Timber & Cattle Company. I live in fear that you might one day want to leave the Company."

"Dakota, why should I ever want to leave?"

"I don't want to pry into your private life, but I want to know something and the only way I will ever know the answer is to ask you a direct question."

"Ask, Dakota, If I know the answer, you will know it."

"Constantina, ever since I've known you, you have always had a smile on your face and seemed happy. Every time I see you, you seem to be happier. Do you have a man in your life who is making you so happy?"

"Well, yes, I do, Dakota!" She said somewhat shyly.

His heart sank. He was smart enough to know that when a girl was in love, she would do almost anything her man wanted her to do. His experience with Kathy Ann and Creager proved that. Creed held his composure and knew he had to respond.

"That's wounderful, Constantina. I hope he is good

enough to deserve you."

She spoke with assurance. "He is."

Creed was crushed. He wanted her to be happy, but he did not want to lose her. Flashing a big smile, he said, "Good!"

It was getting cold, and the staff had stoked up and added wood to each of the fireplaces. They retreated inside to sit and talk. The ambience was perfect. The fragrance of the burning wood was soothing and being around Constantina was always enjoyable.

What a blessing to be warm and cozy in my own house, he thought, but became a little sad when he realized it was his alone and that he wouldn't be sharing with a woman he loved.

Dakota had always thought of Kathy Ann when he was around the smiling Constantina. Now that he no longer had Kathy Ann, he felt himself being drawn closer to this beautiful Spanish vaquera. *What am I thinking? She has her man who is making her happy. I can't interfere with that. I only hope that I can find someone like Constantina someday.*

The next morning after breakfast, Dakota and Constantina rode back to Nacogdoches. Constantina had tried the day before to discuss Bob Randle's request to build his stables and racetrack on the north end of the 80,000-acre tract. The track would be close to Nacogdoches. Dakota's home would be far enough away that it would not interfere with any activity or expansion Dakota might desire.

The first thought that had entered Creed's mind the day before was that Bob would be closer to Constantina. After sleeping on it, his thinking now was that Constantina had probably known her beau for some time before Bob Randle came into the picture. It was evident that Bob was very fond of Constantina and she had told him she liked Bob. He wanted all his employees to like Constantina. He had no reason to be jealous. She was not his, anyway.

"Constantina, I like your and Bob's idea of building the stables and track on the north end of the 80,000-acre tract. You pick out the site."

"We already have. I know you will love it there. It will be close enough for you to come and see me riding in some of the races, and far enough away from the house to not bother you," she said as she smiled.

Creed dropped Constantina off at her boarding house to change clothes. Rascal ran around her feet several times seeking her attention and a pat on his head. Once achieved he ran and jumped into the saddle with Dakota.

As he was riding into Alazan, he was greeted with waves of happiness and respect. Before seeking out the person he had come to see, he went to meet with Francisco Lazerine who became a close friend. After they brought each other up to date on items of mutual interest, Dakota sought out and found Father Raul Montoya.

"Father, I've come for the answer to my question."

"Dakota, hello and welcome, Father Montoya said warmly. I'm proud you came. It is an important question and should be answered in a way that God would say it. The Knights Templar killed not for themselves but for God and his glory. God created man. Man was part of his glory. You said the things you did were to protect yourself and yours, such as Francisco Lazerine. When you were protecting yourself and Francisco you were protecting man, part of God's glory, which is not a sin. Other men might punish you for your actions. but not God."

"Father, I know that I have had sins of thought. I confess

those sins and ask God for forgiveness."

"You are forgiven, my son."

Before Creed left Alazan, Juan rode in. "Creed, glad to see you here! I was on the way to Nacogdoches to see Constantina. Three Gringos cut out fifty head of our stock last night. We gave chase and caught up with them about an hour later and drove them back to the herd. We've got the cattle rustlers tied to their saddles and they're drifting along with the herd. Do you want us to hang 'em?"

"No, bring them to me. I've got some unfinished business with the State Police. I want to see if *they* will hang them. If they don't, I'll take care of it. How long will it take to get them back here?"

"Maybe three hours."

"Are Donny Callaway and Antonio with you?"

"Yes, they are.

"Send Antonio on with the herd and you and Donny bring the cattle rustlers back here. We'll take them to Nacogdoches tomorrow and see what the State Police will do with them."

The next morning Creed, Juan, and Donny rode into Nacogdoches with the three cattle rustlers tied to their horses. They rode up to the State Police office and dismounted.

"I've got three cattle rustlers for you, Officer. What do you want me to do with them?"

"Who's saying they're rustlers?" The officer asked.

"I do! Dakota Creed."

"Did you see them rustle the stock?"

"No, but my men caught them with my cattle."

"If you didn't catch them, I don't need to talk to you. I

want to talk to the men who caught them."

Creed bit his tongue and smiled. "They are right here, Officer."

"You two saw them steal the cattle?"

"No! But they had the cattle with 'em when we found 'em." Donny said.

"How did you know they were your cattle?"

"They all had the Empire Timber & Cattle Company brand on them."

"You own the Empire Timber & Cattle Company?"

"No, but we ride for the brand."

"What the hell does that have to do with anything?", the officer barked.

"Mister, when you ride for the brand, it means everything and you're about to get in trouble by stepping off in some deep water," Donny replied.

"Officer, do whatever you want with them, but cattle rustlers are usually hanged," Creed said, turning away and signaling Donny and Juan to follow. When they got out of sight of the State Police office, they stopped and talked. Both Donny and Juan knew that if the State Police released the cattle rustlers Creed would find a way to hang them.

"Donny, get Jake and Billy to stand watch on the State Police office until the rustlers are hanged or released. If they are let go, have Jake follow them and leave a lot of sign. Have Billy find me."

Two days later, the cattle rustlers were released. A short time later, Billy found Creed and led him to the trail heading west where the two set out to catch up with Jake.

"Jake, you and Billy go back on the trail to Nacogdoches and wipe out all sign to here. I will handle this matter from here on."

As the cattle rustlers swung in the breeze, Creed was making coffee. After finishing his coffee, he raked several sticks out of the fire and put out the flames. When the sticks cooled, he took paper from his saddle bag and wrote a note using the charcoal on the end of the burnt sticks. When he finished, he attached the message to each of their bodies. It read "HUNG FOR CATTLE RUSTLING!"

When Creed re-entered Nacogdoches, he made a special effort to be seen entering from the southeast, the direction from his home. When he rode by the State Police office, he tipped his hat to the officer sitting in the chair on the porch.

The next morning the town was abuzz about the three bodies found hung several miles west of town. Creed sat in a chair having coffee in front of his bank. Twenty minutes later, Creed saw the State Police officer that he had turned the rustlers over to coming toward him in a brisk walk. Before the Officer could speak Creed spoke out. "Looks like you did the right thing and hanged the rustlers."

"You know I didn't hang them, Creed. I want to talk to you about that."

"Did you see me do it Officer?"

"No! But..."

"You need to talk to the one who saw it done, Officer."

"You know you did it or had it done," the Officer barked.

"I don't remember hanging anyone, but I am glad that you saw to it that they were hung Officer. I have never heard of a horse thief or a cattle rustler caught red-handed not being hung. Everyone in Texas will have hats off for you seeing to it that they hang."

CHAPTER~THIRTY~THREE

Sue Ann Yates

Creed went to the bank and told Constantina what had happened concerning the cattle rustlers without going into detail "I think it best that I go to Fort Smith and tell Maxwell about the cattle rustlers and tell what happened to them."

'I've got about an hour before I need to leave."

"I hate to see you go, Dakota, you work so hard. I was hoping you would stay around and enjoy your new home. I will miss you and Rascal. I want to give him a hug before you leave."

"I will drop by at the side door, so you can have your hug with Rascal. *And ... No, I can't hug her! She has her man.*

The weather was cold in Nacogdoches and would get colder the farther north he went. He took along an extra blanket for Rascal to snuggle in when he rode on the saddle in front of him. With only three hours of light left when he left Nacogdoches, he began looking for a shelter for the night.

The shelter was a burned-out cabin that had a standing north wall and an intact stone fireplace. He had seen it before but never had had the need for it, being so near to Nacogdoches. Creed found several pack rat nests and used them to start a fire. He rounded up enough partially burned logs from the cabin to keep a fire burning all night.

Creed was lonesome. He would have been much more lonesome without Rascal. Creed wrapped his blanket around his canine friend and thought how thankful he was to have such a devoted pup.

Creed thought about Constantina. Even though he knew she had a man of her own, that would not rob him the pleasure of thinking of her. He remembered that every time he was around Constantina, she was consistently happy. He wondered if the feelings he was having for Constantina would be the feelings he would always have for Kathy Ann. *That didn't work out. He had to stop thinking of Kathy Ann.* The logs in the fireplace flared up as if kerosene had been poured on them.

Creed set up with a stark realization. From early on, he had been in love with everything about Constantina. He had hoped it would be the same with Kathy Ann because he had made a commitment to her before ever meeting Constantina. Now that Constantina was taken, and Kathy Ann was out of the question, he would turn the world over until he found his own version of Constantina. At least it was good to know what he wanted.

When he arrived in Bowie County, Creed went by Desmond Duke's office. "Bo, I'm surprised to see you here. Where is Desmond?"

"He's in St. Louis. Constantina wanted a progress report before she made a big payment to the contractor. He took Hitch with him. Hitch has Bowie County as peaceful as it has ever been with over three fourths of the people supporting the brand."

"That's good. What are you up to, Bo?"

"Right now, I'm buying all the hay I can find. The herds

are doing well on graze until they get here. They are using different trails getting here but the same one to get to the river crossing. If it had not frozen, we would have one big mud hole by now."

When the door swung open, Creed's hand reached for his Colt. When he saw a striking beautiful smiling girl, he immediately thought of Constantina. The girl was well-groomed and poised. She got Creed's attention with the ribbons in her long blond hair and the light perfume he smelled when she got close to him.

"Sue Ann, where have you been so long?"

"Just got back yesterday from Austin, Bo."

"Sue Ann Yates, I want you to meet Dakota Creed."

"Mom wrote me about you, Mr. Creed."

"Miss Sue Ann, please call me Dakota."

"Sure will, Dakota, if you will just call me Sue Ann."

"I heard you were in school there Sue Ann. How was it?" Bo asked."

"I've learned a lot about bookkeeping and enough to let me know I needed to go to work. Dakota, I'm Bo's next-door neighbor. I live on the other side of Rock Creek from him with my mother. Bo's father and my father were in the War together. My father, Ezra, died in the War. Who is your friend here, Dakota?" she asked as she was bending down to pet the dog.

"That's my sidekick, Rascal. He goes with me almost everywhere I go."

"I love dogs," she said.

Could this be another Constantina? Creed hoped it was. He thought she looked about his age and was about four inches shorter. She talked as if she were educated, and she had the smile and bright eyes that made Creed interested in her. *But Constantina's does have prettier hair.*

"Bo, I would like for you to go to Texarkana with me tonight, and then we'll go to Fort Smith and meet with Ryan Maxwell. I have something I want him to do for me and we can talk to him about crossing the Red with the herds farther west. There should be better grazing and footing for the herd there."

"Any chance I could go along with you, Dakota? I enjoy Fort Smith and I haven't been there in ages. I can pay my way and I ride as well as Bo, and I wouldn't slow y'all down. I could do some shopping while you visit with this Maxwell fellow. What do you think?"

Creed looked at Sue Ann. How could he refuse her? She reminded him a little of Rascal when he would plead for attention to get no more than a pat on his head or to have his ears pulled.

"That's fine with me if it's okay with Bo."

"Bo doesn't care, do you, Bo?"

"No! She'll be good company."

"How long will it take you to get ready, Sue Ann?"

"I'm ready now. We could go by the way of Rock Creek. That way I could tell Mom where I'm going. We could go through Red Water to Texarkana. It's about the same distance. I will buy anything I need for the trip in Texarkana when we get there."

"That's fine with me, Sue Ann."

"Thank you, Dakota."

It was a pleasant trip. As they rode, Creed was constantly watching Sue Ann and comparing her to Constantina. *Their smiles and eyes look so similar. Sue Ann seemed a lot more assertive than Constantina. Constantina might be as assertive or maybe she handled things more smoothly. I wish*

Constantina were here. I'd like them to meet.

Rascal seemed to like Sue Ann but maybe not quite as much as he liked Constantina.

After arriving in Fort Smith and settling in, Sue Ann went shopping, while Creed and Bo went to the Indian Affairs office. From time-to-time Creed glanced up to the window on the second floor when he rode past Judge Parker's gallows. He saw nothing unusual, but he felt his heart beat a little faster.

Rascal stayed with the horses outside and Creed and Bo were immediately shown into Ryan Maxwell's office. A new delivery site was agreed on and marked on the map.

"Bo, I must speak to Mr. Maxwell privately. I will meet you back at the hotel when we are through. Leave Rascal with my horse, if you would, please."

"Will do, Dakota," Bo said as he left the room.

"Mr. Maxwell, fifty head of our cattle were rustled from one of our cattle drives. The cattle were cut out of the herd at night, and we did not realize it until the next morning. Our crew picked up their trail and caught up with three rustlers five miles away herding the cattle west. Before the War, the rustlers would have been hung on the spot. We know that things changed after the War and that the right thing to do was to turn them over to the Texas State Police.

"The rustlers were brought to me and I turned them over to two Texas State Policemen, Captain Livingston Tarver and his Sergeant Linwood Langford, in Nacogdoches. My men and I feared that they would not be hung, which I think is the only way to stop rustlers. To the credit of the State Police, they were hung. The State Police is under a lot of fire from the citizens of Texas for not being able to control lawlessness. Could you arrange for a letter to be sent from the Governor and the President congratulating the Captain and Sergeant on a job well done in fighting crime in Texas, especially related to this case?"

"I sure can, Creed. Not only that, but I'll also get a news story out to be published in every newspaper in the state."

"Mr. Maxwell, it will help our crews to know the Texas State Police have our back."

"You just keep the cattle coming, Creed. I nearly forgot to tell you this, but Western Union just opened a line into Nacogdoches. The line links Crockett to Nacogdoches then goes east to San Augustine and then north to connect to the line in Jefferson. The Jefferson line goes to Texarkana then to here."

"That's great news, Mr. Maxwell. It will certainly make things a lot easier."

Creed went straight to the Western Union office and sent Constantina a long message and stood by for a return message. Within an hour Creed received a reply. While he was reading the reply, he visualized seeing her smiling happy face. *How could I have been so stupid? Falling for the first girl I had seen in four years. If I hadn't, it could have made a difference.*

After returning to Texarkana, Rascal, Creed, Bo and Sue Ann, who insisted on coming along, went up the Red River to inspect the new designated entry point into the Indian Territory. The entry point was on property owned by the Empire Timber & Cattle Company but was crowding the Red River County line. "Bo, let's go ahead and try to buy at least a ten-mile-wide strip of land on the east side of Red River County." Unknown to Creed, this statement impressed Sue Ann.

When Creed was ready to leave Bowie County, Sue Ann

wanted to go with him to Nacogdoches. "I have some private things I must do, Sue Ann. I'll have Bo bring you down sometime soon." Sue Ann pouted. *He had never seen Constantina pout. Why was that?*

Sue Ann had been at his side for ten days. He enjoyed her company, but she gave him no time to think. It was as if she needed constant attention. Creed wondered how often he would think of her when he left her in Bowie County.

It didn't take long to find out. His first thoughts were of Constantina. His only thoughts of Sue Ann were comparing her to Constantina.

CHAPTER THIRTY-FOUR

Creed's Return Home

When Creed got back to Nacogdoches with faithful Rascal at his side, he went to the bank to see Constantina. He was told that she had left with Bob Randle to look at the construction of the stables and track. Creed's desire to see Constantina intensified when hearing this.

"Please tell her I am back and would like to see her. I will be at the ranch."

Rascal was as glad to be back as Creed was. Constantina did not arrive until noon the next day. All morning Creed was looking for her to arrive. *She's not as anxious to see me as I am to see her*!

When Constantina arrived, she came in with that big smile of hers and a copy of a Nacogdoches special edition newspaper. The headline read. "Three Cattle Rustlers Hanged."

"Congratulations to the Nacogdoches State Police for hanging three cattle rustlers," the article began. It went on with the details and that congratulations were from the Texas Governor and the President of the United States.

"How did you pull that rabbit out of the hat, Dakota Creed?"heard she asked with a stern look and her hands on her hips.

"I'll never tell." He said as they both laughed.

Later, they were served dinner and continued their

conversation around the fireplace with Rascal snuggled in Constantina's lap. They talked into the night.

"I'm going to the branding camp tomorrow and plan to go into the Big Thicket the next day. Would you take care of Rascal while I'm gone? The Thicket is a strange and dangerous place if you don't know your way around and I certainly don't."

"Sure, I will, Dakota."

"I'll check back in with Ralph Tillman while I'm gone. Do you need to tell anyone anything down that way?"

"No, I will be back in the bank tomorrow. I will go by and check on Bob on my way back since it's on my way."

Creed did not want to think or talk about Bob. "We had better turn in. See you at breakfast."

After Creed left it was three hours latter that Constantina realized Rascal was gone and a search began.

Creed used the ferry at Marion to cross over the Angelina. He rode west hoping to find Ralph Tillman at his trading post. When he arrived, a wagon loaded with barbed wire was leaving the settlement heading south toward the bridge that crossed the Neches River. The driver told him that Tillman was somewhere on the Trinity supervising the construction of the fencing.

Tillman's bridge was holding up well so far. There had been one flood, and luckily, there had not been any driftwood-build up and no downed trees had hit the structure.

When Creed crossed the bridge, he saw dozens of Longhorns on the face of the hill. As he got close, he could tell that most were mavericks, but many wore the Empire Timber & Cattle Company brand. He saw no other brand.

His first thought was that grasses in the flats were mighty thin and the cattle had resorted to the timberland in search of better grazing. His second thought made him shudder. He thought of the carnage of the Longhorns that would be occurring now if the thousands of Longhorns had not been moved to the Indian Territory. The cattle he was seeing were typical of other cattle that were going through the rigors of winter without extra hay being provided.

A slender column of smoke told him he was nearing the branding camp. They had moved several miles north of the Trinity.

"Howdy, Creed!"

"Hello yourself, Juan."

"Creed, we've increased our branded stock numbers by about seven hundred more than the twelve hundred a day we had been branding. That's close to fifteen hundred more than we need for a drive every five days, and eventually, it will eliminate most of the mavericks. The crews are fighting for the ten-dollar bonus so hard that some of them are getting started each morning before a rooster would crow and working right through the noon meal until the last call for chow at night. We moved the branding camp away from the river to give the branded stock a little more room to graze."

"Juan, have you noticed any reduction of Longhorns coming out of the Thicket?"

"I don't know where they are coming from but there has not been any decrease that I can tell. The vaqueros can throw their riata within fifty feet of the fire and drag in a maverick Longhorn."

"Juan, I'm going to the Thicket tomorrow and see what's going on. I'm hoping to find a trail into the Thicket. I will be looking for cattle and a better way to get to the large spring-fed creek I found before.

Creed saw an abundance of branded and maverick Longhorns along the way to the Big Thicket. He saw fences that Tillman's crews had erected, and high knolls stacked with mining timbers. He bedded down early and planned to start early on his entry into the Thicket. He wanted to get in and out before the sun set.

Not long after he entered the Thicket, he realized that many Longhorns he had seen didn't have brands. Creed's horse started acting up. She didn't seem interested in going farther into the Thicket. He rode the mare out to a flat and hobbled her.

He removed one of his Henrys from the scabbard and put on his moccasins. Wearing his sheepskin coat and carrying his gloves, he eased back into the Thicket on foot with a saddlebag over his shoulder. When he came to the spot where the horse had refused to continue, he stopped and listened for several minutes. He did hear sounds he was not familiar with but nothing that sounded threatening. He eased slowly forward picking out three steps that were cleared of anything that would make noise. He stopped and listened for a moment, then picked out three more steps.

Creed had moved forward about a hundred yards when he froze in his tracks. He had seen movement, big movement. A hundred feet in front of him two large buck deer fought to determine who would have the breeding rights in the area. The fittest would survive and pass his seed while the defeated might die from his wounds or simply leave the area to fight another day.

He continued his trek and stayed alert for what had spooked his horse. There were too many unknowns in the thousands of acres in the Thicket—quicksand, alligators, bobcats, feral hogs, bears, water moccasins, copperheads, cougars, black panthers, and more. One did not want to get lost in the Thicket. Nor did he want to lose Rascal in the Thicket and spend days searching for him.

Creed decided to give up on this trail when it disappeared into the dense forest. He returned to his horse and rode north out of the Big Thicket and bedded down. He planned to hobble his horse and walk into the Thicket early the next morning and find the creek. When he closed his eyes to sleep, his thoughts were on Constantina and she was still on his mind when he awoke the next morning.

Creed found a new way to the creek and paused for a moment to watch the fish darting around chasing smaller fish to eat.

Where could that dog have gotten to! It had been six days since Constantina had last seen Rascal at the ranch. She had given up on finding Rascal. Crying wouldn't help. She returned to the ranch house numerous times hoping she would find him there, but no luck. She dreaded having to tell Dakota.

Constantina was sad and busy in her office with her door closed when a clerk knocked and looked in. "A lady to see you, Miss DeLeon."

"Show her in, please."

"Miss DeLeon, I'm Sue Ann Yates. I've been told you might be able to tell me where I might find Dakota Creed."

"Might I ask your purpose in finding him?"

"Oh! I assumed he must have told you about me. I spent ten days riding to Fort Smith and back with him from Bowie County. He told me he was going to invite me down here someday, but I couldn't wait."

"Couldn't wait for what, Miss Yates?"

"Well, the excitement of being around him."

"I'm sorry Miss Yates, Mr. Creed has not told me about you."

"Well, he didn't mention you either, Miss DeLeon."

"I don't doubt that. He does not tell anyone about his personal business, not even me."

"Is there some reason why he should tell you his personal business, Miss DeLeon?"

"Well, no! If he wants me to know something he tells me. I run the Empire Timber & Cattle Company. I can assure you if he thought it was important he would have mentioned you. After I close the bank this afternoon, I would be glad to take you to dinner and you can tell me all about yourself."

"I would love that, Miss DeLeon."

"Meet me back here at four o'clock, and please call me Constantina.

Constantina liked Sue Ann. She thought she was a little naive in ways but seemed gregarious enough. *Just for fun, I think I will get Bob to go to dinner with us.*

Bob and Sue Ann hit it off just as Constantina had hoped. During dinner they talked of Sue Ann's schooling in keeping financial records and Bob's need for a bookkeeper for the Thoroughbred racehorse business while Constantina silently worried about Rascal and Dakota.

Creed walked along the sandy creek until he came to a slough and followed the edge of the slough for several miles mesmerized by the beauty. The light that crept past the dense foliage suddenly got darker. It was time for Creed to get out of the Thicket. He sat on a log and took time to eat some jerked beef and hardtack. The hardtack was so hard it was not worth the effort to eat, so he tossed it away. When he turned to go back, he realized he had slough water on both sides of him. *It's only around noon, a cloud is shading the sun. It should get brighter shortly.* He was wrong. If anything, it got darker.

Creed started walking toward what he thought was the way out of the Thicket. After walking for two hours, he froze in his tracks. There was a log at his feet and part of a hardtack lying on the ground covered with ants. He was lost. He would stay put and hope for better light. He leaned against a giant magnolia, put on his gloves, buttoned his coat and went to sleep. He was awake most of the night and was eager for the sun to be up. The sounds in the Thicket never ceased. They changed from mellow sweet sounds to sounds of terror. His emotions flowed with the sounds.

The cloud cover still limited light. Creed knew that moss grew on the north side of tree trunks. This would be his only help on directions unless the clouds cleared. The moss on the first tree he examined told him which way was north. The problem was that in the west direction that he wanted to go, was nothing but slough. If he went into the slough, he would not be able to see moss on the tree trunks nor could he determine how deep the water was.

The thought that he knew little about alligators convinced him to stay out of the water. Creed would go north until he could not see water in the west. The day moved along without the light improving. He decided to go west even if he had to swim all the way. The flats of the Trinity would be close, and he had work to do and needed to check on Constantina. He would sleep again until morning and head west.

Early the next morning before daylight Creed awoke with a start. *What was that?* Whatever it was, it was running toward him. It didn't sound like a deer. Creed could not tell how far away it was. He readied his Henry and loosened the Bowie in its scabbard. Creed's eyes adjusted to the break of daylight in the sky. It was still pitch dark near the ground. Creed laid the Henry aside and drew his Bowie and one of his Colts. From out of nowhere Creed saw something coming toward him fast. Instead of pulling the trigger of the Colt or meeting the intruder with his Bowie he threw them both aside and wrapped his arms around Rascal. That mutt that some considered "good for nothing" led Dakota out of the Thicket in less than three hours.

Creed and Rascal took the ferry in Marion and went to his ranch. *That's strange. Who's that girl sitting on the back porch?* Rascal jumped from the saddle and ran to Sue Ann Yates. Dakota was glad to see her but wished it had been Constantina. "What are you doing here and how did you find me, Sue Ann?"

"You can't hide from me, Dakota Creed. I just asked the first person I saw where I could find the most handsome man in the County and they pointed the way, and here I am. I ran into Constantina and she said it would be okay for me to stay in the guest house until you returned. She introduced me to Bob Randle, and I've been having dinner with Bob every night since I've been here. He is a swell guy. He has offered me a job as bookkeeper for the Thoroughbred business. I will be starting next week."

"Sue Ann, I'm glad to see you but I'm really busy. I was lost in the Big Thicket for three days and it has put me way behind. I've got to meet with Miss DeLeon as soon as possible. I don't know if Miss DeLeon told you, but she runs my bank and the Empire Timber & Cattle Company for me."

"Yes, she told me that. She asked Bob to take care of me. She's a sweet girl."

"Yes, she is," said Dakota.

Creed realized he was not jealous of Bob Randle spending time with Sue Ann, and maybe he should be. He liked Sue Ann. It was all rather confusing.

"I told Constantina about the trip to Fort Smith with you and how much I enjoyed it."

"Did you tell her Bo was with us."

"Of course! Why do you ask?"

"Just wondered. I will spend what's left of the day here resting and cleaning up but will have to leave early in the morning. I will be gone for several days. I'll send word to Bob that you will be here alone for several days and for him to look in on you."

"I'm sure he will. He's been checking on me every day since I've been here."

Dakota sent one of the vaqueros to Nacogdoches to tell Constantina that he would meet her at her boarding house and for her to have on her riding clothes. She was to be prepared to be gone for five or six days. He was going to show her the discovery he made in the Big Thicket. "Tell her Rascal is safe with me. I was lost in the Thicket and that mutt Rascal found me."

Creed was miserable. He knew Constantina had a special man because she told him so and yet he couldn't stop thinking about her. By no means did Creed want to cause any problems with the man who made her so happy. Creed was nervous about it, but he was going to tell her, then look for someone who could fill her shoes. Dakota and Rascal arrived in Nacogdoches around eight in the morning. Creed's smile faded when he saw Constantina's face. Something had changed. The smile was still there but it seemed forced. "Glad to see you back, Dakota."

"Glad to be back. I might still be out in the Thicket living off the land if Rascal had not found me."

He didn't want to force the issue of what was going on with Constantina. There would be plenty of time on the trip for him to find out. The first thing that entered his mind was that she might want to tell him she was getting married and would be leaving. Fear raced through his heart.

"We'll pick up a pack horse at the stable and take both of your horses. Rascal will want to go with us in case we get lost," Dakota said, laughing. We'll stock up on vittles at Tillman's Trading Post. I'm going to show you the most beautiful country you've ever seen. We're going to the Big Thicket."

"I'm excited, Dakota. I've heard so much about it."

"Constantina, I'm going to be spending a lot of time at the ranch and I want to spend all the time you have available there with me. We've got a lot of catching up to do."

"That will be good, Dakota. You have been gone most of the time this last year." *I wonder when he is going to tell me about Sue Ann Yates.* She liked being with Dakota. She overcame the occasional twinges of jealousy created by thoughts of Sue Ann.

Dakota saw that Constantina was acting like the woman he loved to spend time with, but kept in mind she had her man. She loved the sights of the Thicket and the antics of Rascal. Dakota still had not mentioned Sue Ann to her and curiosity was getting the best of her.

"Tell me about your ten-day trip to Fort Smith with Miss

Sue Ann Yates, Dakota."

"Not much to tell, Constantina. She was a friend and neighbor of Bo's and she wanted to go along on the trip."

"Well! She followed you home. You must have impressed her."

"I wasn't trying to impress her. I was just comparing her to you, and she took it wrong."

"You were comparing her to me to see which one you wanted?"

"No, Constantina. You told me you had a man who made you happy and I knew I couldn't have you, so I was just keeping my eyes open for someone like you."

"Dakota, do you love me?"

"Yes, I do. I've loved you from the first time I saw you."

"Dakota, will you marry me?"

"What? What about that man who makes you so happy?"

"That man is you! Will you marry me, Dakota?"

"Well in that case, absolutely yes!"

Rascal sat wagging his tail as though he understood everything he'd just heard.

The wedding was held at the ranch with more than two hundred people attending. Father Raul Montoya presided. Those in attendance included Mariana DeLeon, Señor Francisco Lazarine and wife Loretta. A special enclosed coach was sent for them with clan members as escorts. They stayed in the guest rooms of the ranch house. Ryan Maxwell brought his Uncle, U.S. Senator Phillip Maxwell. Texas Governor James Throckmorton attended with a small entourage. They stayed in the two guest houses. Large white tents lined the hill. Cots, wash basins, and chairs were furnished for everyone wanting to spend the night. A large dance floor was installed, and several different bands played, some from as far away as Austin. It was rumored to be the largest wedding ever held in Texas.

Another wedding was held at the ranch just two months later when Bob Randle and Sue Ann Yates were married Sue Ann now had an office in the bank and covered for Constantina when she was away. The two couples became the best of friends.

The first thoroughbred race ever held in Texas was on the track that Bob Randle built and was called the Empire Promise. That day Constantina rode a silver horse named Empire Promise and won by two lengths. In several years, the Empire stable had world-class Thoroughbred horses and competed with the best of the breed. That segment of the Empire became a very profitable venture.

In ten years, Dakota and Constantina had five children… three girls and two boys. Bob and Sue Ann also had five children… three boys and two girls. The two families babysat sat each other's children and often vacationed together.

After just a few years, Juan and Pasqual's vaqueros and Donny's guards and families built their own homes and called the community Goodrich, a name well-suited for those who rode for the ETCC brand.

Rascal had grown tired of chasing squirrels and started chasing Bob and Sue Ann's dog Mertel. Bob put one of his horse trainers busy training a new litter of puppies each year.

The litters were split evenly between the families after training was completed. The dogs were trained to retrieve ducks, quail and to hunt coons, fox, deer, hogs, as well as to herd cattle.

Six years had passed, and Judge Isaac Parker sat in his office playing with the bones of a human foot. A squirrel hunter had found the foot in the woods and had turned it over to the Judge. No other bones could be found. He often wondered who the foot belonged to. He threw the bones aside and wondered what had ever happened to Pico de Mendoza.

A drastic change was taking place after four years with the cattle herds of Empire Timber & Cattle Company. The pure Longhorn cattle were being bred out. There were still a lot of half breeds, but the quarter breeds were increasing rapidly. The financial rewards were significant with the new breeds. Indian Affairs still bought cattle from the Empire as did the US Army.

The same drastic changes were taking place in Southern Illinois where the timber, corn, and hog businesses were exceeding all expectations. As corn crops increased, hog production increased, with the added hogs ready to eat as much corn that was produced. The corn stalks were so popular with the dairy farmers the ETCC built their own silos near Cahokia and put in their own dairy farm.

Dakota and Constantina built a school north of the ranch and hired the best teachers in the state. The teachers were paid more money than any other teachers in the country, plus they could live in the teacherage with all meals furnished at no cost. All of Empire Timber & Cattle Company employees' children could attend and would have supervised dormitory housing with meals if desired. The school had books on a variety of subjects from all over the world. Two favorites of the students were the Western genre novels *Quick Tender* and *Razor Sharp*, authored by Bert Lindsey.

Everyone who rode for the Empire Brand took care of the Brand and the Empire Timber & Cattle Company Brand took care of them.

www.ingramcontent.com/pod-product-compliance
Lightning Source LLC
Chambersburg PA
CBHW070841250626
47159CB00003B/873